THE MARY-SUE EXTRUSION

Four months before, the planet Dellah had undergone a global revolution and shut itself off from the galaxy at large. The knock-on effect of this had been one of destabilizing the balance of power for systems all around – all those threads of interest suddenly cut loose, and whipsawing, and looking for something to which they could attach. Such situations have a habit of spinning catastrophically out of control as the various local and galactic factions fight over a new and different pie. Diplomatic and commercial relations were strained to breaking point, and there were even the first rumblings of incipient territorial war.

And this is where I came in. I was going in, quite simply, as a representative of Pseudopod SA to look after their interests in this new situation, and to salvage what I could from the wreckage.

THE NEW

ADVENTURES

THE MARY-SUE EXTRUSION

Dave Stone

NA

First published in Great Britain in 1999 by
Virgin Publishing Ltd
Thames Wharf Studios
Rainville Road
London W6 9HT

Bernice Summerfield originally created by Paul Cornell

Cover illustration by Fred Gambino

ISBN 0 426 20531 6

Typeset by Galleon Typesetting, Ipswich
Printed and bound in Great Britain by
Mackays of Chatham PLC

Preliminary notes

It's always good to give yourself a bit of cover when you can. In the following, I've tried to give a full account of my involvement in what has, for a variety of reasons, become known as the Dellah Conspiracy. It's those soddy little sons of fun at the New Frontier Adventures yet again . . .

I can only talk about what I personally learnt, what I thought and what I did, and this can only skew the story in a certain way. Then again, so many people have got the facts, as I know them, so completely and utterly *wrong* that this can hardly make things any worse. At the very least, it might make somebody aware that there's an Alternative Point of View. But then again, of course, there always is.

On a vaguely personal note, I've tried to structure this account in a form approaching that of a novel – something of a dead art, but, as a form, it remains one of the best for concentrating lots of human-level information into an interconnected, some-way coherent and easily assimilable lump. It's no accident that old espionage reports really do read like spy novels, and vice versa. Plus it's about as low-tech as you can get without actually reverting to smoke signals – and is so simple and easy to reproduce and propagate that it's almost absurd. A picture might be worth a thousand words, apparently, but, if a single holo-still transfer were a text file, it could contain the complete text of every book ever written a thousand times over and then some.

As a *novel*, of course, the whole thing blows dead rodents somewhat more than a dead-rodent-blowing thing. What the hell do I know about writing novels? I had an editorial package go over it, like they use to smooth out all the lumps on that New Frontiers stuff, and it threw several varieties of violent transputronic fit. Erratic and idiosyncratic grammar, lurching descents into circumlocutory chattiness, utterly unrelated infodumps coming in from far left field, the fact that the whole thing falls apart spectacularly at the end . . .

On the whole I'm rather glad this is not intended for general publication – at least, the sort of publication for which novels were originally meant.

(I didn't take the edit-package's advice. I'd have had to spend half a day, as it merrily changed all the 'fucks' to 'funks' and so forth, checking the corrections to make sure it didn't garble the hard information itself – the hard information being more or less the entire point. And it's half a day I don't have. I've stayed too long in one place, anyway. I have to make it with the happy feet and move. Plus there is, of course, the small fact that I loathe and despise the Adventures of the New Frontier with a vengeance, and I refuse to end up with anything that resembles the bastards in any way, shape or form.)

I said that this wasn't intended for general publication – and there are two ways you could be reading this. If there's suddenly been some big development in the Dellah Situation, you've pulled this out of the relevant files and you don't need any further explanation from me, so thank you, good night and good luck. I hope you find something you can use.

On the other hand, this and a bunch of other stuff comprises the payload for a number of info-bombs I've left scattered around, here and there, as a small form of personal protection. If they're primed and I don't key in the proper protocols at regular periods, they're set to dump a lot of interesting material to various news services, multiplexal in-boxes and law-enforcement agencies. Anything happens to me and they get the lot. I'm not conceited enough to think it's going to bring down planetary governments, criminal syndicates and incorporate boards, but there's enough good stuff to give the, in quotes, Great and the Good, a few nasty and potentially terminal problems. Fuck 'em, frankly.

It's also primed to send it to a bunch of people whom, to various extents, I personally know and trust. So, if you're reading this, and you know me, and I'm not dead yet, could you please come and rescue me?

INSERT QUOTES:

Let's talk about the story of Pandora for a moment – ancient Greek mythology from preindustrial Earth, several millennia away from atmospheric breakout. So for those who don't know, or have simply forgotten, let's run it from the top.

Pandora was basically one of those proto-robo, golem-like automata that keep popping up all over the human mythological landscape – the idea of creating artificial humanoid life being apparently wired right into the human psyche from scratch, long before even the most basic understanding of the processes that could make such dreams a reality. Pandora was created out of raw clay by the god Hephaestus (he of the disfiguring plummet), life was breathed into her by Athena and Aphrodite gave her such surpassing beauty as to make her irresistible to mortal man. Hermes, the messenger of Zeus – and, for 'messenger', read the sort of right-hand-man enforcer who delivers the mail by way of terminal kicking – fitted her out with a generous portion of guile and arranged for her marriage to Prometheus.

Yes, *that* Prometheus. The one that came up with barbecues and napalm gel and Zippo lighters. Prometheus was, of course, a Titan, one of that other, older race of immortals from whom the gods wrested the world, and who in a certain sense balanced the gods themselves up. It wasn't a question of good versus evil as such – both gods and Titans were fully and spectacularly capable of both – but of opposing factions. If the gods did something petty, cruel and devastating in some particular area then the Titans were forced, almost in spite of themselves, into a more or less opposite stance – and vice versa.

In this light, the giving of Pandora to Prometheus might be seen as an innocent and simple gift of reconciliation, a little something to keep the opposition sweet. The fact that Hephaestus – whom the Romans renamed Vulcan – is most closely associated with the forging of weapons, and the fact that he supplied the thunderbolts to Zeus, might have given some small clue to the true nature of his creation.

It was, of course, about as sweet and innocent as the Trojan Horse: it was the precision-delivery system for the mythological equivalent of a weapons package. Zeus was behind it ultimately, of course, being the sworn enemy of Prometheus.

Prometheus had stolen fire from the gods (from Hephaestus's forge itself, as it happens) to make the lives of mortals better, so with a masterful bit of prototypical game-theory, Zeus set up a scenario that would, metaphorically, blow up in everybody's face and make life that much worse. He sent Pandora into the world with a little going-away present: a box containing all miseries and ills. This was, in the purely logistical sense, the payload. All it needed was a trigger.

Epimetheus was the best friend of Prometheus, and a mortal. The moment he clapped eyes upon the goddess-given beauty of Pandora he was smitten in a way that a Titan could never be – he would, quite simply, die if he could not possess her for his own. The fact that in real life he quite obviously wouldn't has no place in the game-theory structure of myth, which is what we're talking about, as opposed to the drama-theory structures of, well, drama. The Rules were that if he got her he'd live and if he didn't he'd die

– simple as that. We're dealing pretty much in binary-notational absolutism, here.

Prometheus loved his friend and didn't want him to die. Prometheus himself would not die if he lost Pandora, so he did what, on the surface, seemed to be the best thing for everyone. He allowed Epimetheus to marry Pandora in his stead. Big mistake. As a mortal, Epimetheus didn't have the power over Pandora to prevent her from opening the box, and we all know what happened then. Misery and ills let loose in the world, only hope remaining, plagues of whatever, wailing and gnashing of teeth, the usual stuff – and Zeus, the mastermind behind it all, stands there with a who-me gesture and gets away with it clean. Pandora's daughter subsequently goes off with the Greek version of Noah, but that's not strictly relevant here.

But what, you ask, is the relevance of all this to archaeology as a science? It's a matter of context. The above is a relatively full account of the Pandora myth, but people never seem to remember it in full – I myself had forgotten that Pandora wasn't, precisely, a mortal woman until I actually went and looked it up. We tend to concentrate upon the easy flash and thunder of an *event*, a discrete and catastrophic node of transition and/or transformation, without a clue as to the complex interplay of relationships and second-order events that brought it about. The Event becomes detached from its context, its relevance to the world in which it occurs, and in which we live, and thus becomes all but meaningless.

In the same way, and without quite realizing that he or she is doing it, the archaeologist is in constant danger of concentrating upon the artefacts – of choosing one as relevant, another as irrelevant – purely on the basis of themselves as objects, as opposed to their relationships to history, the culture of the times, their larger context. We can become focused on the completeness and condition of some unearthed urn, forgetting that our primary concern is in the whys and wherefores of how it came to be there for us to dig it up in the *first* place.

This is such an obvious point that it's almost embarrassing to state so baldly, like a reminder that the pants should be worn inside the trousers – but that's precisely why it *should* be stated baldly, as a constant reminder. We can become so inured to the obvious that we lose it, and, the instant that we do, we fall flat on our collective face into disaster. We become booksellers as opposed to librarians, operating on a level no better than some sad little adolescent storing pristine copies of comics magazines in little Mylar bags. We confuse the content with the form, the pages with the binding, the chocolate with the wrapper – we forget, quite simply, and if you'll forgive the unforgivably trite, what it all should really be about. To bring this back to Pandora, finally: when you're aware of and recall the whole back-story, you can sometimes see the key events in a new light, see how much else is going on and realize that it isn't just about some silly bint opening a box.

– Extract from *Down Among the Dead Men* by
Professor Bernice Summerfield (pub. various)

On looks and appearance

After the court had fallen silent for a moment, Bernardo Bibbiena said, with a smile, 'I remember your saying earlier that this courtier of ours should be naturally endowed with beauty of countenance and person, and with an attractive grace. Well, I feel sure that I possess both grace and beauty of countenance, and that is why so many women, as you know, are madly in love with me. But, when it comes to the beauty of my person, I am rather doubtful, and especially as regards these legs of mine, which do not seem to be as good as I would wish; still, as to my chest and so on, I am quite satisfied. So please explain in more detail about what shape of the body one should have, so that I can extricate myself from doubt and put my mind at rest.'

After everyone had laughed at this for a moment, the Count said, 'Certainly, it is no lie to say that you possess the grace of countenance that I mentioned, and I have no need of any other example to illustrate it, for undoubtedly we see your appearance to be very agreeable and pleasing to all, even if your features are not very delicate – though, then again, you manage to appear both manly and graceful. This is a quality found in many different kinds of face, and I would like our courtier to have that same aspect. I do not want him to appear soft and feminine, such as so many try to do, when they not only curl their hair and pluck their brows but also preen themselves like the most wanton and dissolute creatures imaginable. Indeed, they appear so effeminate and languid in the way they walk, or stand, or do anything at all, that their limbs look as if they were about to fall apart. They pronounce their words in such a drawling way that it seems as if they were about to expire upon the spot – and, the more they find themselves in the company of men of rank, the more they carry on in that reprehensible way. Since nature has not made them the ladies they seem to want to be, they should be treated not as honest women but as common whores and be driven out from all society of gentlemen, let alone the Courts of great lords.

'Then, as for the physical appearance of the courtier, I would say that all that is necessary is that he should be neither too small nor too big, since either of these two conditions causes a certain contemptuous wonder, and men built this way are stared at as if they were monstrosities. However, if one is forced to choose between the two evils, then it is better to be on the small size than unduly large – for men who are so huge are often found to be rather thick-headed and, moreover, are also unsuited for sport and other recreation, which I think a most important aspect of a courtier.

'So I wish our courtier to be well built, with strength, lightness and suppleness, and to be good at all the physical exercises suitable to a warrior. In this sense, I believe, his first duty is to know how to handle every kind of weapon, whether on foot or mounted, to understand all their finer points, and to be especially well informed about all those weapons commonly used among gentlemen. For apart from their use in war – when, perhaps, the finer points may be neglected – often differences arise between one gentleman and another and lead to duels. And in these cases, very often, the weapons used are those that come most easily to hand. So, for safety's sake, it is important to know about them – and I am not one of those who assert that all skill is forgotten in a fight, because anyone who loses his skill at such a time shows that he has allowed his fear to rob him of his courage and his wits.'

– Extract from *Il Libro del Cortegiano* (*The Book of the Courtier*), Baldassare Castiglione, 1528

PROLOGUE

I suppose I might have been a little hard on God. Purely in the heat of the moment and all that. I just hate not knowing things, of simply being told to run along and never *told*, and this was very much the big one. Something about just leaving us here, blundering around in the confusion and the dark, running off and just assuming that we'd work it out for ourselves, still sickens me. The fact that he'd been planning it for years – for centuries – doesn't excuse that. It just makes it worse.

Clarence as religious icon, in the end. Ha, ha, bloody ha. A particularly asinine joke that only God himself got. Well, now we know the power of the image, the punchline to the Shaggy God joke, and it quite simply wasn't worth the working out.

I think that in the end, though, he really was trying to look out for us, in his own mysterious way. They couldn't deny the transparently holy – the effect was too primal, working directly on the reptile brain. It hit those inbuilt, innate switches hard enough, and for just long enough, to break the spell for a while.

But I have the distinct feeling that what I assume to be the New Moral Army were new to their job and their new god. The grip wasn't tight enough, then, to stop us from getting out in the end – but it will be. Maybe tight and strong enough to pull us back, if it ever feels like it. I saw the change in James, the total subversion of identity and will. He lost everything that was himself in his faith, and gave that faith wholesale to Maa'lon. I don't think images of angels could have ever got through to him, could have ever shaken his resolve.

But perhaps the plans of God go deeper still. It would be nice to think that. I think that, in a certain sense, upon levels of which we can never be quite conscious, we *have* to think that. The legacy of the People is, after all, still hemmed in on Dellah. We don't know how many Believers they actually need to achieve an, as it were, critical Mass and achieve breakout, free themselves totally. Maybe they don't have enough.

In any case, I know that I've had enough. I've had enough of playing games and never being told the rules; I've had enough of worlds that die and leave you crawling, sobbing, in the wreckage. And I know what I must do. I'm going to take the Mary-Sue and walk away. I've had enough.

Rebecca is with me almost constantly now, taking care of me while I recover. It's a strange sort of comfort. She was unapologetic when she came back – as she shouldn't be after the way I treated her – but she was gentle and concerned. She was worried about me. She couldn't leave me in that state. She just wanted to help.

When she came back to me, it was like the other times. I'd long forgiven her for all the times she hurt me, the things she'd said and done that split us last time. I missed her so much that it was like a hook twisting in my heart – but I was terrified that I simply wouldn't feel the *love* again, as though a switch had been thrown, a connection broken, something in me dead beyond all resurrection.

And then she came to me and touched me and I fell in

love all over again. I love her. I love Rebecca. And this time I'm going to stay.

– Extract from the journal of Bernice Summerfield, recovered from the ruins of St Oscar's University, Dellah

CHAPTER 1

It's called the Ptolemaeus Staging Port, Puerto Luminae, Earth Station Prime, Heng O's Refuge, Lunaville, Colony One, and any number of colloquial or mistranslated names depending on your culture, language, species, temporal-dislocation factor or religion. The Luna port is one of the major crossover points of the galaxy and as such operates upon interstellar terms. It can call itself anything you like, down to and including an ordered sequence of pheromone markers that could be literally parsed as Place on Big Round Pumice Thing Go Round Origin Big Round Thing of Monkey Bald-thing People Humans.

It's also a kind of glorified orbital interface; it's the point from which the concerns of Earth extend their spheres and tentacles of influence out into the galaxy at large, from the multiplexes with entire worlds as their own personal manufacturing base, to the big commercial shipping lines, to the ratty little chancers who wander the more out-of-the-way places, picking up and moving anything they can get. All of these myriad concerns need people working for them, in one form or another, on a kind of sliding scale of cleanliness – and they're always hiring somewhere on that scale.

That was why I was here, quitc frankly. I needed a job, simple as that. And I wasn't feeling picky.

Let's be clear, here. Planetary cultures, colonies and empires, populated satellites and BDOs, conglomerations of free-space-living life forms around suns – places where there are basically stable populations, in short – can make and enforce their own laws. But in interstellar terms there is no such thing as an overall Authority. And there are no such things as criminals per se. There can't be. An incredibly dangerous and addictive drug to one species might be something that another merely sprinkles on its cereal in the morning. How do you enforce the anti-polygamy laws of your culture when there are species that need three, or four, or in some cases over a thousand, separate and distinct sexes to breed – or murder laws in the face of species that, as part of physically inbuilt cultural hospitality, expect a guest to kill and eat them in a variety of interesting, ritual, gustatory ways?

What there *is*, in the galaxy at large, is an almost infinite number of factions, of various sizes, each operating with its own agenda and to its own sense of morality. Occasionally these factions intersect and there is consensus – piracy against ships of several species will make you an Open Target, say – but there are far more cases where they don't. This was why I was able to swan into Luna, straight off the Wolfram Line, with a bag containing enough refined ginju leaf extract to hook, kook and kill every man, woman and child on Earth if it ever made its way down there, and nobody could touch me for it.

All the same, I didn't feel exactly good about it. Not about the package itself – I really did believe the incredibly sincere bonded seals that said it was destined, ultimately, for Dramos in the Horsehead, where the indigenous and non-human population use it for synthesizing complex antixeno-carcinogens. I didn't feel good because of what the job meant for me, personally.

It was the lowest form of courier work. You carried

something from one stop to another in return for the seat on the transport in which you carried it. It was one step up from sneaking out to the private launch sites, setting your suit comms to a begging frequency and trying to hitch a lift before the air ran out. I'd have preferred to do *that* rather than this, purely out of professional pride – but I didn't even have the small change necessary to rent one of the deathtrap vacuum suits used by people for doing it. I was that broke.

The reasons for my being that broke aren't important. Suffice it to say that I'd had to take the only professional job going to get me where I wanted to go, and try to live down the fact that it would appear on my CV for ever.

I handed in the package at the bonded drop point, chopped the hard copy, jostled my way through a bunch of losers who seemed even worse off than myself and headed down the ramps towards customs. The far wall had a mirrored finish – no doubt specced by some environmental designer with a nasty, knowing mind to show people just how far down they had come. I saw a ragged scarecrow in a stained jumpsuit and a bulky combat jacket, unshaven, makeshift dreads matted and choked with grease, a ratty holdall slung over the shoulder that contained all he currently owned in the world. I almost walked into the mirrored wall before I recognized him.

There are certain things you *don't* sell, no matter what. Wrapped around my left forearm was a small package of customized, electromagnetic artificial neurotechture upon which, even sold second-hand, I could have lived for a standard Earth year – but then how could I ever afford another one?

'Any joy with the Luna systems, Box?' I asked it.

'It's still locked off,' it said. 'Interlocking self-generated quasi-viral blocks. I'm working on them.' For some reason people tend to spend a lot of time and effort making the sound systems of their PDUs sound mechanical and tinny –

the gods alone know why. Maybe it's out of some sort of vestigial racial technophobia. I prefer to concentrate on upping the sensors and the referential response-bubbles – with the result that the thing's all but sentient with a capital S, and sounds more like a real person than I do myself, half the time.

'Keep working on it, Box,' I said. 'Crack 'em and find another way inside, even after they want to let me in.' I'd have automatic access to the Luna comms and data systems, streamed and transponded through Box via inductance, from the moment I cleared customs, but it always pays to keep in practice. Besides, the people I wanted to work for would never take me seriously if I didn't talk to them through a back door. They leave back doors open for just that reason, kind of like a preliminary test.

Customs resided through a kind of partition-baffled archway, over which was stencilled, YOU ARE ENTERING EARTHSEC™ JURISDICTION. WE CAN SEE YOU. HAVE A GOOD ONE. I felt my insides settle as I entered the gravmetic field that, for the duration of my stay in Earth-human-occupied spaces, would give me an apparent weight of Earth-normal. The offset impact-carbon planes of the baffle were built to slow down any sudden influx of people and force them into single file. I sauntered through.

EarthSec are the basic peacekeeping force on Luna so far as humanity's concerned. Ostensibly a private agency, they're funded by a consortium comprising almost all the big commercial guys, and as close to a police authority, in the planetside sense, as you can get. There's a hell of a lot of rivalry between them and the hypercity Adjudicators, naturally, but, since their remit and processes of operation are somewhat different, actual clashes are few and far between. A trooper covered me with a pulse pump while another ran his sensor rig over me – and promptly hauled his own weapon out as the rig had a small electronic fit.

'What the hell are these, guy?' He jerked his head to indicate the items that had appeared on the rig's big graphic display.

I shrugged, just like I couldn't feel the static in the bells of a couple of pulse pumps, which if discharged could burst my heart and turn my brains and other secondary organs to mush. 'Hand-pressurized needle gun, a plasmatic flenser, three or four knives, a concussion detonator and a bunch of neuruptor grenades, I think. I haven't checked lately. I'm a fully licensed security operative. Stratum Seven. Is it OK if I go for my ID?'

One of the troopers nodded almost imperceptibly. 'Slow. Do it slow. I can make you go bang-splat.'

'I'll do it slow,' I said.

A security operative covers a lot of ground and a multitude of sins – remember what I said about there being no such thing as the good guys and the bad guys in and of itself? Likewise, formal ID is almost purely relative in the interstellar sense. What good does it do you to be the greatest and best-respected particle physicist on Earth if you're suddenly stranded on a planet going through its early bronze age? What good does it do you to be the absolute ruler of an entire people, only to wake from some form of suspended animation or a malfunctioning sublight flight to find that every single one of 'em is long dead? You meet some skaghead mugger in an alley – does he care that you've got friends, somewhere nebulous, up in high places? In a very real sense, personal identity is dependent upon who you say you are, when you say it, and how much the people you say it to are willing to go along with it.

A Stratum Seven clearance is, however, an effectively other thing entirely. (There are no such things, incidentally, as Strata One through Six.) It's an indication of certain skills, certain contacts, a certain standing among the people who know about the classification in the first place. And, if they don't know about it, then, hey, you've still got the skills and, if you can find a way to contact them, the contacts.

Telegraphing no degree of threat is an art. To do it consciously, you have to make your entire body move, modulate your voice and even make yourself think things in a way that triggers absolutely no hint of a danger-signal response in others. This can be a tall order, when the simple act of handing over a credit chip in a crowded store can make it perfectly, unconsciously clear by way of body language how you'd like to horribly murder the cashier, the old lady blocking your way, the screaming kid by the jerky stand and everybody else in the immediate vicinity. I made my body do it right as I pulled my Stratum Seven card from my jacket. They're individually keyed to their owners' DNA and morphic pattern signature, locked into subroutines hardwired into the physical ROM of almost every major data system in the galaxy. The cards themselves are almost impossible to duplicate, replace or forge – the very ability to replace or forge them would mean that you're someone who would *have* one of them in any case.

What I'm trying to get across here is that a Stratum Seven clearance might not tell people that you're working for a specific world, or power, or organization – or even which side of any specific conflict you might be on – but in a very real sense it tells people who you *are*. And it confers certain privileges.

I handed the trooper my card. 'There you go.'

He ran it through the scan, nodded grudgingly, and gestured for his friend to lower his weapon. 'Incorporated or freelance?'

That sort of question is the equivalent of asking visiting royalty if there's really a chamber pot under the cushion on his throne. I let it pass. 'Freelance.'

The trooper snorted. 'Figures. We've had a whole pack of you types through here recently. OK, you can keep your stuff.

Just remember, discharge of powered or projectile weaponry inside the dome carries an automatic death penalty. I think I'd like to see that.'

'I'm sure you would,' I said, shouldering my bag. 'Have fun.'

I wandered through that public concourse Luna has, the one that's used in all the holo-sim productions with its distinctive, actual brass and pewter orrery, balls of metal ticking slowly round the inner roof on cams. In real life, even at a distance, you can see the dents and flakes, the imperfections inexpertly painted out.

From the extraterrestrials in the crowd I got the standard reactions to humans in public space. From the humans I got the sort of mix one gives to the kind of semiderelict I looked like: the occasional individual or family nearly losing their luggage in their hurry to get out of the way, the occasional guy doing that little open-handed shrug and mumbled 'sorry'. I think that if I'd been able to afford one of the hideously overpriced lattés from a kiosk, a couple of people would have absent-mindedly dropped some coins into the cup. Mostly I just got those little looks and shudders of low-grade revulsion that, cumulatively, grind your self and spirit down to the point where you really start to believe that all you are, or were, or can ever be is what they think they're seeing. I was getting heartily sick of it.

'Have you cracked the comms yet, Box?' I asked. I was almost prepared to give up and go through overt channels if it had said no.

'I'm in,' said Box. 'I'm running a trawl now. Any preferences?'

'Easy money, paid in advance. Run it through the default profile just to make sure it's not *too* easy. Watch out for trapdoor spiders in the mesh.'

'Gotcha.' There was an almost imperceptible pause, just

on the ragged edge of human reaction, and picked up by me only because of the slight biohancements basic to my line of work – slight because, in my line of work, anything overt can be a positive liability. Human beings move through a world designed precisely, and, by definition, to human dimensions and tolerances. Make yourself any bigger, stronger, faster and smarter than a human can possibly be and you turn yourself, by definition, into the kind of freak that human beings notice.

'I've got one,' said Box. 'High-level, open-ended and a retainer. They're offering an immediate consultancy fee. Want me to dump your CV?'

'Do it, Box' I said. 'Make the best deal you can.' If they weren't interested in talking to me purely from my specs, I'd lose nothing. If they were interested in talking then I'd have instant eating money and maybe enough for a change of clothes. I only hoped the job I'd just done hadn't knocked too many points off the abstract.

'OK,' Box said. 'I'll have to shut up for a minute, now. They're using one heavy mother of a negotiations package and it's like playing chess in nine dimensions.'

As Box fell silent, I headed in the direction of one of the fast-food stands, on the chance that Box would score, half-undecided between ersatz Venusian kinu-sai and the ubiquitously human King McOffal. Two days in economy-class transit, with nothing to consume but chemical-tasting water from a communal cooler and a half-inched fragment of someone else's packed lunch, had taken their toll. I needed something in my system fast, and the extruded, processed semi-predigested materials of fast food would do the job quickest. One of my most overt enhancements is just a minor jacking up of the basic human ability to extract some form of sustenance from anything you can force down your throat the best two times out of three.

On the way to the stands I took an active interest in the

people around me, the prospect of being solvent again now allowing me to view them with something more of a lofty superiority. A gaggle of vapid young girls in halters, blocky shoes and very little else, obviously local – the daughters of Luna service-industry workers but as yet too young to tend kiosks, mop floors or join the elite of hotel receptionists themselves – were hanging by the pillar that supported the orrery, boasting about their various boyfriends in piercing voices that seemed more directed to the world in general than to each other.

A Vononian with hir brood of ambulatory pupae still attached to hir by cartilaginous tubes ambled across my path on complex limbs that seemed more like naturally evolved caterpillar treads than anything else, the pupil of hir single eye revolving around the domelike membrane of hir head in a coincidental imitation of the orrery in the concourse.

A big, blond-haired, suited exec from one of the intercorporate multiplexes (I was unable to read his sigil, his back being towards me) stormed dynamically towards one of the departure gates, firing off instructions to the lithe young secretary walking beside him (I noted my flash of insight that *she* was actually in control of things, the guy being merely a drone, there to act as a target for any strong-arm stuff from a rival concern in whatever deal she was currently putting together).

Various other people stood around or passed by, none worth the bother of detailing. They were predominantly human, this being the human sector of the Luna station. I took them in and filed them away, basically keeping an eye out for any detail that seemed wrong.

'I've got a deal,' Box said abruptly.

'Is it a good deal?' I asked.

'It's a pretty good deal.'

'So go for it.'

Again there was a momentary pause. 'OK,' Box said. 'You're on the payroll for a consultation. The guys are logging you as active now.'

The blaster bolt shot through the space that had been occupied by my chest – professional doctrine: you go for the main mass of the body in the hope of at least hitting something, thereby disabling the target to be finished off at your leisure.

My chest wasn't there, of course. I've been around long enough to know full well the downside to instantaneous data transfer. I'd dropped like a brick and boosted myself back in a kind of supine slide with my heels – the move presenting the smallest possible target to the shooter, and being slightly less expected than dodging or diving to one side or another. The bolt flashed past me and I heard its discharge and a scream.

I felt rather than heard the impact of the second bolt, a tenth of a metre short of my boot. The shooter had had to consciously *think* about it rather than automatically track-and-pop, and had misjudged. That gave me the second in which – still on my back – to boost myself into a small forest of legs belonging to a now panicked and milling concourse crowd, adding to the confusion and tripping several of them up. I hoped for their sakes that the shooter wasn't sufficiently incompetent to try for a third shot.

He or she didn't. After a while I climbed to my feet and looked around. The first shot had hit one of the girls by the pillar. She was slumped against it, white-faced, clutching at her ruined arm while her friends snarled packlike at the complete strangers trying ineffectually to help. Off to one side of them, a wiry, middle-aged woman had dropped her travel cases and was heading purposely for the wounded girl – one of those off-duty nurses who seem to materialize instantly at the scene of any injury, but are in fact entirely likely, an off-duty nurse being almost certain to be among any largish, random cross section of people and their occupations.

The remainder of the crowd was still in shock, but in that dazed sense that crowds have when the danger seems to have come and passed quickly. I tried to look just like another of the sheepish people who had dropped to the floor or nipped behind a pillar the instant they had heard the shots.

Of the exec-type man and his pretty secretary, as I'd expected, there was no sign. They had long since faded out. I heard the screech-alerts and garbled bullhorns of EarthSec troopers as they finally arrived, and decided it was time for me to fade out, too.

ATTACHMENT (SUPPLEMENTARY):

[The following attachments might need a bit of explanation. Some time after the events I've detailed here, when the dust had settled and I was wrapping up the case, I backtracked through GalNet with the benefit of hindsight, access codes and a couple of names to find a number of coded textmail messages. While being relevant, they're not *important*, if you get my meaning, containing as they do information of which I wasn't aware at the time. Had I known it, it might have influenced and altered the entire course of my adventures – but I didn't, so it didn't, so there.

Each communiqué consisted of two separate mails sent to a command-keyed drop-box rented in the Luna Dome datacores – and the coding method is so laughably simple I'm not even going to dignify it with a decryption. I've included them purely in the interests of completeness. Feel free to skip. Nobody's holding a gun to your head and making you *read* the damn things.]

To: brown@135474.346.12.ccserv.dnet.com
From: pubterm@lunet.com
Organization: Archive News Services Bibliotheca
Subject: FYE

Dear Mr Brown

Here is the article as per your request.

----BEGIN----

POLICE TURN THIEVES IN NOVA KANTAR STREETS

Report by DataDay Frontier Correspondent Sela Dane, Nova Kantar, Proximan Chain Sector, G34

The common-knowledge suspicion that the greatest danger to the Law of troubled Nova Kantar comes from the policing services themselves was given new fuel today by the statements of the convicted urban bandit Qunto Milos. Speaking from his high-security cell, as he awaited sentence for fifteen unlawful killings and more than 125 separate counts of armed robbery, Milos painted a grim picture of an active involvement of the authorities in the activities of Nova Kantar's organized criminal gangs.

Milos described how officers of the Militia would routinely take bribes for allowing criminals to escape – even lending armed escort and air support from the scene of the crime. He fully expects, he says, to be killed for his disclosures 'Any day now'.

'Don't mind that, much,' he told me on my most recent visit. 'Blaster bolt in the head. Better than waitin' for the *grija*.'

The *grija* is the common method of penal execution on Nova Kantar. It involves an automated form of hanging, drawing and quartering, and has been described by galactic-rights observance agencies as 'an unusually cruel and barbaric practice'.

[click to download still]

'Before they kill me,' Milos continues, 'I want to make things right. Someone has to make things right.'

Milos intends to make further disclosures, involving the organized trafficking of ginju leaf throughout the Proximan Sector and the involvement of several interstellar-based criminal cartels. The Commander General of the Nova Kantar Militia of the Light of Judgement, Rano Karma, has said that he will visit Milos in his cell, to 'deal with the matter personally'.

Milos's claims will come as no surprise to the citizens of Nova Kantar – where the policing services have been long since seen to be inherently corrupt. Banditry, in the general sense, is acknowledged to be common throughout the society – three months ago, as a result of miscommunication, Militiamen broke a long-standing murder-for-hire ring, almost all of whom were Militiamen themselves, Milos's only crime, it seems, being that of going into business on his own.

– transcript of DataDay broadcast filtered for text transmission by Archive News Services Bibliotheca

----END----

To: brown@135474.346.12.ccserv.dnet.com
From: winwinwin@yourfriend.com
Organization: [type your organization here]
Subject: WINWIN WIN THE LOTTRY!!!!!!!!

WIN ONTHE LOTTRY WITH THESE NUMBERS!!!!!

SEND 10 CREDS AND WELL SHOW YOU HOW!!!!!!

7, 16, 6, 81, 5, 25, 2, 47, 98, 1, 5, 13, 11, 21, 4, 7, 11, 81, 4, 5, 7, 22, 15, 14, 1, 17, 44, 21, 1, 10, 14, 55, 19, 5, 1, 4, 98.

JUST SEND US 10 CREDS AND WIN WIN WIN THE LOTTRY!!!!!!!

[to remove your name from this mailing list, type 'remove' in the header line and hit 'send']

CHAPTER 2

My prospective employers, Box had told me, were a holding incorporation by the name of Pseudopod Enterprises SA. For 'holding incorporation', of course, read 'front' – but even then it's never quite as simple as that.

It's not like centuries ago, when you could more or less sit down and draw a line back from some 'legitimate' cement-and-haulage company that laundered money, via clearing houses, to the gambling, drugs and prostitution rackets of some single and identifiable family or gang. It's not even like the old-style corporations that had a finger in any number of predominantly 'legitimate' activities (there go the little quote marks yet again), but if you sniffed around them enough you'd find some fingers in things a little bit more rotten than pies.

We're living in an age of almost instant informational transfer, now – at least in the major population centres – and what used to be called criminality is spread, thinly and for the most part evenly, through absolutely everything. But, then again, you could say precisely the same thing about building shelters for the homeless, or food production, or Medicare, or funding new, innovative, creative artists in their culturally valuable but immediately noncommercial work.

That's not to say that there aren't individual businesses on the human scale of things, discrete projects, independent gangs of racketeers and so forth – merely that the *interest* in them is spread far and wide. If I were to ask Box for a complete and detailed rundown on the entity known as Pseudopod, I'd get a list of almost everything on the galactic stock exchanges, the only difference between Pseudopod and any other holding incorporation being in the fluctuations of the percentages it actually controlled. And this is why, naturally, these whole vast business-interest amalgams are known collectively as *multiplexes*.

On the other hand, Pseudopod was an entity in its own right, in the same way as a man is an individual, with his own particular likes and dislikes, wants and needs, with an ability to move through the world and affect it, and be affected by it, rather than a mere chaos of cells. This is why Pseudopod was, in the singular sense, an *incorporation*. And, as when dealing with a man, one doesn't focus too minutely upon the processes of the digestive system, or the specific functions of the pulmonary system: one deals with it or him as a whole and decides whether one likes it or him or not.

Thus it was that Box had taken all the tiny details of the Pseudopod operation and integrated them into a gestalt I could properly assimilate. Pseudopod was by no means saintly – decidedly iffy rather than otherwise – but was far from being actively evil. If Pseudopod were a man, it would pick your pockets with a cheerful grin, and fight when cornered, but would never knife you in the back and, if you were a friend, would never turn its back on you. In short, it seemed just that little bit untrustworthy enough to be trusted, and honest enough, ultimately, in an imperfect and dishonest world.

All the same, as I made my way to the Pseudopod SA Luna offices, I took precautions. A lot of it was just on general principle – but the attack in the concourse was still fresh on my mind. I had drawn out my consultancy fee in untraceable credit chips (poised for some further attack the instant the withdrawal registered on the Luna systems) and then headed for the hinterland subdomes, buying what I needed piecemeal in the stores that catered for travellers, following a completely random pattern that would, hopefully, by sheer force of attrition, lose anybody on my tail. In the holo-sims, the hero is somehow, magically, able to spot the people following him out of a crowd of thousands, many of whom just happen to be going the same way. In reality that just ain't so.

I'd fetched up, eventually, in one of those communal public rest-and-refresher rooms that tend to be used for assignatory rather than ablutionary purposes, checked via Box's sensors that the EarthSec securicams had been disabled by the more usual occupants, had shaken the travel dirt off in the ultrasonic shower, politely declined the advances of a middle-aged and vaguely timid intercorporate exec, stuck my head in a depilatory unit and changed into my new stuff – keeping the combat jacket, boots and holdall, which the ultrasonics had cleaned up enough to be vaguely presentable.

The rest rooms had had one of those little concealed cubicles that had once been used by EarthSec for the purposes of entrapment, until the high-profile series of lawsuits a few years ago stopped the practice. I'd picked the lock and chucked my bundle of old clothing inside. I'd no intention of ever going back for them, but it's useful to squirrel things away when you can, balancing it off against the risk of serious forensics being done on them, just in case.

Now I was making my way to Luna's intercorporate sector, working my way through the maintenance corridors and ducts that run through any large-scale installation in the way that the lymph runs concurrent and complementary to a body's bloodstream. The life-support systems were dormant here, and I couldn't turn them on without drawing attention to myself, but the vestigial air pressure was more than enough if I didn't overexert.

There were perfectly serviceable, pressurized access tubes that led directly to the Pseudopod offices – but, as I said, I wasn't taking any chances. The shooting in the concourse could be the result of any number of things, none of them exactly reassuring.

I ran through my impressions of the exec and secretary again – mnemonically – and tentatively revised my estimation of the guy slightly upward. They were a team, with the woman still in control, but the guy had been the actual shooter – I recalled catching the danger-pattern-recognition of the start of his smooth turn-and-draw, before I was too busy with immediate survival to catch much of anything else.

A team, then. A team working for whom? Some rival incorporation, who wanted anyone Pseudopod tried to hire eliminated from scratch? Prospective candidates for the job I was going for, deciding to do a bit of impromptu competition-cutting? A practical test by Pseudopod itself to see if I was up to the job, whatever the job in fact was? Any number of other reasons, down to and including the remote possibility that the guy's gun went off accidentally, and by an unlikely combination of events happened to go off twice, while by pure chance aimed at me, coincidentally at the precise time my name went into the system?

Sherlock Holmes said that once you eliminate the impossible, whatever remains, however improbable, must be the solution – but that's just so much bullshit. Any complicated, improbable, but not *impossible*, explanation you can think up for an angel appearing before you, for example, strumming a banjo and singing 'I've Got a Loverly Bunch of Coconuts', is just one of any number of other complicated and improbable but not impossible ways in which it could have been achieved.

Someone else, whose name I completely forget, once did that thing where you take the precise opposite of something else, turn it on its head, and come up with something that seems to make more sense – until you start to think about it. He said that to call something *impossible* is merely to say that there's something you don't know – and if you gloss over that inconvenient impossibility, rather than building insanely complicated theories to explain it, you come up with a solution that's far more simple, and thus more likely to be right.

Both of these approaches are OK for fiction, where the creator of it has some specific answer in mind, cuts the extraneous matter and makes damn sure that all the clues point to it. In real life, it doesn't work like that at all. In real life, your best bet is simply to run through all the options, factor them into everything you *do* know about the nature of the world and people in it, look for the things that strike you as somehow *right*, and just generally try to work out what the hell is going on. Calling the process fuzzy logic tends to formalize and demean it; the instinctive pulling of the right answer – whether its actually right or not – from chaos is the greatest, perhaps the only, real human strength.

That, when it came right down to it, was the problem I had with the shooting on the concourse. Given everything I knew about the world, none of the options I could think of seemed to fit. The execution of it had been sloppy in the extreme. Quite apart from the fact that it had failed, it had been done in public, in full view of the EarthSec securicams and any number of witnesses.

It had been the work of amateurs – and amateurs who thought nothing of firing into crowds of civilians – but what would those amateurs be doing hooked so tightly into the Luna systems that they could peg me as a target in the process? Maybe they weren't. Maybe one of the big boys was hooked in and passing them orders via comlink – but what would any of the big boys be doing, working with a couple of clowns like that?

The more I thought about it, the more I thought that the attack had been intended to fail – though what purpose that would serve, apart from instantly putting me on my guard, I had no idea. I simply didn't have the data, as yet, to draw any meaningful conclusions. I shoved it to the back of my mind to let the subconscious work on it – merely making a mental note to make the shooters suffer, as and when. There are some things you simply don't do. Letting off projectile weapons in a pressurized environment had been the least of it; these bastards had fired into the *crowd*, and hadn't cared who or what they might hit . . .

Going by the patched-together map that Box had integrated from freely available floor plans and extrapolative guesswork, I judged that we were coming up on the spaces owned by Pseudopod. I went through a hatch and headed up the tube to the main incorporate entrance.

Once through it, I breathed a little easier. The spaces owned by an incorporation are the modern-day equivalent of sacred ground, or the hospitality of a Bedouin. Whoever was trying to kill me, even if it was Pseudopod itself, couldn't touch me here without breaking the – not rules, as such, but the kind of intercorporate détente that allows the entire multiplexal system to operate. I couldn't think of anything heavy enough to risk an all-out intercorporate war by breaking those rules, and certainly nothing that might be connected with me.

Now, the way I've been talking about the multiplexes as entities in their own right is in a lot of ways specific only to me, and people like me, and our specific relationship to them. From it (if you're from one of the more out-of-the-way and backward parts of the galaxy) you might infer that the multiplexes are nothing more than insect hives writ large and abstract, the people in them mindlessly following some overriding process of ur-imperative like ants.

Nothing could be further from the truth. In another and slightly more objective sense, like planetary governments, interplanetary empires or any other economic system, the multiplexes are just extended mechanisms built for the sole support of their human parts – they're machines built for the purpose of allowing large numbers of people to live. Lose sight of that, as the various corporations, institutions and holding companies did back in the twentieth century, and you end up with the sort of lumbering, inhuman monstrosities that proved so spectacularly unsustainable in the end.

The intercorporate multiplexes do not operate upon the same level as the monolithic corporations of before the War. They work like intranets. However far they might extend, wherever any local office might be, no matter what the other local and galactic concerns with which they might coexist, an incorporation is as effectively self-contained, self-governing and insular as any Japanese *shoen*, or fifteenth-century Latinate city-state. They can be positively tribal, at times, and I, and people like me, are and always will be the Stranger at the Gate.

Of course, it's not thought of in those terms, any more than I think of myself as a *saburau* without a plot of land to till, or my business ethics as *Bushido*, but the overall dynamic is remarkably similar. The receptionist looked at me from behind her streamlined, power-sculpted desk as if I was tracking things into the Pseudopod incorporate front end off the soles of my boots. I get that a lot. I was reminded of the only slightly more overtly violent reaction of the EarthSec troopers.

'Let's try to keep things friendly, eh?' I said, simply to annoy her as she ran the name I was currently using. 'What do you do when you get off work?'

'Nothing with you.' Slim fingers moved with intricate grace over a compact data-entry pad that had about as much relation to a keyboard as a theremin does to a piano. 'Please wait one minute, sir.' Never mind cutting ice, you could have brought on an impromptu Ragnarok with the 'sir'.

A cubicle door slid back and a boy of about ten appeared, a little too puffed up and proud in his Pseudopod livery, which told me that he'd only just recently been given it. The incorporations find work for the children within them at all ages. This has any number of planetary-local child-protection agencies up in several varieties of arm, of course – and the multiplexes looking on those planetary-local agencies with blank contempt. How the hell, they say, do you expect children to learn anything other than prison manners, if you just lock them all up together for years on end, with someone shouting multiplication tables and things at them?

'Take the, uh, gentleman to Drop Nineteen,' the receptionist told the boy, managing to rhyme the 'gentleman' with 'scum'. The kid looked me over and then led me down a corridor to the tubes. The visible extensions of them were racked against one of the walls, one side going down, one side going up, each wide enough to accommodate three at a time, or five if they were feeling particularly friendly, each running down to a specific level of the Pseudopod complex. There were twenty of them in all, so Drop Nineteen was going to be either a short one or one of the longest. I didn't get my hopes up.

I stepped into the tube and dropped at something nearer to Luna gravity than that of simulated Earth, it being simpler to use a stock impeller-rig that, on Earth, would give the impression of floating gently down. Even so, the drop was a long one, I was building a fair bit of momentum, and nasty thoughts of sad and tragic 'accidents' were starting to occur before the cushioning field caught me. I stepped out into a shortish, blank-walled corridor with a double door at the end.

'Anything on the other side of those doors I should know about, Box?' I said.

'Just the usual power, servo, comms and air conditioning,' Box said. 'Nothing giving off a weaponry signature, nothing suspiciously unidentifiable. There's six biologicals with a whole bunch of passive implantation and some actives. Maybe seven biologicals – only one of them's moving around much, and it's hard to tell unless they move.'

Nothing out of the ordinary, and nothing particularly dangerous – and let me say right now that all the low-grade paranoia and suspicions I keep going on about are no more than the things that half-subconsciously cross my mind all the time; a constant evaluation and correlation of potential threat, a part and parcel of the work I do. I'll mention them from now on only if they are of actual importance – if I kept on going into the minor details of every little thing that flashes through my mind upon seeing a garbage canister and the possibly dangerous things it might contain, we're going to be here all night and no further on by the end of it.

All the same, I'm chary about going through strange doorways blind, and this was why, when I went through them, the first thing I did was shoot a glance around, behind and up – just in time to catch the flat and razor-sharp edge of a blade as it sliced down.

CHAPTER 3

It wasn't a blade, of course – as I realized in time to stop myself reacting, acting totally inappropriately and having a damn good crack at killing everybody in the room. It was an electrogravmetic privacy field, intended to block remote camera signals, clamp-mike pickups and any other well-known form of electrobased snooping. It demonstrates every property of a solid, apart from that of your not being able to stick your hand through it – effectively a dome of hard light unfurling through the walls around me, and what I'd mistaken, momentarily, for a blade was just its visible and mirror-bright quasi-surface coming down across the open doorway.

While one part of my brain had been assimilating, evaluating and rejecting thoughts of guillotine-instigated death from above, the other parts had been taking in the room in general: domelike, lit by tracking lights that tracked by some retinal-recognition system so that they never shone directly into the eyes, giving the light a shifting but diffuse and sourceless quality. The lighting diffusely and sourcelessly lit a slickly gleaming, genuinely antique inject-polypropylene boardroom table of generally horseshoe construction, the bitten-out bit facing me directly.

Around the table sat five heads of the Pseudopod corpus, in their sloppy sweats, doing their Stanislavsky and

Strasberg exercises and getting into character. The *real* heads of Pseudopod, the men and women in real control, were of course scattered around in offices and complexes throughout the Solar and other nearby systems. For reasons of security, however, and as a result of their personnel-intensive way of doing things, the multiplexes have hit upon an alternative to what would ordinarily be a conference call that, to outsiders, might seem somewhat unique and strange.

Leaving aside the meme-implants, the conditioning from birth and the systems of informational transfer and redundancy that make the process actually work, the incorporations basically employ a bunch of highly trained method actors at each major organizational node, each actor spending his or her life simulating the thoughts and reactions of his or her more genuine counterpart. The end effect is a kind of artificially created, policy-implementing group dynamic, more than up to dealing with the day-to-day running of local interests, wherever such local interests might be – and more suited for the local conditions by its very nature, since the people who comprise it actually live there. Those who've somehow still completely missed the point might think that this would free up the *real* heads to go around water-skiing, sunjammer racing, attending glittery society balls and the suchlike. In fact, it frees them up to run around dealing with the various crises and problems for which the system was never set up and with which it can't cope.

The sixth figure in the room told me that this, the job I was in line for, was one of those problems.

An enormously fat man – fat from growing up in free fall, where matters of weight are irrelevant and one ends up occupying one extreme of the endo/ectomorphic bell-curve scale.

On first sight, he seemed to have been covered in a custom-tailored, human-shaped and articulated cage of gold wire –

but this was merely a personal gravmetic unit that allowed his body to exist and function under Earthlike gravities. His bulk was such that it would injure badly at the slightest fall, and things would herniate and prolapse even if he just stood upright for too long.

The face had that dimpled, smoothed-out, ageless look common to faces with an affluence of subcutaneous fat, but the bone-structure character under it seemed strong and alert, indicating a capable and effective man with eyes that missed nothing, secure enough in his own abilities to relax into them, to suffer fools to a precise and particular point and then no more, like a steel trap buried in lard.

'Good evening,' he said, with a sardonic little smile that told me I could ultimately trust him rather less than I could sling a seventy-kilogram pig. 'I'm glad you could find us.'

'I just followed my nose,' I said. I have no idea why I said that.

I recognized the guy from the incorporate data that Box had streamed me after setting up the interview, plus a general following of the intercorporate news in which he was a player, having the sort of distinctive and charismatic persona that the news people seem to like. Formal naming in the multiplexal overstructure works on the name of original family line from which one derives, given name and modifiers, then the incorporate. Thus, this man was Michaels-Presteign Volan Tiberius of Pseudopod Enterprises Societé d'Anonime. Almost all of that's mere extraneous bollocks, of course – as I said, he's one of the movers, and out of the movers there's only one Volan.

I recalled the précis Box had presented me with: Volan was known for honouring the spirit of agreements rather than, unless in extreme circumstances, delving deep into the minutiae, which was a nice enough thing to know. (The last thing you want when, say, a courier job goes bad in the worst way is to know that your employer is going to walk away if you miss some arbitrary and completely unimportant deadline by so much as a minute. Some have and do, but not Volan.)

He was also known – so far as such things can ever be known – for never having messed up his hands with some of the dirtier aspects of the intercorporate cut and thrust: wetwork, extreme prejudice, scorched-earthing and the like. That was even better to know, in a world where you wouldn't believe how serious the 'hostile' in a hostile takeover can get.

If that makes him sound soft, then it couldn't be further from the truth. There was a touch of the old Medici Prince about him, and people lived or died by his command – the point was that they didn't live or die mindlessly, thoughtlessly or needlessly.

I know the outsiders to the world I inhabit can't see the subtleties, see us as glorified, dirty-working murderers and thugs, working for the highest bidder, switching masters at the drop of a payoff. If that were the case, we'd be no better than the scum we claim to be above – let alone the small fact that if that were the case then the entire system would fall spectacularly apart. The fact is, once we've licked the salt or kissed the ring or whatever, we give our word and loyalty completely for the duration of a job – and this cuts both ways. There is a code of conduct you follow if you want to call yourself a Stratum Seven. And there's a minimum standard of conduct if you want to *hire* a Stratum Seven, and Volan's specs told me he could clear that standard minimum from a standing start. He was, in short, a man to whom I could swear allegiance with a working minimum of honour.

Of course, the question now was whether I could clear his own standards.

Volan gestured, absently, taking in the assembled ersatz heads. 'I hope you don't mind an audience. They won't play any active part in this meeting, but I'd like them to be aware of what transpires.'

I shrugged. 'Anything you tell me they'll know about already. Anything I say is going to be what I want people to hear.'

Volan nodded. 'A commendably candid attitude.' He flowed gracefully under his own personal antigrav to the table and picked up a datapad, glanced at the screen and then looked back at me steadily. 'Under common intercorporate agreement I have to inform you that I am implanted with Grade III psychometric sensors that will monitor and log these proceedings. Do you consent to the use of such methods of personal verification?'

'I consent expressly,' I said, equally formally. Names, reputations, verifiable histories, self-identity, phenotypes and even basic cytoplasmic codecs being as mutable as they are, psychometric implants of this kind are an absolute necessity in these formal situations. They monitor several varieties of physical and mental response, not so much to catch lies, as such, or even to distinguish between lies and truth, but to determine whether or not the 'lies' were self-consistent enough to be solid. A nervous system jacked up to the point where one can pick a fly out of the air is a kind of fundamentally physical *lie*, for example – but it doesn't stop you from being able to pluck a fly out of the air.

Memories and entire personalities, likewise, can be changed with tech-med assistance. Even unassisted, the basic human cell-regeneration cycle means that human beings, effectively, are completely different people every seven standard years. All in all, what with one thing and another, you, me, us, them, anybody and everybody else could have been a completely different individual last year, last week – or even a couple of hours ago – and we'd never know the difference.

Personally, whatever other enhancements I might contemplate, I'd rather blow dead rodents than have the kind of brain change I'm talking about here – but what the hell.

I could have had a brain change to make me the sort of person, in the here and now, who thinks that.

Spin off down that ontological vector too far, of course, and you disappear up your own noumena – and good luck. The purpose of the psychometric implants was, quite simply, to check that I was who I said I was, in the instant that I said it, from which could be extrapolated a model of future probabilities based upon my characteristic gestalt. Volan merely nodded, gave the funny little multiple blink that switched his implants on and looked back at the datapad. 'Your CV says that you're a person of metatemporal displacement . . .'

'I prefer the term time traveller,' I said.

'Really?' Volan raised an eyebrow, a trifle sardonically. 'I was under the impression that you people considered that something of an insult. Far too many connotations with gibbering idiots in flappy scarves, elderly Victorian gentlemen in wire-frame spectacles, stovepipe hats, and so forth.'

'We're reclaiming it.' There are certain people who actively discriminate against those who originate from a time frame other than their own – for no better reason than those with prejudices against anything else. 'It's actually an advantage in my line of work, which is, after all, a basically nomadic way of life. It keeps you slightly out of place, wherever you happen to be.'

'Quite so,' said Volan. 'Pseudopod is, of course, an equal-opportunities employer. You won't find any of *that* peculiar brand of rudeness from my people, not if I have anything to do with it. I merely mention it because, in this particular instance, a knowledge of and experience with time travel might prove decidedly useful.'

There didn't seem to be anything to say to that, so I didn't. The main agenda of this meeting was to evaluate me as a person rather than to dwell on the specifics which, as I said, are ultimately unprovable for absolutely anybody. My responses, or lack of them, to any question, however inconsequential or irrelevant it might seem, were being weighed against some transputronic Ideal at which I could only guess – and all I could do or say was what I felt like at the time.

'You were born at the end of the twentieth century,' Volan continued, reading from the datapad, 'and subsequently disappeared from record at the age of fourteen. Nothing out of the ordinary in that, as so many records were lost in the twenty-first-century social and geopolitical Collapse. There are references to certain, shall we say, problems with the authorities of the time, but those were the times, and it's to your credit that you survived them. You reappeared approximately nine years ago, complete with Stratum Seven clearance, and with a subjective personal age of twenty-five. The activities involved in acquiring a Stratum Seven classification are a given, in general, of course – but is there anything you can tell me about those subjective missing years?'

'Any number of things,' I said, 'but anything you'd be interested in hearing about would be confidential matters. I can't even give you a hint.'

That was slightly untrue – at least about my method of time travelling being confidential. The fact of the matter, though, is that my own particular method was incredibly complicated and, unless explained properly, it tends to knock off credibility points. Here and now, it simply wasn't worth the bother.

'Quite so,' said Volan. 'I understand completely. I'd expect you to extend that same concern for privacy should you work for me.' Volan turned his attention to my public-access files. This is where the double-edged sword of confidentiality comes into play: the files relating to work and not bound by it have disclosure on everything, good or bad. I knew that I was cleaner in that respect than most but, believe me, there are more and worse things I'm ashamed of than taking on the odd low-rent courier-for-seating job. When you skim the highlights, plumb the depths and simply wrap up and discard the run-of-the-mill, I'm not sure how it makes me look myself, far less how it looks to anybody else.

'The business on Dramos,' Volan said. 'Quite impressive. I don't think I've ever met anyone who has literally been given the Keys to the Citadel before . . .'

'All it means is I can walk into the colonist-only recreation habitats if I feel like it,' I told him. 'With a couple of people spraying me with detergent all the time and hoping like hell I don't touch anything.' I shrugged. 'I just found myself up to my neck in one of those big political situations that had nothing to do with me, and I was trying to get out of it alive. It was pure luck that one of the people I ended up saving from the Soldiers of the Light was the half-niece of the Regent Elect.'

'All the same,' said Volan, 'it's nice to have the occasional friendly ear in a high place.' He skimmed onward: 'Mentioned in dispatches and decorated three times in the Hanoth/T'kuulk conflict – two on one side, one on the other . . .'

'Different jobs,' I told him. 'You know how it works.'

'Indeed I do. Recorded vote of thanks from the New Barquentine Provisional Governance – the fact that we none of us knew how *that* particular regime would turn out is neither here nor there, of course . . .'

I shrugged again. I tend to do that a lot. 'What are you going to do? Yesterday's underdog is at your throat tomorrow. That's one of the main reasons, quite frankly, why I don't do long-term contract work.'

Volan raised an eyebrow at me. 'Is that entirely the reason?' He chuckled a little sardonically. 'I myself have never given in to my urge to be a cat burglar – an abstinence that bolsters up my sense of moral worth no end.'

I took his point. 'I said it was one of the main reasons. I'm quite aware there's not much chance I have the mix for people actually offering the long-term work.'

'Don't sell yourself too short.' Volan scanned the pad again, his expression not changing in a way you could point out, but obviously having hit the bits that didn't show me up in what you might call the best possible light. 'Your unsatisfactory performances, in general, seem well within tolerable limits,' he begrudged, at last, 'but two things seem to stand out. Cantor Prime and Golgotha.'

'Cantor Prime was entirely my fault,' I said. 'I fucked up the job, simple as that, and, having fucked up so badly, I should have walked away. Instead, I tried to fix it and just made things worse – catastrophically worse. You and everybody else know how worse it got as well as I do.'

'And how do you feel about that?' Volan seemed sympathetic, for some reason, rather than anything else.

'How do you think I feel about it?' I said. 'I don't know how I feel about it. There's not a day goes by when I don't wonder how I feel about it, but I don't think I'll ever really know.'

This was drifting from the candid into dangerous self-pity, so I changed the subject, a little, to something where I felt, inside myself, to be on solid ground. 'Golgotha, I *won't* hold my hand up to. The basic facts are there, but they don't show my true relationship to them. The people involved set me up and lied when they sent me in, sent retrieval as an afterthought, and after five months in the Skull Maze I wasn't in any fit state to peg the good guys. A lot of the wrong people died. My mistake was in not recognizing my employers' basic incompetence until it was too late. If I had, I'd have done things differently from the start. As it was, I had to improvise with what I had.'

Volan nodded, more or less to himself, as though I had confirmed some inner suspicion – about the Golgotha incident or me, I couldn't say. 'Have you ever thought of, uh, taking up the issue *personally* with the people who sent you into Golgotha?'

'I want to eat at some point in the future,' I said. 'And I'm on enough better-dead lists as it is.'

'A perfectly understandable attitude.' Volan switched off the datapad with an air of finality, and looked me over. 'Yes,' he said. 'I think we can find a use for you in the current situation. Hook your mobile to our transputer base and our negotiators will take care of it.'

The receptionist's name, I learnt, dispensing with the Pseudopod peripheralia, was Liau Mei Chung – a little bit of a surprise for me, being still to a certain extent canalized by an early upbringing that expected an Occidental rather than an Oriental-sounding name.

I'd been perfectly aware of her interest under the hostility, but I was also slightly surprised by the sheer force and enthusiasm of it when it went overt. A few hours after my meeting with Volan, I asked her about it, what she had seen in me. I'd like to say that a significant part of asking wasn't to assure myself that the pickup hadn't been set up as part of some greater plan by Pseudopod or anybody else – the girl being used as the sweetener for a setup – but, what with my well-known, overly suspicious nature, I'd be lying if I tried.

'You walked in like an animal,' she said. 'Like a predator, a panther or something.' She brushed the skin of my arm with a finger, tracing the outline of one of the tattoos I was currently cultivating. 'All those muscles moving under the skin. I looked into your eyes and knew that you had hurt people and you didn't care. You kill people for money. Would you do that to me? If I talked about you, would you kill me?'

I said what she wanted to hear. 'Without a second thought, if it was necessary.' The fact of whether that was actually true or not is quite beside the point – she was obviously speaking to some image of me, who and what I was, inside her head.

After Liau Mei had drifted off to sleep, I extricated myself from the razor's-edge slice of the single bed I was occupying, pulled on my clothes and prowled around her apartment, predatory and panther-like.

Standard young-and-single habitation for the Pseudopod rank and file, decorated in that abstractly homey, modular, interchangeable way reminiscent of a hotel room in one sense, but which always reminds me vaguely of a waiting room – people waited in rooms like these for the Next Step in their lives, whatever that might turn out to be. While she was waiting, Liau Mei seemed to have a thing for ghastly little pewter-alloy unicorns inset with rhinestones, balanced on the outer edges of bookcase shelves.

As I'd expected, the bookshelves themselves were crammed with neatly ordered data-wafer packs, each purporting to tell, the majority in trilogy, some vast, true and magical saga of Outland adventure and romance. These True Life Stories can't even be dignified as fiction – historical records from the galactic Frontier (i.e. anywhere outside of the major population centres) are taken and put through the transputronic spaghetti machine to churn this drivel out, skeening out tales of supposedly real people, and actual events, but having about as much to do with the truth of matters as *The Adventures of Buffalo Bill* has to the man himself, or a Penny Dreadful has to the actual forensics and pathology behind the Grisly and Abominable Murders of Springheel'd Jack.

The good and sedentary people of the population centres, who wouldn't be seen dead catching the real news services and getting some real insight, eat it up. They follow the 'lives' of certain favourite, supposedly factually based characters and even, in some cases, attempt to send fan mail. I've even appeared in a couple of these things myself – or at least a number of stories have accreted around a name by which I once and briefly went, most of them with me as the villain, for some reason. One or two of them even have some minuscule relationship to one job or another with which I've been involved. I noted with a kind of guilty pride that Liau Mei had a copy of *The Matrox Conundrum*, which I sort of enjoy despite myself for its flat-out, barefaced, frankly unrepentant gall. I copied it into Box just for the hell of it.

I noticed, also, that Liau Mei had several paks dealing with the galactic sector I'd be heading into – nothing even remotely suspicious about that, of course, it being one of the favourite sectors for such things in the way that the Old West was a place to find a horse thief. I copied them into Box, too, on the you-never-know principle.

Across the chamber, Liau Mei stirred on the bed and muttered something. She didn't have to be up early and neither did I, but the unspoken, tacit agreement in this deep and meaningful relationship was that she'd wake to find me gone, vanished like some puff of romantically cruel and dangerous smoke.

All the same, I didn't want to sample the dregs of Luna night life, and wandering the tubes until the breakfast bars opened appealed even less. I sat at Liau Mei's rather prim little kitchen counter, poured myself a cup of caffeine-laden cinnamon and hooked Box into the Luna systems. I still had a few things to set up, and put in motion, for my journey into the Dellah sector.

SUPPLEMENTARY INSERT:

. . . a red light was blinking on the dash. It didn't matter what McCrae did now, the car was almost out of power and running on reserve cells. And the sleek black limousine of El Diablo still followed inexorably.

They were nearing the edge of the New Chicago city centre now. If McCrae left it too late, he would find himself involved in a firefight in some residential area, rather than a zone of shopping precincts shut down for the night. Innocent people would die.

'Ah well,' Flint McCrae growled to himself, taking the data wafer containing the Matrox Formula from the shotgun seat where he had tossed it and slipping it in a pocket of his Hunt & Sons dinner jacket. 'Here goes nothing.' He slowed the car, locked the auto-guidance system, shot the doors and jumped. He hit the ground rolling and bounced alert and lithe to the balls of his feet. The Sikorsky V9 Triple-Turbo Hovjet carried on under its own momentum for some hundred metres before slowing, turning and parking itself with neat and automatic precision by the side of the road.

The limousine of El Diablo squealed to a sudden and gear-stripping stop. A black door slithered back and a figure lumbered out. Even in the dim light of street lamps, it seemed too bulky, its movements too lurching to be a normal human being. Flint McCrae pulled out his Spanda

PPX with integral sighting and bonded-rubber grip, optional fastload key-release and digital alarm clock, and shot it, twice.

The Teflon-coated, .38, full-metal-jacket slugs bounced off it with a clang. The figure closed in fast. It was a cyborg, an obscene technological hybrid of steel and flesh. It reached for McCrae with fingers like snipping pincers, the LEDs behind the membranes of its eyes flashing balefully. It seemed that the saga of Flint McCrae had at long last met its end!

Or possibly not – for Flint McCrae, in addition to his expertise in skydiving, cordon-bleu cookery and advanced sexual technique, was a Master of the Technological Arts, a four-year college course which, such was his genius, he had completed on a two-week vacation some years before. He knew everything there was to know about these abominable creatures – and he knew their weak spot. His hand whipped out like lightning and pressed a certain spot in the cyborg's chest with fingers of steel. A small hatch sprang back in the mechanical monster's chest to reveal its wires and glowing transistors. As the cyborg lurched back in alarm, McCrae brought up his Spanda and plugged it squarely in the chest.

The cyborg screamed, and plucked at the sparking, gaping wound, and then exploded in a shower of burning steel and meat.

'I'll take my order from the barbecue well done and with a side salad and a bit of coleslaw,' quipped McCrae grimly.

El Diablo's limousine was circling in for the kill. McCrae knew that the lives of every man, woman and child in New Chicago – maybe even the lives of every galaxy in outer space – depended upon his keeping the Matrox data wafer safe. So he reluctantly held back from dealing out the fiendish El Diablo the justice he so richly deserved. He saw the lights of a metro station nearby – and headed for it, the tensile thews of his thighs pumping like steel pistons.

* * *

In the sybaritic luxury of his limousine, El Diablo toyed with his silver-handled cane as he watched McCrae's dramatic escape. The silver top was fashioned in the form of a naked woman, complete in all anatomical details, and could be unscrewed to reveal the blade of a sword – as many an unwary adversary and several luckless henchmen who had failed him had learnt to their cost.

'Amazing!' exclaimed the other figure in the car. 'This Flint McCrae seems truly unstoppable. What can drive a man like that?'

'Strange impulses that we can hardly even imagine,' said El Diablo. 'A love of truth and justice, friendship and the light of happiness in a small child's eyes. What can it be like to experience such strange feelings, do you think?'

'I doubt if we will ever know.' The other gave a sudden, vicious grin. 'Do you want me to go after him?'

El Diablo thought for a moment. 'Yes, Moloch,' he said at last. 'Bring me back the Matrox formula, and bring me back his head.'

The metro station was deserted. McCrae's footsteps rattled off the white-tiled walls. It would be some minutes before a transit capsule arrived, and so he repaired to the rest rooms to change his face. A master of disguise, he emerged looking completely different from the man known by men and loved by women the universe over as Flint McCrae.

A capsule arrived with a hiss of compressed air. He entered it, noting that it, too, was empty. Just as the doors slid shut, however, a dark figure flung himself at them and levered his way through.

The man was thin and dressed in black, studded leather, grubby with wear and stained with old, dried blood that he had not bothered to remove. His ragged, jet-black hair was slick with grease. His skin was the unnatural white-face pallor of a vat-grown clone, his eyes encircled by pure black. He leered at McCrae – and McCrae's steel-trap mind recognized him. His name was Moloch, a vicious and sadistic killer, who hired himself out to the highest bidder, currently working in Diablo's bloody trade as his right-hand man.

Moloch was well known for preferring the blade, or scratching with his blackened nails, to each of which he'd added some subtly different poison. It was a measure of his fear for a man like Flint McCrae that he had decided to use his gun – a little Matsui Flintlock IV that would have ordinarily have been found somewhere in the bottom of a woman's handbag.

'Time to die now, Mr Hero Man,' he sneered snidely, bringing up his little gun.

The shot was aimed at McCrae's heart – but Flint McCrae wasn't there any more. Even so, even with the lightning reflexes of his dive for the cover of a row of seats, the ceramic slug from the Matsui Flintlock IV slammed into his shoulder. McCrae mastered the searing agony without even so much as a grunt.

Seeing that he had merely wounded his opponent, Moloch jumped behind one of the Plexiglas partitions flanking the doors of the tube, and began firing blindly. As slugs ricocheted off the walls, McCrae knew that one must surely hit him, by pure luck, in the very near future.

The slug was lodged under his collarbone and the wound, though not enough to incapacitate a man like McCrae, was bleeding profusely. With a flash of inspiration, McCrae squeezed the wound, hard, collecting a quantity of blood in his hand. He waited until Moloch fired yet again, and threw the blood in the air with a cry of pain. He then lay still and silent, as though in death.

After a while, gun still at the ready, Moloch approached. He aimed a heavy kick at the supine form of McCrae and, when there was no response, put his gun away with an odious and satisfied grin.

'And for my next trick . . .' quipped McCrae, and shot him in the mouth.

– Excerpt from *The Matrox Conundrum*,
a True Adventure of the New Frontier

[And this is me again.

I was just going to insert this and let it speak for itself, but I can't. I mean, big fat hairy total bollocks or what? Guess which one's supposed to be me. Go on. Have a guess. And the fact that, to the best of my knowledge, I've never been shot in the mouth by way of a gun that does not in fact exist, has never existed and never will, is the least of my problems with the bloody thing.

I mean, Flint McCrae? Give me a fucking break. The guy that this particular instance was based on wasn't Flint McAnything. What he was was a complete and utter tosser. And say hello while we're about it to the only evil cyborg killing machine ever built with a sodding great key sticking out of its back. And just where that little filler scene came from about not getting truth and justice and little fluffy kittens I have no idea.

Anyhow. Interests of verisimilitude. What really happened was this:

It was one of those little bits of commercial by-play that seem amusing on the surface, until you realize that people are really being taken out and shot for it, like the Third World cola wars of the twentieth century, or certain dealings between the pair of jumped-up burger bars. I was working for El Diablo's, a fast-food division of the Matrox Incorporation, tailing some low-rent little chancer who was trying to extort money from them by contaminating the Special Secret Sauce in selected hot-dog restaurants with industrial bleach. The idea's to put the frighteners on him a little and make him stop, on account of how El Diablo's can live without the unfavourable publicity.

I go through hoops trying to get this tosser to notice me – and, when he finally does, he flips out, loses control of his autohov and smacks into a bollard. He then staggers into the metro tube, in the middle of the rush hour, with me hot on his heels. He never even made the capsule.

Now, maybe he's not feeling himself after just front-ending his car, but I think it was just because he was a tosser. When he sees me coming after him, he pulls out this fuckoff-huge handgun and just starts blasting away. Three people die, eventually, and several more are wounded before I close the gap and disarm him. He gets away for the simple reason that I spend the next ten minutes holding on to the carotid artery of some kid until the paramedics arrive.

The guy's still wanted in New Chicago on three counts of murder, various malicious woundings, and another couple of murders that came to light when the cops went back and looked through his life. I took the opportunity, however, when I disarmed him, to slap a little tracer unit on him. The cops are never gonna find him.

It's on such incidents that the New Frontier Adventures like the continuing saga of Dick McPillock and the like are based. I include it, here, just so's you realize precisely how far they can be trusted.]

CHAPTER 4

There's a common misconception that interstellar travel over serious distances takes an extreme degree of effort, peril and time. This is because for the most part, even now, people still have an image in their heads of humongous colony ships rumbling ponderously through space at something like a mile a minute – something that the cruise-liner operators (cruise liners being the only direct experience people for the most part have with space) go out of their way to propagate. Even now, the vast majority of any planetary population have never thought, and will never so much as even think, of leaving the system of their birth. It takes a planet-cracking global catastrophe to get 'em to migrate, and, even then, most of the buggers dig their heels in and refuse to go. However skin-of-the-teeth precarious they might know the universe to be in the ultimate sense, they seem to think of their own personal environments as, somehow, inviolate and absolutely solid.

In reality, of course, you can cross from one side of the galaxy to the other – from one galaxy to another relatively easily – in terms of the physical processes. The basic limiting factor is the sheer cash overhead of processing power capable of calculating the vectors to the correct decimal point, the transputer banks that, essentially, make sure that you're pointing the ship in the right direction. This is why so many man-hours and resources are sunk into data analysis and the transfer of information rather than the more crudely physical sciences. The important things to deal with, now, are knowing where the hell you are, and what you can actually do when you get there. As things stand at the moment, translation across half a galactic spiral arm is practicable. Translations of a higher order are still the domain of neurophysicists with grants and transputer blocks the size of three largish moons.

Time travel as such, on any noticeable scale, is of course, for any number of reasons, still *verboten*. We can talk about just why that is, and my own small relation to that, sometime later.

The upshot is that interstellar travel is about as arduous and difficult as the intercontinental travel I knew about when I was a kid. Intercontinental travel in the planetary sense, for that matter, operates on about the same level – and therein lies the rub. It's the farting around at either end that does the damage and, in the end, it's a matter of making connections. The sixteen hours on the Luna–Proxima Line – that being the major jump en route to Dellah and the surrounding systems – were going to be the easy part. It was after it that things were going to get more hairy than somewhat.

Now I was on expenses – and expenses paid up front – I didn't have to bother with steerage. I spent my first five hours on the Line stuffing myself with complimentary delicacies delivered by the live and humanoid attendants (their revived use in recent years, as opposed to clunky and incredibly stupid-looking Dumb Waiter™ automata, being one of the small joys of intercorporate involvement in day-to-day life) and hit the bar quite hard. It was quite probably going to be my last chance for a while. The rest of the time I spent napping in my seat and reviewing the background specs and support files supplied by Volan:

Four months before, the planet Dellah had undergone a global revolution and shut itself off from the galaxy at large. The knock-on effect of this had been one of destabilizing the balance of power for systems all around – all those threads of interest suddenly cut loose, and whipsawing, and looking for something to which they could attach. Such situations have a habit of spinning catastrophically out of control as the various local and galactic factions fight over a new and different pie. Diplomatic and commercial relations were strained to breaking point, and there were even the first rumblings of incipient territorial war.

And this was where I came in. I was going in, quite simply, as a representative of Pseudopod SA to look after their interests in this new situation, to salvage what I could from the wreckage. When it came right down to it, my job was to find out what the hell was happening, what I could do about it and then *do* it – and, if that all seems incredibly ambiguous and vague, well, hey, if the job could have been summed up easily then Volan would have sent in one of his spanky-suited incorporate drones. That autonomous and open-ended flexibility of action, the ability to take the hits and kick against the pricks, to improvise on the fly towards some greater end, was precisely what I was being paid for.

Hard facts upon the Dellahan situation were sketchy at best. Certain revelations that would later change things far more seriously in the wider sense would not come for months if not years. What scraps of information we had suggested that, while the violence on Dellah had been directed against off-worlders in general, its primary target had been the campus of the University of St Oscar's, an autonomous and interstellar-based concern operating under fief from the Sultan of Tash-wari, a relatively minor province. Whereas other off-worlders had been, shall we say, encouraged to leave, the university had been actively targeted and destroyed.

Quite what a locally well-known but galactically minor seat of learning had done to earn such animosity I had no idea. The place had seemed to have concentrated upon the arts and the softer sciences – and, if that had been a cover for harder research by somebody or other, weapons R&D, say, then I couldn't find so much as a sniff of it. As I skimmed through the faces, names and personal histories, however, one name seemed to ring a couple of bells. There's no way I can say, precisely, what made me skim it, go back and skim it again and then start digging further. It just seemed that this individual was somehow important.

One Bernice Surprise Summerfield, ostensibly a Professor of Archaeology and with enough expertise and practical experience in the field to make no difference if the ink was dry or not on the credentials. In the few years she had been there, she seemed to have been involved with far too many incidents of a certain kind, had a suspiciously large number of a certain sort of acquaintances – and there were strong indications that she had been working for several heavy factions as a double agent. Whether any of these factions had been using her for their own ends, or whether she had been quite knowingly playing them off against each other, remained to be seen.

There was no recorded trace of her life before she arrived at St Oscar's one term, seemingly out of midair – until you took the time lock off your spiders and let them scuttle around on a word search. Then the names leapt out at you – a tracery of references and connections, running back and forth through the last five hundred years of galactic history, from the starting point of some forgotten little planetary backwater taken out and sterilized in the last big War.

As I've mentioned interminably, time travel, though entirely possible, is so relatively uncommon an experience among humans to be the Least Likely Scenario. Far more people did it the hard way via cryogenics and stasis, even accounting for the vast majority of them who didn't survive. People can just have had similar names, or family lines with traditions and so forth that give the surface impression of a single, similar person appearing in different decades, centuries or entire eras. The basic pattern of this four-dimensional tracery, however, was distinctive. Our Bernice had done the real thing, and done it so extensively that it was a wonder she wasn't a walking wormhole. And anybody wondering if this might involve sucking someone into a completely new dimension will, at this point, be shot.

Take it from those who know. For most of us time travel is an accident, a one-way trip with no hope of ever getting back. Bernice Summerfield, on the other hand, seemed to be one of the more spectacular exceptions – but none of the harder records showed her as older than her current biological age. That could mean any number of things, from the possibility that she had now lost the means to the immediately bloody obvious. Whatever the reasons, here and now, Bernice Summerfield seemed to hold the keys I needed. She had been involved in the Dellah situation up to her neck.

From the stills provided it seemed like a very nice-looking neck. I rather hoped I wouldn't end up having to snap it.

An hour out from the Proximan terminal, I encrypted up my notes and shoved the datapack into the package of various other items I'd prepared. I was going to have to lose these items, for a while, for what was coming next.

Of the items left, only two held any kind of immediate interest. The first was a copy of Summerfield's book – an actual *book*, facsimiled up to look like genuine paper and card, which seemed vaguely appropriate for a text attending to the arcane art of Archaeology. I set that aside for later. The sheer alliteration of it all was getting on my nerves quite apart from anything else.

The other item (three discrete objects, but you know what I mean) were the three data-wafer fictions I'd copied in Liau Mei's apartment – proper commercial copies I'd picked up at the Luna Terminal, for the same reason I had picked up all the other untraceable and completely unsuspicious stuff for the trip.

Summerfield, it seemed, was something of a minor star in these tales of outworld life. Each of the copies I currently had seemed to be by a different hand, none of them exactly literate, and they couldn't seem to make up their minds whether they were adventure stories, murder-mystery stories or some half-baked bastard hybrid of the two.

It was an odds-on certainty they'd contain nothing of actual use, about either Summerfield or Dellah – but what the hell! I was in the mood for some brain candy, and I might just hit upon that thousand-to-one chance and glean something useful. I settled back, skimmed the wafers, and the time flew by like a great auk.

SUPPLEMENTARY INSERT:

In an alcove of the Starfire Lounge, Bernice Summerfield nursed her Maldovian boilermaker and scowled as, from the room beyond, there came the sound of shrieking laughter like a red-hot poker being forcibly inserted into a macaw. She was increasingly aware of the weight of the throwing knives, stitched into their graphite-lubricated sheathes in the reinforced armour of her leather combat jacket.

'Parasites,' she spat. She felt a steadily increasing itch to pull out the knives and throw them. Cruise liners were almost exclusively the domain of the rich and well bred, and, in the week she had been aboard the *Titanian Queen*, she had come to know and loathe every one of the other passengers.

'Chinless fucking wonders, Berni.' Across the table, her sidekick and sometime lover, Jason Kane, tried to comfort her by going against his easy-going nature and falling in with her mood. He was a big and heavily muscled lunkhead with a heart of gold and a straight-arm punch that had once stopped a charging Varjaxian rhino. His essentially simple cheerfulness won out and he grinned at her.

Bernice found herself smiling back despite herself. Jason was like a clumsy puppy sometimes, and would follow her loyally into the jaws of death – that was one of the reasons why she liked him.

She tossed back her drink. 'I'm going to get another one. You coming?'

The walls of the Starfire Lounge crawled with gilt and velvet plush in a particularly bilious shade of maroon. The red shag carpet was so thick that Summerfield fancied, if she listened hard enough, that she would hear the distant clanging of bells from the minarets of miniature cities lost in it. Reddish filters over the lights gave the impression that those upon whom the illumination fell had been recently filleted.

At the bar, Summerfield set down her glass and glowered at the barman while she waited to be served. Kane took the opportunity to look around himself with interest – it was seldom that he moved in such circles, and this was something of a new experience.

Off to one side the slumped and slightly ragged form of Mr Roger Awlson, the well-known holomovie method actor and dipsomaniac of no small renown, was regaling the world in general with the apparent events of one evening in October, when he was far from sober, and dragging home a load with manly pride. Some short while after, his feet began to falter, it seemed, and he had lain down in the gutter and a pig had come and parked down by his side.

Beyond him, a Ms Lobelia Romp-Specimen, the Dravish medicated goitre heiress, stood resplendent in a glazed bread mask (which she raised and lowered by way of a miniature silver hoist) and tucked into a plate of slightly lethal-looking canapés, while proffering the occasional *bon mot* to her tuxedoed paramour, Mr Rupert Glome-Rotring. (At one point, before Berni had put him right, Jason had been under the impression that a *bon mot* was a variety of boiled sweet.)

To one side of this pair, the Viscount Jeremy Tarquin Temporal-Lobe was dancing on the little space of floor set aside for that occasion, stripped to the waist and in the company of several like-minded friends, with the occasional happy whoop and with a faintly nascent air of body oil.

Beyond them, at a candlelit table – in the company of a gigolo who had quite obviously fallen upon hard times, had taken the job out of desperation and who was now counting the hours of the days till he was paid off – the large and jewel-bedecked Dowager Duchess of Ghent dropped the glass from which she had been drinking a light Sauterne and clutched a trembling hand at her throat.

The Dowager Duchess coughed, explosively. She retched. And then, with a muffled hissing of the discharge from some fiendish contrivance of a canister, she began to inflate.

Perhaps as a result of his slightly simple-minded nature, Jason's physical reactions were second to none. Without pause for thought he grabbed Bernice Summerfield and, despite her protests that she was in the process of trying to buy a packet of nuts, hauled her under the nearest table.

The now distended Dowager Duchess exploded with a bang – leaving no trace but for the epidermal, visceral and digestive matter spattered around the Starfire Lounge and its occupants. Several slightly scorched lace veils, which the Duchess had affected in her manner of dress, fluttered gently to the floor like dying bats.

After a time, or possibly two times, Bernice Summerfield and Jason Kane crawled out from under the table. Summerfield looked down, and up, and indeed around at the mortal remains of the Duchess, and at the patrons of the Starfire Lounge so understandably shocked and disconcerted by the mode of her departure from this life.

'Possibly some sort of meso-electromagnetic element in the drink,' she mused. 'It disrupted the cumulative internal cellular pressure – and whammo! I think we should go and have a –'

Jason never learnt what Bernice thought they should go and have, because at that moment the door flew open, and through it burst a bald and portly figure of medium height, with a waxed and twirled moustache and his mouth wrapped around a Churchwarden (which was, as Bernice Summerfield explained to Jason Kane, a kind of pipe). This slightly unprepossessing figure was, they later learnt, no less than M. Emil Dupont, renowned the galaxy over as the greatest detective on Nova Belgique!

'There has been a murder here!' cried M. Dupont. 'Murder most foul! The Dowager Duchess of Ghent lies dead, in a rather unconscionably wide blast area, and someone in this very room is responsible!' The Great Detective strode into the room. 'As we are, at this moment, outside the jurisdiction of any reputable judiciary service, I myself will undertake to investigate.'

Bernice scowled, and then shrugged to herself. 'Suit yourself.'

It was slightly later. The Starfire Lounge had been cleared by burly ship's stewards, and Dupont and the suspects had retired to the cabin suite of the late Dowager Duchess, there to further the investigation under Dupont's watchful eye. The suspects included: Roger Awlson, Lobelia Romp-Specimen, Rupert Glome-Rotring, the Viscount Jeremy Tarquin Temporal-Lobe, Ron the gigolo, Bernice Summerfield and Jason Kane.

'Why us?' Bernice said indignantly.

'Was it not just this lunchtime that you became rather more inebriated than is seemly, and declared to all and sundry that you'd see the lot of us dead and screaming in hell if you could get away with it?' enquired Lobelia Romp-Specimen, with happy malice.

'She has a point, you know,' said Jason.

'Shut up, Jason,' said Bernice,

'All right, I will,' said Jason.

Bernice turned away from him, and amused herself by rifling surreptitiously through the late Dowager's movables and drawers, while Emile Dupont elicited information from the other suspects.

'I loved her like a mother.' Lobelia Romp-Specimen ratcheted up her mask and dabbed at her kohl-rimmed eyes with a dainty handkerchief. 'She was like a mother to me, always at hand with advice upon comportment and other subjects of a particular nature. Even the time when, on a whim, she brutally dismembered my pet hamster, Crippin, with a bone saw and served him up in a short-crust pie didn't matter, because I really, really . . .'

The young Viscount, on the other hand, seemed unflustered and perfectly calm under Dupont's probing interrogations. 'I barely knew the woman,' he drawled. 'We moved within completely different social circles. What reason could I possibly have for . . .?'

Bernice Summerfield, meanwhile, had unearthed a large and leather-bound dossier from within the late Dowager's steam trunk. She examined the contents, snorted with barely restrained laughter, and passed it on to Jason.

Jason scanned a page, and then stared at the Viscount Jeremy Tarquin Temporal-Lobe, his simple soul shocked to the foundation by what he had seen within.

'Is that really possible?' he said. 'With the gene-spliced heifers, the electrodes and the pair of Wellington boots? Can you really *do* something like that?'

The interrogations wore on. It transpired that Rupert Glome-Rotring was also mentioned in the shameful dossier – in, as it were, the appendix. When the full and detailed circumstances had been revealed, Lobelia Romp-Specimen had clapped a hand to her mouth and run from the suite, to return, some moments later, looking slightly pale and wan and covered in breadcrumbs from where her hand had broken through her mask.

Roger Awlson, who was in such a state of alcoholic stupor that it was doubtful he was aware of the very nature of these proceedings, then treated everybody to a song, detailing how he had once had occasion to discover that his new bride was a multiple amputee, to the old music-hall tune of 'Side by Side'.

Ron the gigolo then revealed that he had, in fact, been plotting to murder the Dowager Duchess all along, but that her murder had taken place before he had been able to put his own plans into effect.

All through this, there was something nagging at the back of Bernice Summerfield's mind. It was something to do with the actual sequence of the murder, though for the life of her she could not quite pin it down . . .

'*Alors*!' Dupont exclaimed at last, mopping his face with a handy croissant from the Dowager's untouched breakfast tray. 'After such a cavalcade of infamy, I must admit that I am not closer to a solution than before. I am – how do you say it? – at least two stumps short of the wicket!'

He turned his attention to Bernice Summerfield. 'And you, madam, what do you have to say upon this whole unfortunate occurrence?'

Bernice frowned. 'It's Miss, actually. Well I do have something to say, as it happens – but you're not going to like it.'

'Ah yes?' said Dupont. 'And what would that be, exactly?'

'I think I know who the murderer is,' said Bernice.

This elicited a positive gasp of surprise from all who were gathered here – save for Jason, who had become bored and was staring happily at the pattern on the cabin's wallpaper.

'And how might this be, Miss Summerfield?' said Dupont.

'It's simple, really.' Bernice climbed to her feet and wandered about the cabin, counting points off on her fingers. 'I think we can all agree that the unfortunate Dowager exploded. I think we can agree that she exploded with a very loud bang. The thing is, if you didn't see her doing it, you wouldn't know it was a person exploding. We're on a ship and it could have been anything. An airlock blowing out, a meteor strike, the air conditioning backfiring – it could have been anything.

'Furthermore, after she died, the Dowager Duchess was hardly in a fit state to be recognized by anybody. There might be teeth and bits of finger scattered around for a post-mortem identification, but –'

'I think I've got her glass eye somewhere,' said the young Viscount helpfully, rooting around in his trouser pocket.

'Spare me.' Bernice Summerfield walked over to where the shameful dossier had been left on an occasional table, and looked down at it thoughtfully. 'Moreover, it seems that every single one of us had some motive or other for murdering the Duchess – but doesn't it strike you as slightly odd that we were gathered together before this common factor came to light? And will you please stop picking at that wallpaper, Jason!'

'Sorry.' Jason sat on his hands with a slightly shamefaced expression.

'As I was saying,' said Bernice Summerfield. 'There is one person in this cabin who not only knew that a murder had occurred, but knew precisely who the victim was – and was not at the scene of the crime, in the Starfire Lounge, at the time.'

'I admit it,' Emile Dupont cried, falling on the carpeted cabin deck before the startled suspects. 'I admit it all. I would also like four hundred and seventy-three counts of a similar nature to be taken into consideration, including several incidents of matricide, fratricide, regicide and seven counts of cattle rustling, which involved the wrapping of gene-spliced heifers in brown-paper bags – for export to those who deal in depraved practices concerning them, electrodes and a pair of Wellington boots.

'I have roamed this sector of the galaxy for years, slaughtering wherever I go as the whim takes me, and then passing it off upon some innocent bystander who just happened to have a motive for the act. My greatest triumph was in decimating the population of an entire Proximan colony and laying the blame upon an itinerant traveller in medicated goitres. His own medicated goitres, you understand . . .

'But now,' he continued, an evil cunning forming in his features as he leapt to his feet, 'you shall never take the greatest mass murderer in all of Nova Belgique alive!'

With that, Dupont bounded for the door. The various suspects tried to stop him, but he had taken the liberty of purloining the body oil belonging to the young Viscount, and slipped through their grasp. Enraged now, beyond belief, the suspects stormed out of the cabin suite in hot pursuit.

'I suppose we'd better go after them,' said Bernice.

'What?' said Jason. 'Oh. OK. Where are we going?'

They found the suspects in a gangway, crowded about one of the emergency airlocks of the ship. Emil Dupont was within, having attempted to hide here and being brought up by the exterior hatch.

'All right,' he said through the speaker unit that relayed his voice from within. 'I've changed my mind. You can take me alive.'

'I don't think so,' said Bernice, grimly. 'Do you want to do the honours, Jason?'

'Sure.' Jason hit the airlock controls. There was the sound of bolts and outer hatch retracting, an outgush of air and a brief but fading scream.

'Scratch one problem,' Bernice said. She and Jason turned their backs on the various suspects and headed back to the Starfire Lounge for a drink. Hopefully, by this time, it would have been cleaned up.

It had. But that was only the start of the adventures of Bernice and Jason aboard the *Titanian Queen* . . .

– Excerpt from *Ship of Death*,
a True Adventure of the New Frontier

CHAPTER 5

The ship was called the *Star of Afrique* – though, if it had ever *been* a star, it was one well past its days as a matinée idol and with a career quite frankly down the toilet. A raddled old trading scow, barely held together by caulking, welded patchwork and, quite probably, spit and string. A six-man crew, not one of whom I'd trust to stay awake four hours out of five, let alone to do their jobs. Without usable ID, however, it was the only way I was going to get off Proxima IV and to where I was eventually going.

You'd have to look closely at the engine pods, and know what to be looking for, to see that they were rather more powerful than you'd expect – and powerful in a certain, highly specialized way. The docking clamps were likewise modified, servo-adjustable to any number of configurations as opposed to any standard gauge. I'd booked passage on the *Star of Afrique* after leaving the Line by the simple expedient of waving a big wad of cash at the captain, pulling off enough chips for a down payment and stuffing the rest back in my pockets.

Believe me, if you think you can act, you should try acting clever enough to have a lot of money in the first place, and then stupid enough to do something as inexpressibly asinine as *that* in the same breath. I even submitted to a pat-down showing I had no weapons of any kind, just so they could be sure that they could trust me on the trip.

The passenger compartment (SSPASC-spec mandatory for any ship, for, quote, the succour of those bona fide travellers in distress, unquote) had been converted into storage. I laid the dubiously stained sheets of acceleration foam I had been reluctantly given over a line of packing crates of foodstuffs and spread out, breathing deeply despite the standard shipboard odour of stale sweat, oils and urea that seemed even worse than usual, space smugglers and pirates not exactly being noted for their sartorial demeanour or scrubbing behind the ears – or, indeed, anywhere else. The jolt of liftoff as we crash-accelerated to escape velocity jammed me down into the foam, and I felt every vertebra as it skinned against the splintery fibreboard of the crates underneath.

The ship was too small to pack gravmetics, but the acceleration laid in after leaving the gravity well was enough to give some semblance of weight. I lay back and moved my limbs into the posture of sleep, gazing absently at the dalon-mesh securing lines that dangled, swaying slightly, above me, working my muscles and joints through warm-up routines that, to the untrained observer, would seem all but motionless, and from which I could instantly return to complete relaxation.

It was almost exactly an hour and twenty minutes outside Proximan jurisdiction that they came for me: two crewmen, skinny-framed as one has to be for sustained work in cramped and weightless spaces, but with muscles like slightly undersized rugby balls, and the captain himself – doubtless making sure he was going to get his preliminary cut. In any number of senses. They had something like seven knives and a couple of grappling hooks between them, stuck in various places, and there was I, poor little me, completely and utterly alone and unarmed.

The crewmen hauled me off the foam and I looked up, pale and shivering and broadcasting fear on every wavelength. 'You can't do this!' I quavered, in the same kind of cracking easy-prey voice I'd used when dealing with the captain, back on Proxima, but racked up a couple of notches. 'We had a deal . . .'

'Well, now, then,' the captain said, giving me a friendly wink, putting his face very close and menacing to mine. 'The deal has sort of changed, you see.'

'Fair enough,' I said, shrugging an arm out of the grip of one of the guys who were holding me and jamming a splayed set of fingers into the captain's eyes, up to the knuckles. Scratch one problem.

Two problems left, so I dealt with one by wrapping a securing strap around his neck and using his own acceleration-assisted weight to strangle him, and the other by smacking his head a couple of times into a capped and truncated conduit pipe sticking out from the balk. Scratch problems two and three – and if you're after excitingly dynamic descriptions of Whipcord Reactions of Death, gory depictions of people hanging by their faces off a pipe and suchlike, then you can ask someone else. Go and get one of those True Adventure data wafers or something.

Likewise, there was none of this stalking-in-the-dark bullshit about dealing with the rest of the crew. I just hauled up to them under free fall and put them down, a job made so much easier by the weapons I'd liberated from the captain and his pair of friends. I left the guy on the bridge until last, just to make sure that the automatics were sufficient for a single pilot – I knew that this class of ship was rated for that, but I didn't want to find too late that it somehow wasn't.

I left the automatics ticking over, dragged the bodies to the airlock and crash-dumped them, just as they had intended to do to me. The difference between the principles of piracy and privateering might be a narrow one, but it's good enough for me, and I certainly wasn't going to lose any sleep over *these* little innocents.

I then went through the ship and stripped it of every armament – hand-held weapons for the most part, hull-mounted laser blasters, torpedo racks and the like being the province of military ships, which operate more or less like thruster-powered chess pieces in the Game of War. The practicalities of piracy are more concerned with worming up to some unsuspecting prey, clamping on, cutting through, and going in like a squad of combat troops in a planetside guerrilla war.

The various hand blasters, tasers, concussion caps and even a genuine, antique cutlass went the same way as the late crew. I likewise scoured the ship from top to bottom for contraband – this took slightly longer as I wanted to be at least as scrupulous in looking for hidden compartments and the like as a customs official who hasn't had his bribe. Bye-bye, eventually, up to a couple of million shillings' worth of chemicals, potables and perishables, depending on the state of the market for each of them at the time.

Back on the bridge, I looked over the boards again. The bolt-on modifications, again in keeping with the basic function of the ship, were concerned with real-time manoeuvring. The navigation banks had your standard astronomical destinations, preprogrammed and updated on a second-to-second basis on the GalNet subetheric. The only anomalies were a couple of unnamed extra destinations, which I assumed to be the equivalents of Barbary Reef bolt holes, and which I dutifully deleted. I left the ship's transponder codes as they were – the late pirates would have made damn sure that they were clean enough not to arouse suspicion, and they had obviously been a small-time, independent operation. Nobody was going to be actively looking for those codes.

The *Star of Afrique* was now as clean as I could make it without going outside and physically scrubbing off the name, so I turned my attention to where I should be taking it. The decision seemed to have been made for me in this. The Dellah system had been declared a no-go area by Earth Force, the stellar tracking access taken off line.

Now, a planetsider might think it strange that a ship capable of flipping between star systems might be stymied by that, but in a baby-flip-capable heap like that *Star* it was the equivalent of driving an auto and finding that the bridge over the ravine ahead of you is out. It comes down to a simple choice between turning back and trying some other day, or finding somewhere to pull over, leaving the car and looking for some alternate mode of transportation.

The best bet for that latter seemed to be the planet Thanaxos – one of those neighbouring systems I talked about earlier. It had an Earthlike atmosphere and a basically humanoid population – their distinction, to outsiders, being their slate-grey skin and a crest, a bit like a bony Cornish pasty, on the front of their heads. It had a relatively high if newly evolved level of technology and – best of all – some nascent acquaintance with such local intercorporate interests as remained with the disruption of them upon Dellah. It wasn't civilization by any stretch of the imagination, but it would do. I'd fit right in.

I barrelled into Thanaxon airspace on manual, refusing to answer increasingly vociferous ID queries and putting mayday signals out on all channels. I hit the atmosphere rather harder than automatics would have allowed, shearing off a couple of the nonessential superstructures, confusing the heat- and pattern-recognition sensors of any GTA defences that might be pointed at me and, coincidentally, burning off the distinctive markings of the ship's last paint job. I grounded some way out on the spaceport landing field, well away from any official-looking and restricted area, sat tight and watched with interest as a couple of disaster-control trucks headed for me, slackening their pace as they realized that my landing had been under control and there was no immediate danger.

As the fire appliances slackened off they were overtaken by a medium-sized troop carrier, a brightly coloured lump of prismatic-fractured steel and Teflon that sped ahead on cantilevered treads. This was, quite obviously, going to be my welcoming committee, and the last thing on their minds was camouflage. I slid out from the pilot's cradle, shot the hatch and strolled down the gangway, just in time to see the transport pull up and several figures pile out. Armed Thanaxon troopers with their pale, matt, slightly marbled faces, their uniforms reminiscent of functionally evolved, nineteenth-century Hussars, though without the silly hats. I kept my hands where they could see them as they covered me with weapons of some local design, but obviously based upon the galactically common blaster-bolt principle.

A rather snotty-looking adjutant with a little clipboard came forward and demanded to know what I was doing, violating the airspace and soil of Thanaxos without permit. I spun him a story of how I was a humble trader, set upon by privateers, but who had managed to escape after they had taken my cargo. He then asked to see some form of identification. I told him I didn't have any identification. I might have got a bit irate about it. I may or may not, in fact, have spoken my precise mind as to the treatment I, a civilized man, was getting at the hands of some crappy little excuse for a backwater planet and its obviously stupid and incompetent officials, in the most insulting way as was possible . . .

In any case, by dint of my well-known, innately polite, commodious and easygoing nature, I managed to turn what could have been a perfectly ordinary encounter – and one that might have given me some basic if restricted access to the facilities of Thanaxos – into an interpersonal disaster. If

I'd been a diplomat it would have been a Diplomatic Incident. They impounded my ship, strip-searched me on the spot, declared me an undesirable alien and dragged me off to the detention camps pending a hearing that, I gathered, would be several years in coming, if at all. They weren't particularly vicious about it, but they weren't that gentle either.

As a trooper slapped the manacles on me, and another one gave me a kick for good luck, I succeeded in holding back a smile. Everything, so far, was going precisely according to plan.

BACKGROUND INSERT (PERSONAL FILE):

Scenes from an Ordinary Childhood I

After three hours of waiting, watching through brittle, grey and nicotine-encrusted net curtains, the signal finally came. Leaning on the broken iron stump that was all that remained of a lamppost, on the corner of a street dripping spraybomb and crawling with tangles of razor wire, Joey lit a cigarette. Joey was a heavy smoker, when he had a stash, and he all but ate the thing.

I splayed my hands, first one and then the other, until the tendons cracked, shoving out the tension-cramp of waiting, and glanced back into the room at Annie, who was sitting on the bed with her knees rucked up and cradling a sick-looking nine-month-old child – not hers, though Annie being sixteen, a year older than I was, it wouldn't have been unremarkable if it were. The girl from whom we'd borrowed it was, in fact, a couple of months younger than myself.

The way we lived, in those years after the Collapse, women tended to have babies as soon as it was physically possible. From the lofty heights of a historical perspective, people can talk about a reassignment of biological imperatives in response to environment – but that's just a poncy way of stating the completely bloody obvious. We lived from day to day, and we never knew if we were going to see another one. You had kids early if at all.

With her halfway freeish hand, Annie was flipping absently through a book – a yellowed but pristine copy of *Now We Are Six*, one of a small pile she had taken from a bookshelf in the corner. The room itself had obviously, once, been the domain of a child much older than the one she held, preserved after it had gone like a kind of shrine.

'Things are moving,' I said. 'Are we ready to go?'

Annie nodded and climbed off the bed, holding the child to her in the firm but careful way of one who knows the thing won't break, but has been given it in trust. Keeping her shadow off the window, she backed to the door and slipped out through it. I turned my attention back to the street outside. A squad of dogboys were coming up it, taking advantage of available cover, their combat shielding activated and their smart systems tracking like nobody's business. Fat lot of good it would do them, on account of how military-based technology tends to operate on a kind of constantly elevating, narrow bandwidth. The sensors hooked into these guys' heads were useful only for picking out the energy signals of weapons on the same comparative level as their own – and in that sense the dogboys had the only game in town. My antique Armalite with solid optic sighting slid right under it.

Two years before, the dogboys had been soldiers in the proper sense of the word – soldiers of the Emergency Military Government that had taken control of Britain, as a whole, in a last-ditch attempt to hold things together. Now they were cut from the main body of the corps and just another faction, just another set of people trying to take control of and hold a blockaded city in a country – in a world – piling like a ton of bricks over the lip of the catastrophe curve and with the infrastructure quite frankly fucked. The names aren't important now. There are hyper-cities floating over it all now, and nobody remembers the name 'Birmingham' as anything other than a historical footnote. The important fact was that the dogboys were the faction with the heaviest firepower, and that meant that all the other factions, however they might squabble among themselves, had to be against the dogboys to survive.

The window was open a bare crack. I loosed a round to get my bearings, leaning into the recoil as I'd learnt, compensated, fired again, tracked and fired and fired again.

I snapped a conscious look at the scene below, as opposed to mere instinctive track-and-pop. Two for four. The first target was already on the ground and bleeding, a round having gone straight through a power mesh designed to counter state-of-the-art energy bolts as if it wasn't there. The second was still in the process of spinning – caught in that instant of my attention as if by time-lapse photography. One round had mostly taken his arm off at the shoulder, the other entering at a downward angle, just left of the sternum, to blow his renal system out of his back.

Good enough. Moving slowly and easily – a sudden movement, even at this distance, would have acted like an electromagnet for the eye – I pulled the business end of the Armalite back and sank back from the sill. Sweat was pouring off me now, and the rifle nearly slipped out of my hands. Out of the line of sight from the street below, I could move faster: a knee-skinning scrabble across the floor, up and out of the door, down a bare and shabby staircase (noting, in passing, the change in tone from the pristine, maintained neatness of the dead child's room) and taking the Armalite apart as I went, tossing the lumps of scratched and slotted metal to Mico, who was waiting in the hall with Annie and the baby. They shared that cramped space with the iron-and-enamel bulk of a baby's pram that was older than all of us combined. The pieces of rifle slotted easily into holes cut in the expanded polystyrene foam that lined its bottom.

At this point, of course, Joey would be outside, spread-eagled on the street while a slightly depleted squad of dogboys gave him the once over. Joey, at least, would be completely and utterly clean.

'Everything OK?' I asked Mico, jerking a thumb towards the interior door behind which were the actual occupants of the house, an elderly couple called the Theads, I think it was.

Mico nodded. 'Tight. I tied them and belted the old guy a couple of times to give him an alibi. They'll come out of it OK. No problems.'

I didn't bother or need to check that things were just as Mico said. There were people who'd have used a knife (bullets being slightly hard to come by, dontchaknow) out of cold witness-losing ideas of professionalism, but in fact because they got off on it. I mean, how the hell can you be a professional insurgent? This was why, even then, I worked freelance, never allying myself to one particular movement or another – and I worked only with people I could personally trust. Mico and Annie were two of the few, and for certain other reasons than professionalism.

Annie finished piling blankets and suchlike on an Armalite-and-baby club sandwich and gave it a peck on the forehead. 'Are we ready?'

'As we'll ever be.' I gave her and then Mico a rather more extensive kiss than she'd given the baby. It might have been the last chance we'd ever get. You gots the stuff, you puts it where it do most good. 'Let's go.'

Mico and I headed back through the house while Annie went out through the front door. In the period of confusion after the shooting, if they didn't simply fire on her for being a moving target, Annie had a better-than-average chance of sliding past the dogboys before they got themselves together enough for a house-to-house. As for Mico and me, we went out through a back garden long gone to seed, hopped over an ancient fence and wandered up the alley backing on to the terraced rows, talking vaguely about the strange shots we'd heard, beer and its current woeful unavailability and wondering how we were going to get the smell of creosote off our hands.

I lit another roll-up and coughed as the recycled draw from old charring, saltpetre and any other amount of contaminated crap hit my lungs. I could just about remember the time when cigarettes came in the precisely packed cartons, their straight clean lines like little dreams of the perfectly evolved good-stuff dispenser. Of course, when cigarettes looked like that, and not like something left behind by a miniature dog with a training problem, I'd been too young to even think about smoking. And doesn't that just sum the bloody world up?

'Forget it,' I said, 'it's just not possible.'

'What about that guy with the lawn-mower engine and the home-made microlight?' Joey said. 'He got over.'

'What about the twenty other people who tried to copy the idea?' I asked him. 'They went down in flames.'

'You're just frightened.'

'Too bloody true,' I said, looking out at the expanse of rubble and wire, the vague shapes of armour and artillery moving at a crawl in the middle distance. 'Last of the great yellow hunters, me. Note how I never set up a hit until I'm damn sure I can get away from it with my skin and the sweet-young-girl laugh intact.'

'Right,' said Mico, who when you came right down to it was as complete an utter coward as I.

'We missed a couple of easy targets doing that,' said Joey, thoughtfully.

'We'd miss a fuck of a sight more if we went in without taking care and got our heads blown off. Or worse. Shit.' The scavengings-and-bible-paper fag had fallen apart on me. 'Anybody got any more?'

'Here.' Annie tossed her stash over. It was almost fresh and almost full since she tended to use it for currency rather than consumption.

I took a carefully measured pinch. 'You want some of the booze?'

'Sure,' she said, a bit flatly, and I handed her the quarter-bottle of black-market-liberated NAAFI Scotch I'd acquired in return for a couple of favours, none of them worth bringing up here and now.

Annie sipped a minute quantity. There had been something odd about her voice, and it was a moment before I got it. You have to understand, in the world in which we'd found ourselves, that simple pleasures like alcohol and tobacco, things you could buy elsewhere without thinking about it, had become as precious as gold and jewels and suchlike. It was like in prison – and while we can get our heads around the idea of an entire city, an entire world being a prison now, in those days the condition was relatively new. You don't go throwing such stuff around – somebody gives you a snout and they damn well expect to be paid. I had done that automatically with Annie – and realized only belatedly that she had offered me her stash as a genuine gift of friendship, and had been hurt a little by my instant offer to pay. I felt embarrassed, and tried to think of something to say that wouldn't call attention to it and make things worse.

I turned my attention out on to the wastelands again. You don't need a wall to block off a city, in the end: you just need the will. And minefields and 105-millimetre seven-pounder cluster-frags, of course.

We did this every now and then, Mico, me and Annie and Joey when he was alive, hanging just back from the very edge where the forces outside would take a pop at us from general principles, taking in the perimeter of the blockade as you would take in the view of a mountain or a chasm. It was like a geographical feature, a piece of the world as it was, and one of these days we'd find a way across.

'There's worse things than having our heads blown off,' I said. 'We could be taken in alive.'

'Not me,' said Mico. 'I'd kill myself first.'

'Doesn't work like that,' said Joey cheerfully. 'They hamstring you first chance they get. I suppose you could do it with a suicide pill or something . . .'

'Where the fuck would we get something like a suicide pill from?' I snapped. Changing the subject back had brought it around to the one that distressed me most, on some deep level, for reasons I could not quite name. In the months the EMG had held the entire country as a single and coherent power, they had concentrated their Psychological Warfare, Biochemical and other Research and Development divisions here. Indeed, that had been a major factor in isolating the city when things fell apart – the process had begun already to turn it into a prison of a different kind, a testing zone for new processes.

The R&D people were still holed up here, in the building that had once been the Festival Hall, and took care of anyone captured alive by the dogboys. That was why the dogboys didn't automatically shoot to kill. It wasn't as if there were desperate and heart-rending screams coming from the place night and day or anything – the acoustics of the building had been modified to produce an almost perfect soundproofing. That was part of its special terror. There's something simply terrifying and wrong about a building, obviously occupied and full of activity, that seems to broadcast silence.

It was a pretty safe bet that those taken in were interrogated and used as test subjects of some kind – though what kind of tests precisely nobody would ever know. People went in, people never, ever came out.

'Look over there,' said Joey, breaking into my mood. 'Someone's trying his luck.'

Way off to one side, a figure was making its tentative way across the wasteland. At this distance it was too far to see if it was a man or a woman. You couldn't catch any clue as to his or her state of mind, either – all you could do was think of how you'd feel if it were you.

'Ten'll get you seven it's the mines,' said Mico.

'I call the snipers,' said Joey.

'I'm not playing,' said Annie. 'It's sick and I'm not playing.'

That left me with the shells, so I didn't say a thing. We watched the figure for the sake of something to watch. After a while there was a detonation and a distant squealing. Depending on how much of the lower body had gone, it could be any time before he or she actually died.

'It's almost always the mines,' said Mico. 'That's why I always pick 'em.'

'That's why you always nip in quick with them,' said Joey.

One of these days we'd crack it. One of these days we'd get out. And one of these days pigs would be taking airfare.

CHAPTER 6

The trouble with writing a subjective account is that it's a constant balancing act between recalling what I knew at the time, and the true facts of matters as they eventually came to light – indeed, have in a large part become, if not common knowledge, then at least incorporated into the mythos of our common interstellar world. I've mentioned a few famous people – Figures of Historical Importance, even – and you, reading this, are no doubt wondering whether anybody could possibly be so dense as not to have noticed it at the time. The point is, as I say, I'm talking about what I or anybody else knew of them at the time.

Likewise, you have to dance a line between simple exposition and the overexplication of every single thought, impulse and self-contradictory motive that goes through the head with even the simplest of acts. The reasonably attentive reader might, for example, be wondering why I had chosen to begin my mission on an entirely different planet and in a manner that seems so superficially *dumb* in almost every respect. The reasonably attentive reader has a point. Why go to all that trouble just to end up being dragged off in manacles?

Well, the first reason was, as I've said, that Thanaxos was relatively advanced in the sense that it had connections to the galactic networks. The lines of communication were basic, but they were there. This was something of a blessing and a curse – at least it was a factor that I had to take into account. Anything I did on Thanaxos overtly was going to be known, the instant I did it, by anyone who had an interest. The tortuous route I'd taken, the scrupulous cleaning of identifiability, was an attempt to slide out from under that for a while, in the hope that it worked well enough for long enough.

The second reason was far more concrete. Bernice Summerfield seemed to be the best lead I had; I wanted to talk to her; and the last recorded thing that anyone had seen of her was in escaping Dellah. The vast majority of those escaping had hit Thanaxos as their first port of call, had been treated as stateless refugees and promptly placed in mass detention. Subsequent official records of them were buried.

I had no idea, at this point, whether Summerfield was alive or dead, but this was the best place to pick up the trail. My major intention, in arriving upon Thanaxos in the way I did, was to put myself on to the precise same track and see where it led. It had to be finely judged – I had to come over as some easily disposable off-world annoyance, but not such an annoyance or active threat that I'd be liquidated on the spot. And, if I say so myself, I made a damned good job of it.

The reason I've gone into the whys and wherefores of my plans, here, in all their exhaustive and tedious detail, is that said plans went tits up in remarkably short order. It was my fault entirely. If there's a flaw in my otherwise perfect, rounded and almost entirely laudatory nature, it's a touch of that special breed of arrogance that what you might call a galactic sophisticate has for planetary cultures in general. You might have noticed. The sort of thing where one confuses the tourist quarter of a city for the city itself, or will blithely walk out into a planet's polar regions in sun hat and shorts on the basis that said planet is famous for its tropical beaches. Or you might wander through sacred burial grounds, secure in the knowledge that the local religion is extremely silly and couldn't really be taken seriously by anyone. The sort of thing, in short, that in other times and climes had the Little White Rajahs thinking of the Sepoys as nothing more than wilful children, and certainly incapable of posing any kind of serious problem to – quote – civilized men.

Everybody's got a tang of this to some extent, and the nasty thing about it is that it creeps up on you unawares. In my case, in my first dealings with Thanaxos, I made an error in my thinking so fundamental that I didn't see it until it was too late – and it damn near gave me my comeuppance.

The off-worlder detention complex didn't have a name as such – you need at least two of something before it needs a name. The various boroughs and townships and hamlets of Thanaxos dealt with criminals in their own ways, and the majority of those ways, not to put too fine a point upon it, tended to make places for long-term incarceration unnecessary. The off-worlder complex had been built, on the one hand, to avoid the stellar-level censure that would result from the full-scale execution of undesirable transients and, on the other, to prevent said transients infecting the local population with their undesirable foreign ways. It consisted of a floating platform, held up by huge and impermeable tungsten-shell pontoons full of helium, tethered to what had once been a petrochem rig, a hundred miles offshore of the land mass that accommodated the Thanaxon global capital.

Look at it on the map and you'd think – as I subconsciously had, looking at it on the *Star of Afrique*'s datapack schematics – that getting off the thing and back to dry land would be a doddle. Look down at the cold and raging sea below, and you realized the truth of the matter, the fact that the only way in or out for anything was by airlift. The choppers came once a local week (six Earth days, more or less) to drop off new detainees, take rather fewer of the old ones away, to dump a load of foodstuffs and other consumables and to top up the helium. The second week, I hung off an aluminium honeycomb girder and watched them do it, by way of a kind of narrow-gauge and flexibly segmented metal pipe, manoeuvred by an arrangement of rods and wires that made it look like a puppet elephant's trunk on a string. Good for a laugh, if you were that way inclined, but way out of reach for any thoughts of grabbing it and hanging off it for an informal trip back to shore.

The week before, I'd assured myself that there was no hope of getting close to the chopper when it actually landed to exchange detainees. Those going in were blindfolded, booted out of a hatch while still four metres in the air and hustled off the landing pad before they quite knew what was happening. The chopper then put down and those going the other way – those who survived – were taken to it under guard and under watchful weapons-tracking systems.

There was only one way on to the pad, a gantry twenty metres straight, and anyone who tried to cross it without matching the record-stills of that week's discharged prisoners precisely, or even went near it save at that one time a week, would be shot on sight. A list of those to be discharged for their hearings was posted in the complex every week by the Guard Service – and, if you happened to miss your particular week, well tough luck. You were stuck here for good.

In the years since Thanaxos had opened up to galactic trade, the detention complex had evolved into a kind of self-enclosed community in its own right – a violent and incredibly dangerous community given the nature of most of those who were dumped here in the first place. People don't realize quite how easy it is to slip into a kind of collective madness when you're bottled up in close proximity to others, self-contained, with no way of judging the appropriateness of an act other than in terms of itself. In the small scale it's called cabin fever, and guys chop up their companions with an ice saw. On the larger scale you can see it in those centuries of chronic warfare you tend to get on planets before space flight, subsets of the species fighting over a finite amount of territory. I first saw it directly back when I was a kid, in the blockaded city in which I'd grown up. You lock people up together and the next thing you know they're at each other's throat, the step-by-step process from one state to another seeming so low-key and natural at the time that you don't quite notice what you're doing till it's done and the blood's all over you.

The lack of high-power weapons that could have turned it into full-scale slaughter meant that the situation in the complex operated at a cutoff level of violence, from which it couldn't escalate. Effective power was in the hands of gangs, who fought constantly for supremacy, and the only way for the common run of any new intake to survive was to be adopted by one or another of them. As for the guards themselves, their only duty was to prevent people from escaping. They watched the access point and patrolled the perimeter with lethal force, but left those within to stew in their own compounded juice.

Personally, I did what I've pretty much always done. I declined the offers of various clans to join them, dealt with their reaction to that, and then dealt with their slightly more extreme reaction to my dealing with the first one. I made sure that I didn't actually kill anyone – the last thing I wanted was an intermural vendetta on my hands – and let it be known that I would entertain one-off jobs for food and in return for being left alone. The trick, as ever, was to make it just that much more preferable, to every faction, to leave me walking around as a possible resource rather than to wipe me out as a possible threat to everyone.

* * *

In the third week after my arrival I was hauling myself along the underside of the structure by way of ropes, clamp hooks and crampons I'd devised from the local materials. In addition to food, the Thanaxon authorities supplied a minimum degree of resources that would keep the prison-economy ecology of the complex ticking over, and the specific stuff I'd used to make this makeshift mountaineering equipment isn't important. Plaited blanket fibre, shapes cut out from tin plates with shears, crimped and slotted together to strengthen them, that sort of thing.

Below me, the sea heaved. Between me and it, something like a hundred metres below, curved down one of the tensile steel lines that tethered the entire complex to the oil rig below. I suppose, if one judged the fall right, one could have simply dropped off, grabbed the line and slithered down it. That is, if one wouldn't mind having one's arms wrenched out of their sockets trying to grab the line, maybe even lopped in half by it if one hit it badly, skinning several kilograms of viscera off on the slide down and ending up lying, with every bone in one's body broken, tangled up in the wreckage of an on-site petrochemical refinery and with nowhere else to go from there. The good news was that I didn't have to look out for Guard Service fliers, but that was simply because they knew that nobody was stupid enough to be down here in the first place.

I'd done a number of odd jobs by this time, small-scale stuff and nothing worth mentioning. A bit of bodyguarding, a bit of leaning, you know the drill. This job was of a higher order, so far as that was possible in this microcosmic world: a snatch job – or possibly a resnatch. The R'Kanrak clan had lost someone who was under their wing to the T'galk clan and they wanted him back. (Those names mean precisely sod all, incidentally, except in the absolutely literal sense of 'three small lemur-like creatures of a certain sort found only on the distinctively shaped peninsula of the major southern continent of Zarjax' and the like. The neural webs grafted to the neocortex that allow me to pull meanings out of any number of different languages are set to simply stream them to me as the basic sounds.)

The guy I was after had been 'won' in one of the ritualized interclan battles as a kind of hostage-wager, and the R'Kanrak were adamant that the T'galk had cheated in some abstruse way. I couldn't give a toss about the quasi-legality of it, personally. The reason I was interested was that this guy was one of the refugees from St Oscar's, a research chemist – and the value of such people to the clans was in their ability to find uses for the diminutive resources of the complex, from brewing ethanol from bread-and-water rations to the fashioning of primitive power weapons. His value to me, of course, was as a source of information, and possibly a lead to the elusive Summerfield.

Thus far, for all my searching and asking around, I'd found no trace of her. Possibly it was my own personal response to the cabin-fever-like mass psychosis I've talked about, or maybe it was brain-chemistry imbalance brought about by the bad and vitamin-free prison diet, but over the past weeks Summerfield had gone from a simple place to start, a lead to follow just to see if it led anywhere, to a kind of emotional Grail.

I kept a kind of vision of her in my head, a composite of the stills from the data files: the long and slender neck, the quirky, slightly too-big mouth that seemed perpetually caught between solemnity and a spontaneously wicked grin, the eyes that were ... inexpressible. Even in the stills something informed them, lived behind them; you couldn't talk about the slightly wounded look they had, the hint of mischief, the potential for a sudden flash of anger, humour or spite, for the simple reason that you can't detail every single shifting of mood and expression, over the course of years, of a person that you've known for years.

I don't mean I fell in love with Bernice Summerfield from her pictures or anything, or that I'd become obsessed by her, but she'd become a kind of Real Person in my head. A sort of imaginary mental friend, who helped me through the misery and friendless life in the complex.

Objectively, of course, she was still just a person I wanted to find and pump for information. I really wanted to meet her, though, on the purely personal level. I pictured her in her leathers and with her throwing knives, her quick wit and full-on lethal response to any threat of danger. That tended to preclude the idea that she had even been here in the first place, though. If even half of the stories about her were true, and she'd been here, then, far from dying some nameless and anonymous death, she should have been damned near *running* the place by now.

One thing was for sure: that muscle-bound dimwit Jason didn't deserve someone like her . . .

The sanitary arrangements of the complex had been designed to be as simple and as maintenance-free as possible. They were, quite frankly, a series of wide and strategically placed pipes that ran straight down through the structure to dump, as it were, into midair and then the sea below. They were wide enough to fit a human body – the Thanaxon designer realizing that a primary danger of blockage would come from people trying to stuff human bodies down holes that weren't quite wide enough. I crawled along until I found one that, by my reckoning, should take me up directly into T'galk territory, putting me past their guarded perimeter, and began to climb up it. And the less said about that the better.

The name of the ex-chemist was Professor Sabron Jones. I found him in a cell guarded by a couple of minor-league and inattentive T'galk bravos, whom I dispatched by the simple expedient of smacking the brain stem, first the one and then the other when he came over to see what was going on. One of the bravos was basically human, with the minor variations that come from a colony gene pool: bony temple-ridges and greenish mottling down the sides of the throat. The other was a Draal from one of the ocean-world colonies – a kind of bipedal arthropod, it's body and limbs covered with a jointed, crab-shell carapace. You can deliver a disabling or killing blow, however, by using soft-karate techniques to transmit the force into the soft matter beyond.

I wasn't about to kill anybody here – but let's be clear about this. The idea that people can wander around getting smacked in the head, plunging into blackness and then waking up just in time for the Next Exciting Episode, is complete and utter toss. A head injury severe enough to make you lose consciousness does brain damage, to some extent or other. As I said, I didn't want to kill anybody, but then again I didn't want them getting up again any time soon. I hit the bravos hard enough to ensure that they weren't going to be much use for anything afterwards.

Professor Sabron Jones wasn't looking good. He might have been valuable to the T'galk in one sense, but in another he was just the kind of overrefined, eggheaded weakling that they would innately regard as a victim. He had not been treated well. In late middle age to start with, he was emaciated with the catastrophic weight, teeth and hair loss of active starvation, as opposed to mere chronic malnutrition. The flesh of his cheeks had shrivelled to a kind of thin and bloodless membrane, the incipient stages of that catastrophic weight-loss condition that eats holes in them.

Short rations weren't the worst of it: he had suffered a series of severe beatings, both at the hands of his original captors and now these new ones – he was covered with contusions and welts. Some were half healed, and the only thing that stopped the later ones from being stomach-turning was that his body was too wasted to kick in with the various biological damage-containment processes that can make injuries look worse than they are. It might seem strange, given my line of work, that I can get queasy about such things – but the point is that such things have to be done cleanly, and sparingly, and always with some purpose in mind. The damage to Jones was just brutal, clumsy and mindless. This had been done simply because he was weak and it had amused someone stronger to do so. My better-dead list notched up a number of new candidates on the spot.

Jones cowered away from me, gibbering, and so I went into my nonthreatening routine: 'It's OK, Professor Jones, I'm a friend. I'm here to help you.' One of the common mistakes in reassurance, incidentally, is to say you're not going to *hurt* someone and the like – which instantly concentrates the mind upon the word in question. 'I'm here to help.' I told him. 'I'm here to save you.'

The combination of posture, tone of voice and cumulatively meaningless platitudes seemed to mollify him. He looked up at me with the kind of trapped eyes you normally only see in the terminally senile, his mouth working feebly. A vague murmuring came out that my translators tagged as 'indistinguishable muttering' and filtered out.

Time to push my own agenda a bit. 'Before we go, I have to know some things. You were on Dellah. Something happened on Dellah. What happened on Dellah, Professor Jones?'

He flinched each time I said the name, as though I had physically slapped him. The interrogational law-of-three, however, the repeating of a key trigger word, did its job and something spilt out:

'My prize begonias,' he said in a faint and reedy voice.

'You what?' I said, momentarily nonplussed. This didn't seem to have any relevance to Dellah, chemistry, metallurgy or anything useful at all.

'My begonias,' Jones repeated, in the calm, chatty and surprisingly precise tones of the profoundly shocked, the mind latching firmly on to some specific thought as a kind of talisman against pain. 'I grew them from seed, you know. As a hobby. I won prizes for them. I kept them in the gazebo by the Botany Department – and didn't old Chalmers make a fuss about that! Contamination of local flora and fauna indeed! Well I showed him . . .' Jones trailed off into a little senile-gleeful chuckle at a minor victory in some long-gone interdepartmental tussle.

I went along with him. 'You grew begonias as a hobby?'

Jones nodded happily. 'I won prizes for them.'

'I thought begonias were extinct,' I said. 'How did you grow begonias, then?'

'A bunker,' Jones said. 'A bunker on the Moon, an emergency storage facility for Earth's DNA, lost and forgotten. For thousands of years. They had samples of genetic material there, for transplanting on the colonies. Embryos from ocelots and elephants, seeds and bulbs of plants. Buried and forgotten. Some of the samples were still viable. Miss Summerfield dug them up and –'

'Summerfield?' I cut in sharply, despite myself. 'Bernice Summerfield?'

'Oh, do you know her?' Jones said brightly. 'Lovely girl. Lovely girl. She gave them to me. She knew that fool Chalmers wouldn't be interested – oh no, not Chalmers. Far too interested in keeping local food chains absolutely clean . . . I . . . she gave the seeds to me. I grew them as a hobby. I won prizes for them, you know . . .'

There was, at this point, one question and one alone that could be asked. 'What happened to your begonias?' I asked.

'Gone . . . all gone. When the university was . . . it was, it was there, you see. I won. And then it was . . . We didn't *know*. Things were there, sleeping. Gods woke up and walked and razed the university to the . . .' Jones worked his mouth, blatting at it with a withered and trembling hand. I'd diverted his thoughts to the one thing he didn't want to think about, and it was as if he was trying to force out something too big for his mouth.

'You got out,' I said. 'You got out and came here. What about the others? What about Summerfield?'

I don't quite know what I was expecting – but I was utterly surprised by his reaction. Abruptly Jones stopped shaking, and smiled at me with a kind of mad and deep and beauteous joy.

'She's gone now,' he told me with absolute solemnity, but with an underlying sense of what I can only describe as rapture, like he was imparting to me the kind of Truth that has pairs of people knocking on your door the moment you've got into the shower. 'She's in Heaven and with God. I saw her go, lifted up within the arms of an angel.'

Background Insert (Personal File):

Scenes from an Ordinary Childhood II

One of the weirder things I remember from old science-fiction as a kid – the sort of stuff that said, in the Future, with a capital F, we'd all be zooming around in hyper-wobble ships, eating chocolate made by nanites out of old socks and living on Uranus – is not just the fact that they got things wrong, but how they got things wrong in a certain and specific way. They turned things, almost exactly, on their heads.

On the one hand the basic, animal humanity of people was given a superficial, bolted-on exoticism – we'd have all evolved physically impossible telepathic powers, we'd have slightly anodyne and by-the-numbers, polyamorous sexual arrangements that had every good point about them and none of the bad, we'd have every single one of us achieved Enlightenment and stopped being racially, sexually and all sorts of other kinds of bigoted on the dot of noon, 12 May 2154, and so on.

On the other hand, we'd spend our lives being utterly astounded by the simplest and most basic facts of the world around us. 'Gosh,' we'd go around saying, 'have you heard that the new recycling plant and combined heat sink is going on line tomorrow? That will help the power levels of this particular part of the city immensely!' Or, 'Aha! We are living in an age of true galactographic expansion! Even now the mighty behemoths of starships ply the ghusty depths of space! The Manifest Destiny of the human race awaits!' Or, 'Dear me, how tedious it is to live in this totalitarian state with the guards going by in their armoured trucks, clunky Bakelite television sets on poles and nothing to eat but week-old cabbages . . .'

Neither and none of which, quite frankly, are what people actually do. We're still just people, after all. We're far more interested in the latest catchphrase that's doing the rounds from some amusing holoshow: we're more interested in smacking in the face of some creep who's just annoyed us by looking at our girl in a funny way, or whether there are actually going to *be* any cabbages in the shop this fortnight. The basic conditions of the worlds in which we find ourselves fade into the background. If those conditions are even remotely computable with life as we know it, we just get on with it and live it. It's only when we have some basis for comparison that we feel as though we want to die.

By the summer after Annie died, the EMG curfew was more or less a formality. If you just happened to be out, and looked as if you were minding your own business, the dogboys were as likely to let you run as to shoot you on the spot. I kept an eye out for street cleaners – and, believe me, in our world the term took on a slightly different meaning than some guy with a mobile trash bin and a broom – as I made my way towards the Night Market. My name was known, by now, and my face was on the files. I took precautions.

Crawling over rooftops by way of sneaking up and down the drainpipes and fire escapes that hadn't been scavenged for their iron might sound incredibly dynamic and exciting, but if you have to actually *do* it then it's just slow, interminable and tortuous pain: I'd started across the city at twilight and it was long gone midnight by the time I reached the Night Market. The smells of gasoline and cooking meat, the lights and the sounds of warm bodies told me I was near before I was even close.

The Night Market was situated in what had once been the Bullring shopping centre. It was a free-zone, a place that was allowed to operate after dark and, if we weren't too blatant about it, a place where you could get black-market goods in from the outside world, via the various nefarious ways that black-market goods just seem to suddenly appear all the time. Even the dogboys had finally cottoned on to the fact that places like this simply have to exist, as a way to blow off steam, like knocking a hole in a can of something before you chuck it on the fire. They policed and regulated it, and policed it hard, but they allowed it to exist.

It was a building that had been erected – on the cheap – on the bomb site that had been its predecessor, and several floors had fallen in to give the place a cavernous aspect, lit by the flickering light of braziers and the jittery light from banks of headlights scavenged from derelict cars, hooked up to the sputtering bulk of a slightly malfunctioning generator. (I remember a time when I was a little kid and I was taken to a funfair. The generator here reminded me of those that powered the rusty and clapped-out-looking rides that, even at that age, I knew better than to even want to go on.)

Even so, even now, when I go through some low-tech-world bazaar, my first thought is of the Night Market. Makeshift stalls were piled with bolts of cloth and rugs and complicated strings of trinkets. Stacks of battered old books and third-hand clothing, old and easily portable bits of furniture and *objets d'art*. The scent of sizzling contraband meats, from chicken and lamb to genuine horse, swept over me; saliva spurted into my mouth, my stomach yawed and I felt that I might almost faint from the hunger. I wasn't here to eat, however – or, for that matter, to take advantage of the rather fetching array of young women and boys who were on offer, ranged in their own corner in cobbled-together damask and fur and cracked scraps of jewellery.

I was here to meet someone on the fringes – that strange little edge-world that lives between the sort of commerce of whores, drugs and violence-for-money, and the sort of commerce that buys you your food, power and house. This is the sort of world where you can buy bongs, say, when cannabis-derivatives you could smoke in them are illegal, an aromatherapy massage equidistant between the clinical and the sexual, and any number of things that are, when it comes right down to it, about as much use as a chocolate nob.

I'm talking about a world where you pay over the odds to have someone slap down a ratty pack of pasteboard cards and then say Death doesn't really mean death, literally. A world where some ineptly riveted-together amalgam ankh suddenly jumps in value by a couple of hundred per cent, because somebody's spit on it the right way and tuned it to your aura. A world, to cut it short, where people make their livings by selling dreams made out of shit.

Believe me, I'm not knocking it. On a hundred planets, under regimes and conditions you couldn't imagine unless you've been there yourself, I've seen people selling those kinds of dream – and known that, however bad things might be, they could have been one hell of a lot worse. It's a sign that people want and need and can still make things, even if they make them out of nothing.

At some point, a bunch of old railway sleepers had been dragged into the Night Market, and piled up in a kind of crazily interlocking ziggurat. The patched-together construct was longer than it was broad, and along one long side of it were pitched the dealers in the intangible: the holy idiots, prophets, soothsayers and fortune-tellers. Even here, there was a pecking order – it was like one of those streets you get in any city in miniature, one of those streets devoted to a single product or craft, the better side of it at one end, the lowest of the low at the other.

I walked on past the ragged and skeletal wretches with bowls to catch crusts given in pity for their psychosis, past the hellfire-and-damnation crowd and the speedy-looking cybermancers, with their cargo-cult mosaics of techno-garbage that didn't work, and found myself before a kind of open tent, built from sacking stitched with astrological signs and supported by the kind of desiccated bamboo poles that might once have adorned some nice little suburban garden.

Within the relative murk of the tent, lit by squat and dribbling tallow candles that seemed to make it darker than anything, was a woman. She was well past middle age – which in the world we lived in made her something like an Elder if not an actual Ancient. She was wrapped up in a ragged sari, threads of fuse wire weaving in and out of the cloth. Her hair was brittle, coming loose in patches from the scalp above a lined and somewhat scaly forehead. Her eyes were sharp. It was her that I had come to see.

She flicked her sharp eyes towards a three-man dogboy patrol working their way through the crowd, judged that they were too far away to be a consideration, turned her attention back to me and nodded almost imperceptibly. I sat down on the splintered sleeper-wood before the tent. 'Evening, Megan.'

''Allo, pet.' Megan leered rather theatrically at me, exposing yellowed stumps of teeth, and gave me a broad wink. 'What brings you out on this most star-crossed night? A philtre? A yen for knowledge of things to come, of which a mortal man should never ken? You want me to make you up a chart?' In a time when accents meant anything, hers was a strange kind of cross between the Wolverhampton and the Welsh – with a large dose of sarcasm thrown in for good luck.

'I'd rather have my hand felt, Megan,' I said.

'My lucky night. Come close.'

I shifted forward and held out my hands. She felt the palms, kneading them a little, first one and then the other, with dry and strangely scratchy fingers.

'Now that's a lifeline and a half,' she said cheerfully. 'Years left yet in you? I think so . . .'

'Pigs fly, Megan,' I told her.

'New shipment came through. And look at all those breaks in the heart line. You're playing fast and loose. You playing fast and loose with your best girl, lover?'

'As if I would, Megan,' I said. 'Source?'

'You are that. Old Provo cache. One of those Mickey Mouse outfits that wouldn't take a telling after the ceasefire.'

'Ceasefire?' I said.

'Way before your time. You wouldn't understand. They were going to take it out on to the streets personal, like, but they never got around to it. Yes, those are definitely the hands of a heartbreaker, young fella me lad. The stuff's thirty years old if it's a day, but they greased and wrapped it nice and tight. It's usable.'

Across the Market, the dogboys were homing in on some guy selling salted fish from a tray. There didn't seem to be any reason for it rather than the hell of it. Maybe they'd seen the doomed look about him – or maybe the doomed look had come upon him when he'd seen them coming.

'Anything I can use?' I asked Megan.

'I know what calibres you've got, and I know how many favours you're owed. Fifteen rounds, point thirty-eight, and you're getting the best of it.'

'Good enough,' I said sourly. If it hadn't been good enough it would have just been tough shit. 'Want me to cross your palm with silver?'

'What do you think?' said Meg.

The trick here, incidentally, is to do it slow, relaxed and

smooth. You want to talk about something, you talk about it in the exact same way as you'd talk about anything else. Likewise, the package Megan had passed me had been in plain view for quite a while – at least, I wasn't trying to conceal it in that kind of guilty way that draws the eye like a magnet. It was just something I happened to be holding.

Now I put it in the pocket of my jacket, and came back out again with a coin. I forget precisely what it was, and it was absolutely worthless in any case. Nobody used cash any more, and you could find bits and pieces of it scattered around all over the place. It was the *posture* of transaction, the fact that it was a token of my paying back a couple of favours to various people, that was important. I tossed the coin to Megan, who plucked it from the air and peered at it critically.

'I can remember when that would buy you a big meat pie and a bus ride,' she said.

'What days they must have been,' I said.

'Don't knock 'em,' said Megan. Abruptly, she became serious. I was a little startled. I'd never really seen her without her ingrained patina of sod-you irony before. 'By the way, I've heard a little bird. There's people looking for you.'

'Same as ever, Megan,' I said.

'I mean seriously. Actively. Asking around by name.' She looked at me – and I got one of those little flashes you get, when you realize that someone you just happen to know and banter with genuinely likes you, and is concerned for you. 'You be careful going home.'

As I walked off I saw that the dogboys were still kicking at the fish-seller, who had long since lost any sense of coherence and was just sort of squealing that it wasn't his fault, over and over again. I knew how he felt.

It was nearly dawn by the time I made it back to the fire-gutted tenement I was currently calling home. There was that greenish nimbus on the skyline that was one of the results of all the weird things that had been done to the atmosphere of Earth in the last few decades, from the cumulative releasing of chemical weapons into it, to the detonation of dirty-cobalt bombs inside it. The greenish tinge, I later learnt, was a result of fallout from a nuclear detonation in one or other of the new Western Europe city-states in the last two weeks, and it might have been a good idea to get under deep cover and get qualified medical help as soon as possible. There was none of either available, of course, and I didn't know I should have them in the first place.

Besides, as it turned out, I wouldn't have had the time to take advantage of them in any case.

Megan's warning had hit home. I thought I'd perfected the knack of moving inconspicuously through the world, but I had stayed in the same place for too long. Keep on moving and you knock back all those little threads of association that accrete about you – not by anything you do, but by the simple fact of being there and alive – without even being aware of it. It was long past time to tie the spotted hanky on the stick again and blow.

If people were looking for me, my best bet would have been to simply walk away from it, to pick a direction from the Night Market at random – any direction other than the one where I actually lived – and just keep on walking. The problem was that my weapons cache was there in the house, and how many years would it take to accumulate a new one? It wasn't as if it had been easy for a civilian to get firearms in the first place, even before the dogboys sealed the cracks. Standard punishment for so much as carrying one, let alone intent to trade, was a waistcoating – and if you don't know what a 'waistcoat' is then, believe me, you never want to. It had taken over as their favourite from necklacing, the rubber inner tubes of old tyres being increasingly hard to come by. Plus there were still some bits and pieces Annie had given me in the house – nothing much important, but I didn't want to lose them if I could help it.

I don't want to come on like I went back to pick up my stuff out of some kind of doomed and noble sentiment – I mean, the house was where I'd started from on my trip to the Market, and the people who were looking for me would have been looking for me even then. I just simply decided it was worth dropping back in before I moved on. I clambered over a low wall of fractured brick, slid back one of the loose boards over a window and slipped inside.

A couple of dogboys were waiting inside. It was almost pitch-dark, but I knew they were dogboys because they were fitted out with snoopers. In the holomovies, someone kitted out with the things can move through the dark with complete invisibility, but in real life that isn't so. There's a tiny and very faint glow of visible light, back-reflected from the phosphor in the eyepieces through the lenses, and a little electrical hum that is utterly distinctive.

I just had time to recognize the little glow and hum before a muzzle-flash went off to knock out all my rods and cones and something detonated in my guts. I might have lived for up to half an hour in that condition, as I'd seen people do, but the shock of it stopped my heart, and killed me stone-cold dead.

CHAPTER 7

Just my pissy bloody luck, basically. I'd come to Thanaxos, miscalculated completely and ended up in this hellhole for almost a month, only to be told by this mad old bugger that the one positive lead I had was a complete dead end. Professor Sabron Jones was looking at me, his flash of rapture wiped away as suddenly as it had come, to be replaced by stark and abject terror. He'd no doubt caught the flash of rage that had me wanting, above all else, to give him a smacking that would make his previous beatings look like a chuck under the chin.

I quashed it instantly. It wasn't Jones's fault that Summerfield was dead, and he could hardly be blamed for the experiences of the last few months turning him to religious monomania. Besides, I had a job to do.

'Come on, chum,' I told him, lifting him up by the scruff of the neck and dragging him from the cell. 'Let's get you back to where you came from.'

'Are you taking me home?' he said, in the kind of plaintive voice that had me picturing his visions of going back to his childhood, his childhood home and his mother, as if they were my own. I resolved there and then that, once we were out of T'galk territory, I would hide him somewhere rather than take him back to the R'Kanrak clan. I'd tell 'em I'd been forced to eliminate him, and sell it as being necessary to keep him from falling back into their enemies' hands. It would be a dangerous move – and the last thing I needed in this place was a hanger-on with an extra mouth to feed – but what the hell. Sometimes things stick themselves in your face and you just can't walk away. Besides, looking at the wreck that had once been Professor Sabron Jones, I judged that he would last only another couple of days, tops, in any case, and I might just be able to pump out some last dregs of information before he died. I'm just an incredible softy old git at heart, basically.

I hauled him back to the waste disposals, unhooked one of my makeshift ropes from my shoulder and tied one end to a bit of exposed stanchion pipe. Jones caught on to the idea as I tied the other end around him in an impromptu sling. He started to struggle, so I was forced to simply shove him down the hole and grab the rope before he fell too far, then lowered him until the slack was taken up. With a bit of luck, he'd now be hanging off the underside of the complex, twisting merrily in the wind and waiting for me to haul him in when I emerged from the bottom of the pipe myself.

Some hopes. The line was too short and he ended up hanging in the pipe itself and wailing. I wouldn't have thought a man, and especially a man in the condition in which Jones had been, could have made such sheer noise. Almost instantly I heard other noises that might have been quieter, but crystallized the attention far more than the noises coming from below. Through the twisting corridors and openings of T'galk territory came the stirrings and shouts of puzzled and waking alarm at hearing Jones's cries. I heard running feet, and shouting; caught the first flicker of movement in a doorway. There was no time to make a secure line for myself so I did the only thing that was possible: I jumped into the pipe.

For maybe twenty metres I slithered down it, splaying myself and bracing forearms and the fleshy flats of shins against the sides. In the end it was Jones who saved me – or, rather, the tension of the rope from which he was hanging against my chest – it skinned it royally, but it slowed my momentum until I could find stable purchase on the pipe. Now, if you're wondering just precisely what I could find to grip on in a smooth pipe, then just think of how a toilet occasionally gets when you don't scrub it on a regular basis and don't ask me again.

Above me, amplified and reverberating so that they were almost a match for the wailing below, I heard the sounds of confusion and anger. The T'galk were awake, had found the state of the guards and the missing state of Jones. Fuck 'em, quite frankly. There was nothing they could do about it now.

Of course, there *was* something they could do about it. I will swear to the death, under torture, brainwashing or taking me back in time to physically prove it isn't so, that the T'galk cut the rope that was tethering Jones. It wasn't a question of my making it too weak – I wouldn't have trusted it with myself otherwise – and it wasn't due to the extra stress I'd put on it by my own descent. So far as I'm concerned, they just knew it was supporting Jones, his re-abductor or both, and so they just cut it.

Either way, the broken end of the rope whipped past me and made me lose my grip for a couple of metres before I managed to slow myself to a stop again. The now almost constant wailing of what had once been Professor Sabron Jones suddenly switched to a kind of diffuse and fading scream as, below, he dropped out of the tube and fell to his death in the sea below. Maybe he was sliced in half by one of the wires that anchored the detention complex itself, as I'd worried that I would be. I don't know. The screams had Dopplered away to nothingness, even to my own personal aural enhancements, long before that point.

Either way, if I had thought that I had anything left to

learn from the guy, it would have to wait until I was lifted on high upon the wings and in the arms of an angel myself.

I'd love to say that I got out of the detention complex by dint of the courage, resourcefulness and sheer stick-to-it genius that are my watchwords. I'd love to say that, with a mind like a tungsten trap, the eye of a hawk and the perseverance of a minaret-building weevil of Galos XIV, I spotted the fatal flaw of its construction and its infrastructure, bided my time and then, at the propitious moment, via precise and complicated and incredibly heroic means, made my escape.

Reality don't work like that. In reality, I got out by onc of those *deus ex machina* events that happen to us every day but, if this were fiction, nobody would believe it for a second.

The death of Sabron Jones, though unfortunate, didn't mean much in the scheme of things. There was no comeback from the R'Kanrak, his death suiting their purposes almost as well. It didn't do them any good, but it tipped the balance back from the T'galk's unfair advantage. In the normal course of events I would have simply shrugged it off. On top of everything else, though, it was the final straw. It was as if I'd somehow returned to some abstract of a trapped and hopeless, brutalizing childhood . . . and what came after. Everything I'd seen, or been, or done had come again to nothing and there was no way out. There would never be a way out.

And so I reverted. Something inside me just turned up its toes and gave up. I gave up on any pretence of working, stole food from people when I could and got into a series of vicious, pointless fights. I didn't actually kill anyone, but I came damned close to it a number of times. The days blurred into each other and I lost track of time; I had no use for it, any more than a snow leopard prowling the tundra needs to know what day of the month it is. I didn't care who I offended now, and if I'd known that there were prison contracts out on me then my reaction would probably have been 'Good! When?'

It was in this general mental state that I was wandering through one of the communal areas, a hall-like space packed with tiers of scaffolding, in which the inmates came to trade whatever sorry wares they had. A scrap of meat for a handful of raw tubers. Trash metal fashioned into tools for a tobacco stash. Sexual favours for protection. The postures of commerce and barter, even though there was next to nothing to barter with.

I walked through the crowd, aware, without putting much importance on it, that people were getting the hell out of my way. I grabbed a stick of jerky from some guy or other and was automatically cuffing him as he protested, when I became aware of a commotion over to one side.

Guards were spilling into the chamber in a kind of double wave, the first front shoving back the crowd with billy clubs and riot-gear shields, while those behind covered them with automatic weapons, should some bright spark decide to try his or her luck. It wasn't really necessary: the crowd was offering no resistance – not out of surprise so much as a kind of collective astonishment. The difference between the two was the fact that this happening, the appearance of guards this deep in the complex, was so utterly at odds with the way things *were* that people seemed at a loss as to how to react in any way at all.

'They come to kill us!' squeaked the guy from whom I'd taken the food. 'Come to kill us all!'

The knock-on effect of his fear took hold in those around us – it's quite interesting to watch it as it spreads out from the starting point where you happen to be. It's like a sort of sonic version of watching ripples on a pond. I found myself shoving through the crowd, trying to get a closer and better look at what was going on. The fact that this would put me closer to any hypothetical firing line didn't even occur to me; this was the first *event* after weeks of violent drudgery, and something inside me was starving for it.

After the guards had cleared a space, a group of other figures came through the hatch – human holocam and sound technicians in those bright, fluorescent, orange coveralls that mark them out the galaxy over as noncombatants in whatever war, upheaval, civil disturbance or societal purging they happen to be covering. A news crew from one of the big outfits, DataDay or FNN, one of those guys. These people can move through situations that would kill the rest of us stone-cold dead with an almost complete impunity. One reason for this is that, in the purely physical sense, they remain entirely impartial – they might show a burning baby, and say precisely what they think about that, but they wouldn't put it out. The other reason is that they have the backing and resources to make people, let us say, regret attacks upon their person – by way of the sort of reprisals that stop just short, on the scale of lethality, at Extreme Prejudice. Those incredibly distinctive and unmissable coveralls I mentioned are of a precise hue that the camera can't pick up – and that's as good a metaphor for the interesting societal dichotomy that these people represent.

(Note to self: It's far too early in the morning to ponce on about interesting societal dichotomies. Don't do it again.)

The technician fussed around for a while setting up, and then a final figure emerged from the hatch. Dark and female, dressed in sloppy-looking combat greens reminiscent of a guerrilla, but cleaned and pressed and couture-designed to within a micron of their lives. The living spit of a hard-bitten trouble-spot journo that takes two hours in hair-and-make-up and a couple of crocodile clips around the back to get right. In one hand she held an overlarge and archaic-looking mike that, over centuries, has become a kind of Sceptre of Office rather than serving any kind of functional use. She conferred with the main cameraman for a moment, then positioned herself in front of his rig for a run-through.

If you've ever faced a gun and survived, or been jerked back from a precipice from which there was no hope other than to fall, or jumped back from the path of some speeding twelve-ton truck, you'll have some idea of how I felt at that point. The miasma of depression into which I'd sunk burst like a detergent bubble and the light was back on again inside me, just like that – a positive *surge* blasting from the pit of the stomach to fill me to bursting. I only now became aware of how withdrawn I'd become, how remote from the world around me and the specificity of it, when I snapped back to it with a bang. It was the nearest thing I'd ever come, I think, to the kind of rapture I had seen in Sabron Jones.

Other people were still crowded and pressed against me. I shoved them away without noticing or caring who or what they were. I stuck my hands in the air and waved them. 'Sela!' I shouted at the top of my lungs. 'Sela.'

Several guards reacted first, swinging their weapons round to track me. I saw a couple of them making ready to move forward and haul me out and deal with me.

Then the woman's face snapped round. I was too far away to see her eyes with any detail, but it was obvious from the way her body jerked that she had recognized me, too. She turned and stalked over to one of the armed guards, obviously their squad commander, and hurriedly conferred with him. He glared at her with taciturn suspicion and the discussion became more heated, on the woman's part at least, with a little bit of arm-waving thrown in for good measure. Eventually the captain of the guard nodded, though he didn't seem too happy about it. He motioned to three of his men, and they broke formation, heading towards me through the crowd and clubbing anyone who got too close with their rifle butts. The weapons were attached to them by lengths of chain, but I'd have personally left them behind. I hated to think what might happen if the mood of the crowd chose this moment to change from puzzled shock to anger. Fortunately it held.

What with one thing and another it took several minutes to haul me back through the crowd and into the guard perimeter. By the time I got there and the guards released me with bad-tempered shoves, the woman was back in front of the camera, speaking into her nonfunctional prop mike: '. . . sources in the Thanaxon parliament have remained reticent as to the true nature of conditions for off-worlders in what has been described as the "best-kept secret on Thanaxos". I now pass you over to our roving reporter, uh, Humphrey Pipkin, who has been working undercover these last few weeks to get a picture of the current situation. Humphrey?'

The cameraman tracked his rig to me, and I noticed with some relief that it wasn't uploading in real time. I'd be able to get to the storage wafer before it shoved my bare face out on to the galactic net. 'Well, Sela,' I said, sliding my face, voice and posture into the persona of a noble member of the journalistic profession, haggard but quietly undefeated after a job well done – and making a small mental note to pay her back in spades for the Humphrey – 'I first became aware of what was happening here when I . . .'

ATTACHMENT (SUPPLEMENTARY):

To: brown@135474.346.12.ccserv.dnet.com
From: pubterm@lunet.com
Organization: Archive News Services Bibliotheca
Subject: FYE

Dear Mr Brown

Here is the article as per your request.

----BEGIN----

MASS RELEASE HAUNTS THANAXOS

Report by FNN-DATANEWS Correspondent Dick Chancey, Rakath, Thanaxos, F45

M'rago Tan, a bar owner in Rakath, recalls the days when transient control on Thanaxos was lax, and brawls and murder were commonplace.

'The fights and murders were commonplace,' he says. 'We had just opened up to galactic contact, and we attracted the scum of the galaxy, looking for a fast buck. Murderers, thugs and all sorts. I never knew if I'd have a bar by the end of the night or a knife in my chest.' Tan lifts his shirt to show the scars left by, he says, 'a late-night meeting with a Thraal machete'.

Now, it looks as though these days are coming back. Following the intervention of Sela Dane of DataDay News, together with her so-called 'special correspondent', Humphrey Pipkin, it seems that the Thanaxon policy of detention for galactic undesirables is up for review.

News of this impending mass release has brought a dramatic increase in tension to the increasingly fractious Thanaxos – already beset by problems due to the Dellahan Blockade and its effects upon legitimate trade – as the fear grows that the population, when confronted by this wave of hardened criminals, will take the law into its own hands.

The Minister for Justice Pursuant to the Advisory Council of the House Royal, K'narom Veed, is sanguine. This will be merely a procedural review, to ascertain the facts of matters in each particular case.

'Pressures of administration mean that proper procedures were not always followed,' he says. 'Although we believe that many of them are guilty of wrongdoing, we are obliged under the norms of basic law to release them. If evidence then emerges confirming their guilt, we will, of course, detain them again.'

His rival in the coming Advisory Council elections, A'toth Nar, is less forgiving. 'Make no mistake, the vast majority of these people are killers.' A'toth Nar believes that the incumbent members of the Council are lying when they say they lack the evidence to detain these suspects. 'This is a political decision, not a legal decision.'

An officer of the guard at the off-worlder detention complex confirms that reactions to this move, among those who will be forced to deal with it, is hostile. 'These people are scum,' he says. 'They're just scum. They should all the lot of them be put down.'

– transcript of DataDay broadcast filtered for text transmission by Archive News Services Bibliotheca

----END----

To: brown@135474.346.12.ccserv.dnet.com
From: winwinwin@yourfriend.com
Organization: [type your organization here]
Subject: WINWIN WIN THE LOTTRY!!!!!!!!

WIN ON THE LOTTRY WITH THESE NUMBERS!!!!!
SEND 10 CREDS AND WELL SHOW YOU HOW!!!!!!

18, 2, 6, 61, 12, 8, 2, 1, 5, 57, 1, 22, 6, 14, 10, 11.

JUST SEND US 10 CREDS AND WIN WIN WIN THE LOTTRY!!!!!!!

[to remove your name from this mailing list, type 'remove' in the header line and hit 'send']

CHAPTER 8

I'd first met Sela Dane when I'd been hired by DataDay a few years back, to retrieve her and her crew from a collection of White Fire terrorists out in the Cool Star Hegemony – who simply hadn't been able to get the rules and had taken them hostage. The ins and outs of that affair aren't strictly relevant here, but suffice it to say that we went through a lot back then, and she saved my life a couple of times to my maybe twenty of saving hers – but what the hell. I was getting paid to do it and she wasn't. We formed an attachment.

Ostensibly, I was one of her so-called criminal-world 'contacts'. You know the sort of thing in the holomovies: hot young journalist or private dick comes running in saying, 'My contacts say there's a contract out on Angelface McBumfrey 'cause of what he did to the Don's sister,' and the like. Thing is, things like that work both ways: it's like a symbiotic relationship, not parasitic, and if you want to hold it together then you're ready to help each other out at the drop of a homburg with a press ticket stuck in it.

After hooking up with Sela, getting out of the detention complex was simplicity itself. I did my bit to camera, improvising about nothing much, secure in the knowledge that nothing was going to make the final cut. The point was just to be convincing for the guards. Then someone from the crew found me a coverall, I hung around while they did the location work and then just trooped off with everyone else to the helipad and the waiting DataDay chopper. The fact that I was a nobody, one of the 'disappeared', the basic fact that had made escape impossible for a month, now worked in my favour. Nobody cared either way if I lived or died, and I simply wasn't worth the trouble for any guard to make an issue of detaining me now that my apparent status had been redefined.

All the same, the prison-lag had really got to me – I didn't realize quite how much until we'd taken off and laid in a course to the mainland. I just found that I was shaking, and couldn't seem to stop myself. It must have looked worse to Sela than it really was, because she stopped rapping with the techs about the footage-editing, slithered over to the seat next to mine and held herself to me.

'Jeez, boy!' she exclaimed after a while, shoving herself away from me with a scowl (I was strapped into my seat, remember, and she wasn't). 'You look and smell like shit on toast with extra shit and no toast. Don't you come near me.'

I got that feeling where you want to cry, but don't dare start because you're not sure, if you do, that you'll be able to stop. I looked down at myself and did that very gentle breathing through the nose that lets you smell something of yourself. Up until that point I really hadn't realized how bad I had got.

'I could do with a bit of a wash and brush-up, I'll admit,' I admitted. 'Humphrey Pipkin?'

'More like a shave, a sandblast and a sluice, mate,' said Sela, wrinkling her nose and gagging in a way that seemed theatrical, but only because the genuine reaction was so extreme. 'I think I've caught lice just from looking. I had to make a name up off the top of my head, didn't I? We get back to the hotel and get you cleaned up, we're gonna have to burn those clothes and then the room. We're gonna have to get another one, and it's your fault, so you're fucking paying my old son.'

I honestly don't remember much about the next twenty-six hours; I know what happened and what I did, but there are just jumbled flashes of it happening and me actually doing it. So in quick and point-to-point order:

Sela scrounged a bunch of munchies and carob and candy bars from her crew and I wolfed them down, hardly stopping to chew; I was ravenous. I like to think that the sweet-stuff counteraction of my delayed-shock reaction balanced out the insulin-shock of gorging sweet stuff after a month of all but starving. The DataDay chopper hit Rakath, the capital city of the main Thanaxos landmass, and landed on the roof of the hotel – one of those swanky interstellar travellers' chain jobs frequented by those swanky interstellar travellers who didn't end up getting shoved in the poky the instant they landed. Sela more or less dragged me to her suite and dosed me with antibiotics and glucotics from her field reporter's kit, then stripped me off, shoved me into the Jacuzzi and slathered me with depilatory, insecticidal, antifungal and dermal stimulation creams to deal with the worst and most embarrassing effects of my month of incarceration. I then, apparently, spent two hours wolfing my way through four of the set high-protein meals of the sort intended for honeymooners to keep their strength – which must have induced a number of dark suspicions among the room-service staff as to Sela's lifestyle – before crashing out into a sleep so deep and dreamless that Sela was on the point of calling paramedics before she found a pulse.

I woke up feeling better than I had in weeks. The various medications and my bio-modifications had done their work: I had bulked up and the surface of my skin felt raw and fresh, pricking with the stubble of new hair. It was late afternoon. Through the window I could overlook the Rakath conurbation: a number of high edifices, with those slightly uneasy, squat and blocky proportions that tall buildings evidence when built on soft river-valley loam rather than a granite island, interspersed through a sprawl of the more common two- to four-storey structures. The architectural landmarks had a kind of triumphalist quality, an abstract use of human forms, like the tomb of Oscar Wilde set on its side.

I buzzed up room service, pointedly ignored the liveried waiter as he hovered by the door waiting for his tip, and settled down to a trolleyful of all-day breakfast. My metabolism was still hiked up in a healing cycle and I was still ravenous.

Half an hour later, Sela came in. Her technical support were now off doing whatever technical support do when they're not technically supporting. She was still in the designer combat gear that was her DataDay trademark, its artfully contrived folds and rumples more pronounced and slightly greasy after a day of hard work. Tomorrow she'd discard it and select another of the nearly twenty identical sets of working clothes hanging in the closet. In one hand she held one of those minicams a journo uses when going solo, and draped over the other arm was a crinkly vegetable-cellophane bag in which was sealed a dark, and off-the-peg suit. She tossed both items on to the bed, wandered over to me and planted a kiss on my stubbled head.

'The sleeper awakes,' she said.

'As he's ever going to be,' I told her around a mouthful of the local equivalent of bacon, which seemed to consist of vinegar-cured donkey. 'You shouldn't have let me sleep like that. There's things I should be doing.'

'Yeah, well, I tried to kick you awake this morning before I went out. You were completely dead.' Sela went over to a bureau and pulled out a recorder pack. 'Hang about for a few minutes, will you? I've got to download.' She wired the pack into the socket behind her ear. 'Don't worry, I'll edit anything sensitive and confidential out and EM-pulse it.' She smiled. 'I've messed around with my journalistic ethics too much for you already for it to make a lot of difference.'

All DataDay front-end correspondents have their optic nerves and aural centres wired to implanted storage wafers, which store everything they see and hear on a rolling twenty-six-hour basis, like a jar being filled from the top as it empties from a hole in the bottom. Given that, you might wonder why they still have to mess around with other cameras and complete news crews. The simple answer is, of course, that the implants show the scene from only one point of view, you can't get shots of yourself with them – and there are cases where the intimidation factor of a bunch of technicians comes in incredibly useful. Sela hit the switch on the recorder, and her face relaxed as the implant dumped its cache. There was a kind of animal stillness about it when she did this, a sense of perfect repose. I looked on her strong, sharp features, the innate set to the muscles under the mocha-coffee skin of her face, just for the pure enjoyment of it.

The download ended. Sela blinked and turned her head with no sense of transition or disorientation. 'Nothing much there, of course,' she said. 'Just a bit of vox pop and background. It's just a waiting game till things go bang.'

'What brought you here in the first place?' I asked her. I was genuinely interested, but, having been out of the loop for so long, I also needed a quick way back in – and Sela had the knack of pulling out the significant details of a situation and giving them a shape. That was one of the reasons she was so good at her job – the fact that the camera translated her beauty into something that made anything with a hormone system lie back and howl was just a bonus.

'We're here to cover sentient-interest issues,' she told me.

'Agreed-rights violations, tacitly sanctioned murder, people driving tanks over protesters, just the usual stuff. That's one of the reasons we organized a visit to that prison complex you were in. The local authorities have promised a full review of the procedures, by the way. Amnesties and repatriation under interstellar-conclave observation.'

I thought of the people in detention who had actually deserved amnesty and repatriation who had not survived – or would never survive – long enough to take advantage of it. I shrugged. 'That's nice to know.'

'Don't hold your breath,' said Sela. 'There's some silly dick from FNN going round and talking like a horde of off-world killers are going to be let loose tomorrow, but it's not exactly a high priority at the moment. And all this rights-violation stuff is just the ostensible reason why we're here. I could name you a thousand planets and colonies just as bad and worse. They've jumped over the last few months, and that's the hook we've hung it on to get here – but the point is that they've jumped in a specific way.

'Our psychometrics people have run the figures, and the result is that this stuff is happening because the whole society's putting itself on a war footing. It's this Dellah thing. It's really jacked up in the last month or so – you can smell the tension of it on the streets.' She grinned at me, rather nastily. 'Now it's no place of the news services to attempt to precipitate this sort of thing, just for the sake of all that lovely footage, but there's no crime in going to the right place and waiting for the right time . . .'

'Like a crowd of orange jumpsuits jumping around the place, and loudly wondering when the first attack starts, isn't going to make a difference?' I said. 'Like people aren't going to pick up on that?'

'Yeah, well,' said Sela. 'What are you gonna do?'

'So when do your psychometrists tell you that the various balloons are going up?' I wandered over to the bed and fiddled absently with the cellophane-wrapped suit. It was, as I'd known already, just my size.

Sela waggled a hand noncommittally. 'Medium-soon. We're talking order of weeks, as opposed to days or months.'

I stripped the wrapping off the suit. 'Then I think it's time I got back to work.'

Thanaxos was a basically monarchical society, which has one thinking of splendid pageantry and plumage, royal crests on every available surface, state processions, monumental statuary, household guards in endocephalically silly hats and all the rest of it – and so it was, in the tourist quarters. The mistake is to think that it is nothing else. It was also a post-industrial, interstellar-capable, globally cohesive and complex humanoid society. The streets and structures of Rakath were as functional, advanced and diverse as in any other capital city you can name. The only difference between this and, say, Aeon Flux on Mars was in the minutiae of the details – the uniforms and ranking-system of the cops, the design of the street lamps, the language on the signs.

The street lamps were on by now, gas-powered with a faint, pervasive tang you get because they're methane-powered from some distant recycling plant. There were more official-looking uniforms around than otherwise, maybe two to a street on average, but they were obviously the uniforms of civilian policing rather than military.

The lack of an obviously military presence on the streets, of course, was not a particularly reassuring sign. It just set the mind wondering as to where, in fact, all the soldiers might actually *be*.

All the same, I thought I could detect that war-footing smell about which Sela had spoken. I can't point out what caused it specifically – and maybe it was just because Sela had put the thought in my head – but it was a definite impression I got, in the same way you know whether or not you're going to like a bar the moment you walk through the door. There was a kind of violence-tension in the air – not that of an impending riot, but more sort of self-righteous and directed, if you get what I mean. Just feeling it around you, you could imagine all these people thinking, Hah! If that dastardly Johnny Hun tries anything here he'll get the shock of his life, and we're just the chaps to give it to him! – and suchlike. I suppose the word I'm groping for is jingoism – though directed at whom or what I couldn't say.

The native Thanaxons looked at me a bit suspiciously – as if, as a stranger, I might be a spy or something – but not with the flat-out hatred upon which they'd look at an Enemy. My experience with detention had left me with the subconscious impression that I'd stick out like a boil here, but I was only one of several off-worlders around, dressed better than most in my spanky new suit, and I wasn't being treated any differently.

My translation implants don't deal with the written word very well, in the sense that they flatly refuse to do it. I knew where I was going, though, from having memorized the route from a public map unit back at the hotel – and the small fact that such places are prominent, well lit and open twenty-six hours a standard day and have huge illuminated signs in languages that I can recognize.

GalEx Courier Services pride themselves on being able to deliver a package to anywhere they have an office, unopened and intact, under absolute guarantee. They use only full Stratum Seven operatives and they're the nearest thing in an imperfect world to perfect certainty. (Every so often, some bright local spark will catch on to the fact that this is an obvious route for locally illegal materials and try to shut them down – only to be met with extreme and obliterating reprisals. The GalEx setup is something like a physical law, like gravity – and you might not like gravity when it drops things on you, but just try living if it wasn't there. Its advantages outweigh its disadvantages – it's something you have to deal with, rather than try to change.)

GalEx rates are astronomical, of course, but my Pseudopod clients could afford it, and when I had decided to head for Thanaxos I had sent a package on ahead. And if you think it shows any kind of foresight to send said package to the GalEx main office in the city centre of the Thanaxon capital, within easy walking distance of the hotels where all the off-worlders stay, then you really ought to get out more.

I ran through the scans and keywords that told them who I was, and took the package to a private booth. I strapped on and concealed the various tools and weapons around my person and suit, making a note to get something custom-fitted the next day, when I went out to buy a new pair of boots. Sela always seemed to see me as a cross between a dance-hall instructor and a mob enforcer from an old movie. Then I fired up Box and strapped it to my arm.

Box chimed a couple of times as it booted and hooked itself into the data stream. Then: 'Hi there. Long time no see. A rather suspiciously long time no see, if you get my drift. Is there anything I should be aware of?'

'Nothing much, Box,' I told it. 'Hook in with the Pseudopod people and let 'em know I'm still on the case. No real updates on what they got before, but let them know that the Summerfield lead is dead.'

'Total and confirmed?' Box asked.

'Dormanted and hearsay. I don't think I can follow up. I want to find a way to Dellah now, so check with 'em what parameters they're happy with, up to and including buying my own ship on a legal basis and their money. I don't really want to do that. Check, specifically, if they're happy with me contracting out for local piecework that might take me there as part of it – there's no point in letting it go to waste if there is. Plus there's the question of cover stories to be considered.'

Box had been working on what I said as I said it, so there was no processing break. 'They're up for hiring a ship rather than buying,' it said. 'Blind-financed from a numbered account. They're happy for you to hire yourself out but don't, quote, forget who you're working for in the end, unquote.'

'Fair enough,' I said. 'By the way, hook into the credit houses and divert some into the account of Sela Dane – friend funds and completely above board. Don't make it look like a payoff or anything. It might be nice to find a local florist and have them send a bunch of something. She's staying at the Connaught Transient.'

'Sela Dane?' Box said. 'I like her. Lovely technical package. I have to tell you that they don't go much for flowers, here. Local specialities are a variety of chocolate ginger and leather goods made from the skins of ghouties, which are a sort of cross between a donkey and a three-toed sloth.'

'Even better. Have someone send some chocolate ginger, rather than the leather goods.'

'Are you sure she'd prefer that?'

'For the moment. We can explore that other particular avenue later.'

'I'm sure we can,' said Box, with an arch and Turing-envelope-pushing bit of artificial interaction.

'For the moment, Box, I want you to put out a trawl for that piecework deal we talked about. It's got to be one-off, short-term and it's got to get me in and out of Dellah. Those are the only things I care about. Only let me know if the job is on an immediate-reply basis. Store up anything else that comes along and I'll go through the file later.'

My route back to the hotel took me past a row of mismatched

tourist shops, each open late and lit up, each selling an almost identical selection of local-speciality leather goods and all of them, in all probability, owned by the same concern. Now that my attention had been drawn to it, I saw that the workmanship and the stuff itself was of a genuinely high quality. I spent a happy half an hour picking out the combat jacket and boots I had promised myself next day, paying tourist prices for what I'd probably get for half that much if I spent hours rooting through the back streets – the point being that *not* spending hours rooting through the back streets was what I was paying for. This made me a few minutes late for the hotel bar, in which I had arranged to meet up with Sela.

The bar was pretty much the same as you'd find in any better-class transient hotel anywhere, in the sense that it had been ponced up as an anodyne abstract of just about anything you can name rather than a bar. The lines and fixtures of this one were attempting to be suggestive of an early-twentieth-century cruise boat. It was called the Captain's Cabin. Manfully fighting the urge to go out and hunt down interior designers with a big gun, I carried my bulked-out tourist shopping bags to the counter, ordered a beer and looked around for Sela.

I couldn't spot her, but that wasn't worrying in itself. We knew each other well enough that she wouldn't have stormed off if I was ten minutes late, and neither would I. She was just running late. I settled down on a bar stool and scanned the light early-evening crowd in more detail. Just your basic bunch of commercial and recreational travellers, interspersed with locals: a few general acquaintances of guests, a few subtly provocative good-time boys and girls, plus a smattering of boys and girls running the key-game scam and who had to advertise more blatantly so that the clueless idiots who could be taken in by it could be caught . . .

My head snapped round so hard that I almost sprained my neck. My reflexes had cut in far too belatedly to more than catch a glimpse of the couple who were walking out of the door, with the studied, casual haste that had set off my internal alarms. I caught only a glimpse of them – a big, blond man; a smaller, dark-haired woman – but the pattern-recognition smacked into me like my synapses were electromagnetic bolts.

I'd seen this pair before. The last time had been Luna, when they'd fired on me through the crowd.

Supplementary Insert:

The House Royal has remained, over the course of centuries, the official residence of the Kings of Thanaxos and their courts – indeed, has been so since the Enlightened Consolidation (TB 1542) that united Thanaxos under one rule. The most elegant and sumptuous palace in the sector, it has been much imitated by foreign rulers and the equivalents of many off-world species. Originally a hunting lodge, some way from Rakath, it was rebuilt massively over successive years and now resides towards the centre of the still-expanding city.

The baroque forms of the palace itself are complemented by the extraordinary spectacle of the formal gardens, designed by the celebrated Sanguinity P'tantang, in TB 1687, who arranged innumerable statues, vases, fountains and floral clocks throughout the grounds. The addition of the amusement park, complete with parking space for more than fifteen thousand carriages, has been especially themed to carry on the spirit of this noble work.

Throughout the grounds are situated smaller, subsidiary enclaves, each designed to form, so much as is possible, a haven of tranquillity and a distinct environment in its own right. The most applauded of these so-called 'Little Gardens' must surely be the Shon-Thu garden, with its elegant sweeps of powdered coral and samphire, and its exquisite tearooms of lacquer and jade, in which refreshment may be purchased for a reasonable price.

Within the House itself, many rooms are open to the public, containing the riches of almost half a millennium. See the footstool, upon which the notorious Vertog IV was resting his feet as he signed the death warrant for Mara, Queen of the Woods. See the sumptuous majesty of the Ballroom, with its unsurpassed and painstakingly annotated collection of balls. See the chambers of Hairy Rolf XIIV and marvel at the carefully preserved contents of the convenience under the bed . . .

– Excerpt from *The House Royal – 473 Years of Thanaxon Splendour*, available from Ye Olde Royale Gift Shoppe

CHAPTER 9

Sela's suite was on the fifteenth floor, the direct route being taken by brass-cage elevators that were deliberately slower than their potential, to give the hotel patrons a kind of luxury-hotel elevator 'experience'. I took the emergency stairs. Quite apart from their being faster, the physical exertion helped to divert me from the realization and shame of my utter stupidity, which if I'd thought about it for an instant would have crippled me completely.

It was only when I saw the couple in the bar that I realized, truly realized, what I had been doing. After a month held prisoner I was suddenly free, and had been going through the reaction to it without so much as noticing. I had been farting around stupidly and with a stupid grin on my face, stupidly forgetting the job and being too stupid even to watch my back – and I had ended up doing something so utterly and unforgivably *stupid* that there was no way I could ever take it back. I'd linked Sela Dane to me, while on an active job, giving out the hotel where she was staying and everything. I'd killed her with a free box of chocolates thrown in.

I hit the fifteenth floor still breathing easily but with a singing in my tendons telling me that the lactic acid in my muscle tissue was doing its work. Ah well. Poor me. I wrenched back the fire-escape door and pigged on down the corridor, knocking aside an unattended room-service trolley with a shower of used cutlery and plates.

Here's a little trick. Hotels tend to be security-minded. The doors to rooms are heavy and solid – more to give the impression of security, of course, in this temporary home from home, rather than anything else. You don't, whatever you do, attempt to force them open with a shoulder. Not unless you know how to shove it back into its socket unassisted. What you do is this: you lie on your back and slam at it with the flats of your feet. This (a) gives you all the force of the most powerful muscles in the body, (b) directs said force into an area that the door designers didn't expect, and (c) means that whoever's actually *behind* the door finds themselves facing a target-profile somewhat out of the ordinary, and so is somewhat slower to react. The door gave on the second kick, the hasp of the lock bursting from the frame, and I rolled out of the line of fire – fixing the image before me in my mind before I bounced to my feet and came back round the doorway to do something about it . . .

All very dynamic and heroic, naturally. On the whole it was a bit of a pity that the image consisted of this: Sela was sitting on the suite's chaise longue, wearing that little black dress some women have as a secondary sexual attribute and dalons, unconcernedly sipping at a cup of coffee. Two men were in the room with her, two soldiers – but soldiers in the dashing if faintly ridiculous dress uniforms of the Thanaxon House Royal. All high collars and sabres, frogging and braid. I'd seen little models of them in the tourist shops and on the stalls in the hotel lobby. They were in the process of reacting to the door as it burst open, but there was something in their posture that suggested a chivalrous impulse to protect a lady from some possible assailant rather than anything else.

Sela raised a perfectly plucked eyebrow as, rather sheepishly, I walked back into the doorway. I noticed that she'd spent a lot of time on her face, while I was gone, applying make-up in the precise and seamless way that can accentuate a basic beauty without making one look like a painted doll. I wondered who she'd been planning to meet after having a drink with me.

'These guys would like you to accompany them to the House Royal,' she told me, flicking an amused glance at the soldiers, who were backing down from their reaction and replacing it with the kind of slightly contemptuous suspicion that, as I've said before, I tend to get a lot. 'Someone wants to talk to you. What have you got yourself into now?'

The Thanaxon House Royal was situated off to one side of the Rakath tourist quarter – on the one hand for its public spaces to be relatively near enough to rake in tourist credit, and on the other to be as far away from bloody tourists as possible. We were taken there by the Thanaxon variant of an automobile, a kind of modernized hansom cab, a black polypropylene shell over tungsten-carbide chassis, drawn by a small team of engines operated by steam superheated by passing it over radium. Slightly out of the ordinary, but no more inherently stupid than an internal-combustion engine, or having to keep a bale of horse feed in the boot.

By 'we' I mean the two palace guards, Sela and myself. Upon learning that I was to be taken to the House Royal she had demanded to be taken along – and I had flatly refused. It was an odds-on bet that this was just a setup, that these so-called guards were going to just drive me somewhere secluded and put a bolt in the back of my skull. The two guards had taken extreme umbrage at this, which didn't prove a thing – that would be precisely the act they'd have gone into if they *were* going to leave me lying in an alley somewhere.

Sela had refused to be budged. She had pointed out, at the top of her voice, that if removing me or herself was an option we'd be dead already. There was quite possibly a story in this, at some point, and she was damned if she'd let herself be muscled out of it. Besides, she had added, it would be safer to take her along. Cleaning up some grubby little chancer into something over his head was all very well, but taking out a bona fide member of the press into the bargain was something of a completely different order. (Sela could never quite get her head around the levels upon which I operated, thinking me not much more than a pawn in the underworld game with delusions of grandeur. What the hell. She might well have been right.)

Sela had then turned to the guards and stated flatly that if she didn't come along then neither would I. This had led to a hasty conference via portable radiophone – the hush-field activated so's I couldn't hear what was going on – with the result that she would be allowed to come with me, subject to confidentiality protocols that meant she wouldn't broadcast or divulge the material she gathered without express consent. Sela had had the forms already punched up on her datapack.

Her presence in the cab was something of a mixed blessing. It meant another random factor, another person to look out for, but, even so, it was nice to have a friend around. It was what I needed after so long isolated, a reminder on the deep subconscious level of the connections that hooked me to the wider human world. Plus the fact that her perfume, together with the feel of her in the seat beside me, where we touched, was doing things to my limbic and hormonal systems that I thought I'd forgotten about.

The two guards sat in little pull-down seats and with their back to the driver, regarding us stonily. This made my bolt-in-the-head ideas slightly more unlikely – they'd have tried to bracket me if that were so – but they remained uncommunicative as to whom we were going to see and what it was about.

The House Royal resides in a geodesic dome, in the centre of a landscaped garden of surpassing elegance and tranquillity. A guidebook I'd skimmed as part of general research made comparisons with Babylon, Blenheim Palace and the Forbidden Citadel rolled into one. That may be so, but we didn't get to see any of it. The cab took us through an unlit section and deposited us by a rather scuffed and utilitarian-looking side door of the palace itself. One of the guards rapped on it and it was opened, after some wait, by a frail-looking and elderly footman.

'Ah, yes,' he said, in a papery little voice that reminded me uncomfortably of the late Professor Sabron Jones. 'You'll be the visitors the Minister is expecting.'

'If you say so,' I said.

The footman led us down the corridor, the guards in tow. I don't know why they followed, rather than going about some other duties. I felt that very faint electromagnetic hum, on the very edges of perception, that told me we were being scanned by the House Royal security systems seven ways from Sunday. Maybe they just wanted to make doubly sure we weren't going to steal the ornaments – and there was even less chance of that. The corridor was incredibly shabby and unadorned save for some ratty items of furniture and a few crumbling egg-yolk paintings that looked as if they would fall apart to the touch.

'People don't see this wing of the house,' the footman explained, as if we'd asked him about it directly. 'All the choicest items are arranged in the public areas, on display. This is where we keep such things as are of no real value. They took everything else away. It's a crying shame, casting things aside and leaving them to gather dust when they could so easily be brought back to their former glory. That's a genuine Flotgrang, that is . . .' This to a table by the wall that looked something like a plank nailed to a couple of sawhorses. 'Bit of lacquer and a French polishing and she'd come up lovely, so she would.'

He gestured towards a picture frame so choked with the gunk of ages that it was impossible to discern more than vague shapes beneath. '*The Little Sisters and the Nine Wide Swans*, by Meechum, you know. I remember when you could see the brushwork clear as day. Do they clean it up? Of course they don't. That would be far too much trouble for them and so they just dump it here . . .' The footman continued what seemed to be an automatic, querulous litany and I tuned it out.

'What's that one?' Sela said abruptly, pointing to a frame. It seemed rather newer than the decrepit antiques around it and was partially obscured by the leaves of an overgrown potted aspidistra, as though hidden away out of some unconscious embarrassment. Through the leaves I caught the distinctly unprepossessing features of a youngish man, a protruding set to his ears, an even more protruding set of front teeth and a jaw you could swing off, giving it the aspect of the cruellest caricature imaginable of inbred Royalty with a capital R.

'That doesn't look old and worn out enough to be discarded,' Sela commented. 'Rather ghastly, but not exactly old.'

'Ah, well, that particular piece is something of a special nature,' said the footman, his automatic enumeration of disapproval at the capriciousness of the world momentarily derailed. 'That was painted by the Artist in Residence to the Court to commemorate the occasion of the Young Prince's twenty-first birthday.' You could hear the capital letters in the old man's voice, a kind of ingrained sense that the 'Young Prince' was an entity set apart, a personage to which the common human responses and values did not apply. It was the modern-day equivalent of a mediaeval serf knowing, deep in the bones, that the King held appointment directly under God, and could not be looked at, no matter how many cats actually did just that. Given that different basic way of thinking – a way of thinking that hardly a one of us has any more – a fable like 'The Emperor's New Clothes' takes on a new and slightly different poignancy.

'A quite unfortunate affair,' the footman continued. 'I gather that the artist in question is still in the Tower, awaiting his excruciation . . .'

'Not a good likeness, then?' said Sela.

'Not exactly, but it's something one shouldn't really be – Aha! And here we are.' The footman had led us onward with a new haste, as though trying in as seemly manner as possible to put some space between us and the unfortunate portrait of the Young Prince. He announced our arrival, at a stout set of double doors, with something like relief.

The palace guards took up position on either side, poker-faced as ever. The footman went through one of the doors and held it open for us.

Sela started through. 'Ladies before gentlemen.'

I grabbed hold of the back of the dress and pulled her back, not quite hard enough to tear it fetchingly, but hard enough to make it quite clear that she wasn't going in. 'Ladies went before gentlemen in the days when gentlemen didn't care if ladies got eaten by a cave bear or trod on a mine. I go first.'

'Oh but you're just so butch and manly,' Sela muttered sarcastically. 'My hero.' But she let me go ahead.

The chamber was a conference room, reminiscent of the one I'd encountered back in the Pseudopod offices in Luna. The details were different – the table was oblong and covered with archaic-looking paperwork, the lighting was a variety of gas lamp, the décor was baroque and antique – but there was something about it that recalled the Pseudo-pod boardroom right away.

This something was the figure who was waiting in it, leaning against the mahogany conference table with a relaxed if slightly studied nonchalance. Others were in the room, seated at the table, but they contrived to be mere background to this one man.

It was Volan.

CHAPTER 10

It wasn't Volan, of course, not in that sense. For one thing, he wasn't quite as fat, and for another he was quite obviously of native Thanaxon blood. The impression was there, however, a sense of recognition so powerful that I'll swear that I knew who he was, essentially, even before he so much as mentioned that he was one of those counterparts I talked of earlier, the embodiment in spirit, if not in fact, of Michaels-Presteign Volan Tiberius of Pseudopod Enterprises Societé d'Anonime.

'A good evening to you,' he said, a trifle sardonically. 'I trust that you are quite recovered from your unfortunate experiences in detention. Had I but known of your professional status and predicament, or even your existence, I'd have arranged for your release immediately. I'm afraid that your, uh, methods of entry into our jurisdiction were rather too unorthodox for our poor resources. We're a little off the beaten track, here, you understand.'

'And who might you be to take such an interest?' I said, playing it cagey – I didn't know the situation, yet, and the last thing I wanted to do was blow what might or might not be a cover identity.

'Oh, the name I went under before my employment with Pseudopod Enterprises – that being my occupation *ex officio* – is neither here nor there. In my actual job of work

I'm the Thanaxon representative of an incorporate head by the name of Volan, and the name of Volan will suffice.' The ersatz Volan waved an airy hand – he seemed to have the manner off pat, if a bit overcharacterized and affected. 'You meet me now, however, in my capacity of Minister for Foreign Affairs Pursuant to the Court of the Thanaxon House Royal.'

This told me two things in short order: that I didn't have to dance around Volan's connections with Pseudopod, but that it wouldn't be a good idea to say how I was working for them as well.

'What, really?' I said. 'Doesn't that knock into your time a little bit? Not to mention the question of a conflict of interest?'

Again that rather studied wave of a Volan hand. 'Not at all. The one does not preclude the other. I am a distinct individual, a man of substance, prominence and good standing, with influential business contacts in the galaxy at large. What better choice, as a Thanaxon by birth, for election to the Council?' Volan gestured towards a military-looking gentleman seated at the table and bad-temperedly knocking back a glass of spirits. 'To say otherwise, you might as well say that Field Marshal G'ran here should not be Commander in Chief of the armed forces because he's an old soldier.' Volan turned back to me with a little smile. 'Believe me, if I were to promote my own personal business interests, or the interests of Pseudopod Enterprises, at the expense of Thanaxos, the people would have something to say about it – as would what you might call my rivals in the incorporate world.'

What he said rang true. I've already mentioned my blind spot when it comes down to the minutiae of planetary politics, but I was generally aware that, while the monarchy held the power here on Thanaxos, the administration was in the hands of an Advisory Council that was, ostensibly, democratically elected. These administrators worked on an effectively part-time basis and were not expected to give up their outside interests – the idea being that this (a) kept them in contact with the real world, and (b) didn't give them the time to get bored and so get up to all kinds of bureaucratic mischief. If I could have been bothered to research further and learn the faces and the names, I would have known from the instant I walked into the room that I was in the presence of the people who basically, when they had a spare moment, ran the planet.

I fixed the faces in my mind, now, of the twelve people in the room apart from Volan. Four women, eight men, nothing particularly worth relating about them save for an air of late-night, shirtsleeved tiredness. Cups of the local equivalent of coffee were in evidence, and Field Marshal G'ran wasn't the only one who had moved on to something stronger. I shrugged to myself – it was their planet; they could do what they liked with it.

Volan turned his attention from me and nodded to the footman. 'Thank you, Gnatbeadle. You may go. I do hope Gnatbeadle hasn't been boring you with his tales of antiquity,' he continued, somewhat more chattily, when the servant had withdrawn. 'In happier days he was quite the expert on the wing that houses these chambers, and he's never quite come to terms with these harder, more pragmatic times.'

He then turned to Sela and beamed with what appeared to be genuine pleasure. 'Ms Dane! It is always a pleasure to receive a visit from a member of the news services, especially one so accomplished and, dare I say it, charmingly attractive as your good self.'

'Thanks,' said Sela vaguely. 'Just pretend I'm not here.'

'But of course,' Volan said smoothly, as if both of them didn't know that this was complete toss. Administrative discussion of death-camp quotas, riot-control procedures, off-world annexations or the like was simply not going to occur and everybody damn well knew it. 'As it happens, though,' Volan continued, 'we are here to discuss a matter with which you might like to be personally involved. That was, of course, the foremost reason why we allowed you to –'

'Look, can we get on with this, Volan?' snapped a harassed-looking and middle-aged Thanaxon whom I later learnt to be the Under-Secretary for Agricultural Development. 'I haven't been home before midnight in a month and the kids are forgetting what I look like. Can't we just move things along?'

'My apologies, D'nar,' said Volan. 'To the matter in hand, then.' He turned back to Sela and me, speaking to us both: 'As you're no doubt aware, relations with the planet Dellah have been somewhat strained of late . . .'

Field Marshal G'ran snorted. 'If by strained ye mean shut off entirely, and without so much of a by-your-leave. Damned impertinence, I call it. Buggers should be taught a –'

'Yes, quite, Field Marshal,' said Volan hurriedly. 'Be that as it may. The fact of the matter is that such a sad state of affairs cannot be allowed to continue. Now it just so happens that we have received a communiqué from the Sultan of one of the Dellahan principalities, offering to broker a deal for the re-establishment of diplomatic contact . . .'

A little thought was forming in my mind. 'That wouldn't be the Sultan of Tashwari, would it?'

'As a matter of fact it would,' said Volan, with a meaningful little don't-push-your-luck-sunshine look. 'We'll be sending a diplomatic mission to Dellah within the week.' He turned to Sela. 'Obviously, the eyes of the world – the world of Thanaxos and the galaxy as a whole – will be on such a venture, and I would deem it an inestimable pleasure, Ms Dane, if one such as you were to join the diplomatic party as an independent observer.'

Sela's enhanced eyes lit up at the chance of an exclusive. 'Full access?'

'Within agreed limits. Our negotiations packages can handle the specifics. Your reputation for even-handedness and integrity of fact is well known, Ms Dane, and our interests coincide in that we are only interested in the facts.' Was this edition of Volan so blatant as to actually wink, or did I just imagine it?

Sela nodded thoughtfully to herself. 'Do I get to take my crew?'

'Subject to file vetting and veto.'

'Fair enough. I'll talk to my people at DataDay and see what they want to go for.'

'I await their response with bated breath.' Volan turned his attention back to me. 'Of course, the actual negotiations will be handled by fully trained diplomatic staff – but the mission itself must have the sanctioned validity of the House Royal. To this end, it must be under the titular command of a member of the Royal Family. Sadly, the King himself is of such age and infirmity as to make such a venture impossible in person. In the light of this, we have decided to call upon the gracious service of his Regent, the Young Prince . . .'

A kind of murmur ran through those assembled in the room. It had a note similar to that recognition of otherness as evidenced by the footman, Gnatbeadle, when he had mentioned the Prince – but tinged with something more. I couldn't quite put my finger on it, but the tone seemed decidedly uncomplimentary.

'Security,' said Volan, 'is thus of paramount importance – and, while our military forces are more than up to the task, one cannot be too careful. It would be a disaster unsustainable, a loss beyond our bearing were we to lose such a splendid national treasure as our Young Prince.' For some reason, I got the distinct impression that the Minister for

Foreign Affairs was flatly refusing to meet the eyes of the other members of the Council. 'In this light, when we learnt via the datanet that a security operative of your calibre was accepting commissions, it was too good an opportunity to resist. This is why we have brought you here – I trust you understand now why we have brought you here in secret.' Volan struck the slightly fey but nobly heroic pose of a man hell-bent on doing his best for King, or even Prince, and country. 'Would you, sir, be willing to accept a contract as the personal bodyguard of the Young Prince, for the duration of this mission?'

Which was of course my cue. I didn't want to overplay it, so I just sat there for a while, as though in serious thought. 'It would be an honour, Minister,' I said at last.

Volan sighed with barely affected relief. 'Rest assured, you will be rewarded fully commensurate with your expertise. For the moment, though, I think it might be well you meet your charge.' There was a small ivory bell push on the table, which he depressed. After a while, he depressed it again, for rather longer this time. 'Where is the little –' He appeared to catch himself. 'I mean, I'm sure the Young Prince will be arri–'

Off to one side a door swung open, and a figure blundered in, tripped over the carpet and fell flat on his face. I had been partially prepared by the glimpse of the portrait in the hall but, even so, the reality was worse, far worse, than I could have ever possibly imagined.

It was wearing what might have been a splendid military dress uniform, had it been buttoned up the right way, or indeed at all, and if one absent-mindedly chewed epaulette wasn't hanging off it by a thread. The addition of trousers and underwear might have also been a help. The apparition stumbled to its feet and beamed around itself with the cheerful, drooling, self-important idiocy of a complete and congenital idiot.

'What-ho, chaps!' he exclaimed. 'I waited a really long time, don't you know! Then I had to take my pants off 'cause I was *dirty*.' He nodded solemnly at this last; being dirty was obviously a very, very bad thing indeed.

From somewhere behind me I heard Sela snort with barely suppressed laughter. Volan stared grimly and rigidly into the middle distance. Around the table, various members of the Council put their hands over their eyes.

'Allow me to present,' Volan said, in a voice so tight it occasionally squeaked, 'His Most Excellent and Puissant Highness, Prince G'jimo, Regent of the Thanaxon House Royal. This man is here to look after you, Jimbo. Keep you safe. Say hello to the nice man, Jimbo.'

'Bingo!' Prince G'jimo – Jimbo – bounded over to me, stuck out a hand and then, as I shied away from it despite myself, absent-mindedly wiped what I could only hope was dribble off it and on to his tunic. 'Hallo.' He looked at me sideways, conspiratorially. 'I saw a monkey, today. It was a funny monkey. It was wearing a hat.'

SUPPLEMENTARY INSERT:

Oh Ye Believers,

Fellow compatriots in this noble and most excellent venture to bring the Light of Truth into the eyes of the Infidel, as sanctioned by and in the Name of the All-High Gods of the New Republic;

Peoples of New Tashwari, that finest of all citadels under the Gods that shines in the dark night like the most precious and costly of all jewels;

Peoples of the most estimable and Revolutionary Republic of New Dellah, that beacon of Holy Light and Hope that shines in the firmament's dark, bring light to the souls of all Believers;

True Believers and converts everywhere, though we know your numbers are lamentably few, living as you do under the iron boot heels of the worshippers of false gods, the slavers of commercial enterprise and the lies of propagandists;

Fellow travellers, who might yet be taught the errors of your foul, unsanitary and hell-bound ways;

Infidels –

I welcome you to this triumphant and most glorious venture that shall bring the Light and Truth to those Infidels who even now pollute the heart of our blessed and most beautiful republic with their heathen and noxiously animal presence.

(*Stormy and prolonged applause from all Believers gathered here.*)

All glory to his mighty and most regal excellency, the Sultan, father, his palace staff and his Guard, who under the All-High Gods has made their will known and provided the facilities. And especial glory to the caterers.

(*Stormy applause.*)

Long live the glorious and triumphant Republic of New Dellah, which inspires and organizes all victories for the Believer under the magnificent and splendid auspices of the All-High Gods! Divine will lights our destiny and causes us to perform prodigious feats for the benefit and Enlightenment of all Believers!

(*Stormy and prolonged applause.*)

In the name of Malon and His Brethren

(*Stormy and prolonged applause and cheers.*)

Coffee will now be served for fifteen minutes in the hospitality lounge.

Was that all right, do you think?

(*Realizes microphone is still on.*)

– Thanaxos–Dellah diplomatic mission: transcript of opening speech by Dellahan Chief Consul

CHAPTER 11

The ruins of St Oscar's lay around me: smashed terracotta and ash as far as the eyes could see, the broken stumps of buildings protruding jaggedly through it like a misshapen set of bloodstained teeth. Or teeth with the enamel stripped, to show the dentine and the bloody pulp below.

Here and there the glass and metallic scraps of scientific equipment, the scorched remains of papers, the general personal detritus of the four thousand or so who had lived and breathed and eaten and worked here while they got into tussles about it being forbidden to grow begonias in the greenhouse. As with any large-scale massacre or destruction, the magnitude becomes too great to really feel it unless you fix on some specific, someone or something you know, something that can bring the full impact of it home to you – and I was stuck with Sabron sodding Jones and his bloody pot plants.

Prince Jimbo was sitting on a small pile of pottery. 'Uncle Mumfrey said I could go to university,' he proclaimed with idiot pride. 'The moment I learnt to tie my shoes. And I can. Look!' He climbed to his feet, took one step forward with the laces tied together and fell flat on his face.

I have no idea what the Thanaxon diplomatic party were expecting from Dellah and the Sultan of Tashwari, but I very much doubt if it was what they actually got. It was made perfectly clear from the start that we were all the lot of us Hated Foreign Dogs of Unbelievers, but, under Dellah's code of cultural hospitality, we were to be afforded the status of Honoured Guests for a time up to but not over three local days and nights. We were offered every service and comestible, by sweetly smiling and quite resplendent servants, whose sweet smiles nonetheless contrived to suggest what would happen if we outstayed our welcome by so much as a nanosecond.

The diplomatic function itself would take place in a kind of splendid, gilded rococo auditorium, in which the Thanaxon envoys would sit and be harangued in the sight of a crowd of the Faithful as to their Godless, decadent and warmongering iniquity, never being allowed to rebut, refute or indeed make any kind of reply at all.

Before the upheavals and the Earth-imposed blockade, as I understood it, the spiritual life of Dellah as a culture had been expressed through something similar to Hindu Buddhism – the specifics were different and it was more complicated than that, but that was the nearest analogy in human terms. Now, and almost overnight, it seemed that things had shifted into the equivalent of some fundamentalist Islam. There seemed to be a new god in town – or rather, multiple gods, the specific nature of which remained unspecified. Maybe someone told you their names when you became a Believer. These various All-High Gods were the only gods, and if you didn't Believe you might be pitied, but you certainly didn't deserve to be allowed to live. You couldn't *fart* without exhorting, in the most boastful terms imaginable, the glory of these gods, the Revolutionary Order of New Dellah and its Glorious Leaders, both coming and going, whose unstinting efforts for the betterment of humankind had made the fart in question such a triumph for New Dellahan Order. Like as not with all around you breaking into wild spontaneous applause at how triumphant – as a splendid example of the glory of the All-High Gods and the revolutionary New Dellahan Order – that fart in fact was.

Thing is, while the dogma and constructs of Islam evolved so that what appeared, on the surface to outsiders, as a simple trotting out of platitudes could in fact convey nuance and true meaning, a defining of relationships, this new Dellahan dogma seemed a bit bolt-on. It was as if they were going against the grain, trying their damnedest, couldn't quite manage it and so were doubling their efforts to try to get it right. This tended to beg the question of who, or what, was watching them to make sure they did.

On the subject of going through this diplomatic farce, the Thanaxon delegates had decided to do it – hoping by their calm and reasonable demeanour to make an impression and win on moral points. Personally, I thought they were on a hiding to nothing.

Prince Jimbo, they had tactfully agreed, would take no active part in the proceedings, and it was tacitly agreed – on oh-so-civilized and respectful terms – that my job was to keep him the hell out of the way. It was yet another example of that curious double-think I'd encountered in the Council chamber on Thanaxos and again on the jump into the Dellah system in the Royal Yacht, as everybody had tried their level best to ignore the fact that he was pawing the flight attendants with the mindless persistence of a priapic stoat with a lobotomy. Everybody knew the guy was a blundering little inbred tit, with the personal habits of a bare-arsed baboon and the mind of a plank, but nobody was going to be the first to come out and say it.

Ah well, I'd thought – as I sat back in my acceleration seat and tried to tune out the happy burbling to the effect that it was amazing, wasn't it, and that we must be travelling at more than a hundred miles an *hour* – if anyone was going to try to knock the little bastard off, it was me who'd have to be lucky all the time, and they who'd only have to be lucky once.

I remembered a certain call I'd got . . .

The call had come the night before we were to leave and take our respective places in the diplomatic party. Sela had stirred, and muttered something unintelligible that sounded a bit, to me, like 'Monkey on a stick'.

'It's not for you,' I told her, recognizing the tone of the bleeps. 'It's coming from Box. It's for me.'

I disentangled myself from her and padded over to the little truncated hallway and door that separated the bedroom of the hotel suite from the lounge area, snagging Box, from where I had left it hanging from the back of a chair, on the way.

'Incoming and private,' Box told me as I entered the lounge. 'Audio and visual. Want me to put up a resonance field?'

'Yeah, do it,' I said, plugging Box into the suite's comms monitor. I'd swept the place for bugs and suchlike, but there was the possibility that Sela might wake up properly and come in to hear something that might jeopardize her. Box set up the field that would counter electronic and physically sonic eavesdropping and, from the outside, make the air haze so that the movements of my mouth could not be read.

A face popped up on the monitor, wearing that little subconscious look of irritation of someone who's made a call and has being waiting for the other end to pick up – the look that's the first thing everyone sees, and has seen since the days phones first got screens.

It was Volan. Not the latest fake one, the one who helped to run Thanaxos in his spare time; the one who helped run Pseudopod all the livelong day.

'Why am I not surprised?' I said. 'I thought the setup had to be too good to be true. That other Volan might talk about keeping his responsibilities separate, but we all know what's really pulling his strings.'

The real Volan's features assumed that smooth insouciance that I had come to realize was his defining characteristic – having seen it aped so actively by his local counterpart.

'Actually,' he said, 'the setting up of it was a unilateral decision by my counterpart. I only became aware of it when he conferenced me to get the all-clear. Too good an opportunity to miss, I understand – but I must admit that the end result is entirely more fortunate than otherwise for us all.'

'Yeah, whatever,' I said.

'The reason I'm calling,' Volan continued, 'is that I'm after your opinion on this matter. Now, my counterpart swears blind that this so-called "diplomatic mission" –' you could hear the little quote marks around the term '– is absolutely in good faith. He makes it sound plausible – but then, I know myself, and plausibility is my middle name . . .'

'What? You've got yet another one?' I said.

'I am,' said Volan, 'a remarkably substantive person.' His expression became deadly serious. 'So, in your professional opinion, is this "diplomatic mission" a genuine attempt to salvage a working peace in the face of a potential war, or is it just a bit of window-dressing before the first shot is fired?'

'It's window-dressing,' I said. I didn't even have to think about it.

'All right,' said Volan. 'I'll take that into account.'

'What, that it's window-dressing or that I just *think* it's window-dressing?'

Volan beamed. 'What do you think?'

'I try not to, much,' I said.

'Good man. Now, the matter of guarding this Young Prince. I know you people take your work extremely seriously, but I want to be clear about one thing. Protect him from harm, by all means, but not at the expense of your prior commitments. I want you to know, for what my word's worth, that there will be no comeback should the Prince suffer an, as it were, unfortunate accident that you're unable to prevent.'

'Volan,' I said. 'It's late and I've just woken up. Tell me if that's meant to be any kind of hint.' I pantomimed putting a gun to a head execution-style and cocking it, for Box's visual pickup.

Volan looked at me a little angrily. 'Absolutely, positively not. All I'm saying is, if push comes to shove, you remember where your prior commitments lie.'

I had expected to have problems getting away from the Sultan's palace. We might be here as guests and our persons sacrosanct, but I was far from sure how far this would stretch if we started sticking our noses in where they weren't wanted. In the event, though, I needn't have wondered. In some way that, at the time, I couldn't fathom, both Prince Jimbo and I seemed to do something odd to the Dellahans' perceptions.

It wasn't, quite, that they didn't see us: it was that they didn't notice us. You could get a tray of food from one of the servants, say, if you asked for it forcefully enough, but, if you didn't keep following him and reminding him about it, he'd forget about it and wander away. It was like looking at something, deciding you're not interested and then putting it out of your mind – but on a deeper, stronger level.

I learnt why this was happening sometime later, of course, and the slightly different reasons for it – but the fact that it seemed to affect only me and Jimbo scared the hell out of me. I kept poking at it with my mind, like a tongue pokes at a broken tooth, trying to find some similarity between myself and this drooling moron that could explain it, and which wouldn't want me to immediately stick a gun to my head.

In any event. I had hung around the conference hall for maybe half an hour of day one, in the equivalent of a Royal Box, munching the complimentary delicacies – which had been laid out beforehand, in anticipation of the arrival of some important personage, as opposed to an Invisible Idiot – and looking down upon the stormily applauding crowd as yet another Dellahan delegate made yet another quarter-hour-long speech to announce what his name was before I decided I had had enough. I had a job to do.

Prince Jimbo seemed happy enough, having found a piece of string from somewhere, which had kept him amused since breakfast. Possibly it was just me, but I got the distinct impression that, on leaving Thanaxos, he had reverted even further from the cheerful drooling idiot I'd originally met to an actual moron with the mental capacity of a small dog and the mental age of a toddler. Maybe it was just that he had been extensively coached for that first meeting – but I couldn't shake the feeling that there was somehow more to it than that . . .

I debated whether to just leave him here – he'd probably be safer than if I took him, if only on account of not being noticed – but there's such a thing as professional pride. I might be using this job as a cover, but it was still a job and, while I'd have rather pitched the little sod over the rail and into the crowd below, I'd been contracted to look after him. I couldn't let him out of my sight.

I sighed. 'Come on, Jimbo,' I said shoving him rather harder than I'd meant to in order to get his attention. 'We're leaving.'

A look of petulance crossed Prince Jimbo's face for having

his fun with this marvellous bit of string spoilt, and then he forgot about it. 'Are we going somewhere nice?' he said, a childish hope briefly animating his slack-jawed features.

'We're going somewhere,' I admitted.

The petulance was back again. 'Don't want to go if it's not somewhere nice.'

I sighed. 'All right, Jimbo. It's somewhere nice.'

'Bingo!' The imbecilic, sunny joy of the terminally retarded burst from him. And then his face changed yet again.

'What the hell are you doing now?' I shouted.

Prince Jimbo had clenched his fists and face and stuck his elbows out in a horribly familiar-looking little tableau of inner strain. He relaxed again.

'Uncle Mumfrey told me to always go before I go somewhere nice,' he said proudly. 'And I just have.'

Professional pride has a hell of a lot to bloody answer for.

We had simply walked out of the palace, unaccosted, unremarked upon and, apparently, barely even noticed. The city outside was your usual hubbub of urban sprawl, and you'd have to be a new arrival from where conditions were slightly better – even a Thanaxos soft-shoe-shuffling itself into a war footing – to catch the impression that a faint patina of seediness and grubbiness had only quite recently come across this scene. And that, by degrees imperceptible except over the course of months, the trend was going down rather than up.

Now there are any number of travel journos, outworld correspondents and the like (Sela wasn't one of them) who will tell you that, when you visit a basically theocratic culture, you can smell the raw Faith with a capital F in the streets. No you can't. Raw something else, perhaps, but not raw Faith. What you're smelling is the fact that mere, prosaic things like building things, repairing them and keeping them clean are done in a cursory, slipshod fashion, because the effort, attention and time of the people who should be doing them is eaten up by the protocols of the intangible. Likewise producing any kind of art outside the prescribed bounds, or thinking up new gadgets to do things, or ways to make sure that almost everyone is pretty-much fed.

As I'd seen in the palace, Dellah was in transition – was willing this transition – but the cultural lag of a billion-odd people trying to get their heads around the same idea meant that by my lights things could have been worse. It would be quite some time before the beggars outnumbered the people giving alms. For the moment Dellah retained some semblance of the development it had achieved before the blockade.

There were hover cabs, here and there – and the thing about hover cabs was that with their floaters and the working-life perpetual engines that kept their maintenance down, they were, effectively, all-terrain vehicles with no limit on the distance. It was but the work of an increasingly infuriating hour to drag Jimbo through a crowd that kept bumping into us unawares, locate an empty cab, plug Box into it and short the controls to manual. I could only hope that this strange sense of obscurity we possessed didn't somehow extend to the fact of this large lump of metal and moulded resin barrelling through pedestrian-crowded markets, streets and combinations of the two. Fortunately, it didn't.

There's a long, long tradition the whole galaxy over, upon the various planets of the galaxy at least, of cities deriding the open country and vice versa. The city, says the country, has cut itself off from Nature and wallows in its own decadence and filth, while the country, say the city dwellers, stands up to its collective knees in the shit of its farm animals and shags them. In fact, from the outside, you can see the two planetary states as being roughly equal – the cities merely being scrunched up tight and the country being laid out flat. In any case, after getting out of the city and its declining but still relatively high levels of wealth, I got to see how the other half were living under the revolutionary New Dellahan regime. They weren't doing very well.

I gather that it used to rain all the time on Dellah – the result of the Sky Pylon, a vastly extruded, monomolecular cable that physically connected the planet to its orbital space station and disrupted the weather patterns. Now the Pylon and the station were gone, and the world was reverting to desert. There were sad little clusters of sandstone huts that looked like outhouses. The outhouses, of course, were non-existent. Each grouping was surrounded by a scraggy patch of cultivated land that I assumed was the equivalent of a vegetable garden – but if they were, the lot of them wouldn't have produced the garnish for a tub of coleslaw.

I saw figures in the landscape, just standing there as if they had been dumped – I recalled those faceless, spectral creatures you see, in the murk between the Futurism and the motorways, in a lot of Nazi art. The land itself seemed half dead as I drove through it. I was just following a direction as opposed to actual directions, for there was no road, paved or otherwise. It was all scorched foothills and flatlands well on the way to becoming desert, a crazy paving of eroded trenches, the skeletal remains of cattle in the pastures that they'd overgrazed.

Prince Jimbo just sat there, gazing out of the window, his mind seemingly switched completely off. He'd had another accident, and even with the cab's air conditioning – working, for a wonder – on full blast, the smell was getting to me.

It was almost a relief, in the end, to come upon the devastated wreckage of the university.

* * *

The immediate area was secure in that this sector of the ruins of St Oscar's was deserted. There's a kind of specific tang to a place – if you get what I mean – where once you know who's there and have counted noses, you know, deep inside, that there's no one else.

Of course, the fact that Box's sensors showed no body-heat signatures or movement was a help as well. There was absolutely nothing. Even animal life, such as might have survived in this drought-struck desert, didn't seem to want to enter the wreckage. I left Prince Jimbo trying to work out what was wrong with his shoelaces and went for a wander.

The trick is, sometimes, not to think about things too much, let your mind go and just go where your feet want to take you, let your eyes fall upon what they want to fall upon, your hands pick up and feel what they like. I found what I was looking for some fifteen minutes later. Mind you, I didn't know what the hell I was looking for until I found it. It could have been anything.

It was four big, crosslike, impacted indents in the ground, obviously the landing gear for a ship, maybe a planet-hopper but far more likely a small cruiser of some kind. The depth of compression within the indents told me that this ship had rested here for some time – it was impossible to be sure, but we were talking weeks if not months. The fact that there were shards of red pottery driven into the ground, of course, told me that this ship had come, and stayed, and gone away again, after the university had been destroyed.

I walked up and down, picturing the ship in my mind. If I were a ship this big, depending upon which way I was facing, I'd have an exit hatch either here or here . . .

I picked the wrong direction first and had to backtrack. The other way led into the broken remains of one of the potlike buildings. Just the place, if you wanted to make camp, to go back and forth between the ship.

The broken remains of a sign clattered under my feet. It read:

DEPARTME
O
ARCHAEOL
AN
XENOARCHAE

Off to one side, piled up against the inside of the outer pottery wall, was a makeshift shelter, built from old support beams and a large board, which had once served as a reference map for the surrounding buildings, and now served as a kind of slanting roof. It couldn't be to keep the rain off, and the lee of the wall protected against the sun – it could only have been built out of that innate desire for something sheltered and enclosed that has people making tents and pulling the blanket over their heads.

I clipped a little mesmetic pinlight to my teeth and went inside. A bedroll and an archaic-looking Primus stove. A pile of empty and discarded military-spec ration packs. A smaller, neatly stacked heap of same that were still full. Various other items of a generally personal nature, a littering of little yellow paper scraps and so forth. But my eyes were immediately drawn to what was on the bedroll . . .

It was a largish, ledger-like and new-looking book – a genuine book, bound in synthetic leather, with gold tooling and everything. Inside, precise lines of scrupulously neat handwriting marched across unlined, rag-bond pages smooth as vellum. The materials and craftsmanship, the condition, the sheer effort that must have gone into its neatness, combined to give it the aspect of some precious object in its own right. I closed the book gently, and carefully opened it from the start to read the title page:

– A Journal –

Bernice Surprise Summerfield

'Slightly Problematic' to 'You Never Know'

SUPPLEMENTARY INSERT:

. . . and for hours after we left the space station Rebecca just piloted the ship in a stony silence. The weals on her face and neck slowly darkened to actual bruising. I wanted to say something, but I was obscurely ashamed of myself, full of so many other conflicting emotions that I couldn't quite bring myself to open my mouth. Of course, I rationalized it – it was Rebecca, after all, who wasn't talking to me, and if she wasn't I'd be damned if I started the ball rolling.

Eventually, I decided this was silly. 'Look, this is silly,' I said. 'It looks as though we're going to have each other's company for some considerable period of time yet so we might as well find some way to pass it in as friendly manner as possible.'

Rebecca snorted. 'Yeah, right. Let's play a little game or something.' She peered rather theatrically through the canopy of the little craft. 'I spy with my little eye, something beginning with S. Your go. I spy with my little eye, something beginning with S. Your go. I spy with . . .'

'I *mean*,' I said, rather more cuttingly than I had meant, but she had annoyed me – oh, Goddess, how she could get under my skin and annoy me. 'I mean,' I said, 'that we could just talk. Tell each other what's been happening with our lives and so forth.'

'Fine,' Rebecca said uninterestedly. 'You go first.'

I have to admit to being caught a little wrong-footed, even though I had laid myself open to it. I think it was because of that unconscious egocentricity that everyone has – I had unconsciously expected *her* to know everything important about *me* as a matter of course. Seen in that light, having put myself on the spot in that manner, it was hard to think of precisely what to say. What could I say, what had I done, what had happened to me in my life that could ultimately, in some final sense, *define* it . . .?

. . . I'd forgotten about Gerhardt. He'd died. No, let's be honest, here if nowhere else – I'd killed him less than an hour before. Perhaps now, Gerhardt's mother or lover or sister was sitting, waiting for the news. Did any such women exist? I'd lived with him for three months, but didn't know anything about him. He must have had family, though. Across the world, women were sitting in houses and factories, waiting for their men to come home, dreading the fact that they might not.

Rebecca was in the same situation, of course. I didn't quite know how to feel about that. Sympathy? Sorrow? Gratitude and love? Guilt at what I was putting her through, what she was going through? Such little worlds but they encompass an entire world . . .

. . . the conclusion that there *is* no single root source. I think that, in the end, all those stock elements you find in children's stories come from *two* distinctly different realms of human experience, at the very least. Things like elves, gnomes, goblins, pixies, you can draw a through-line back through racial memory, to when we were all bushmen in the Kalahari, and we shared it with gibbons, baboons and other, smaller primates. Anyone who's seen recorded instances of a bushman tricking a gibbon into finding water for him – he puts the stone in a crevice, an inquisitive gibbon grabs it and finds he can't get his hand back out until the bushman frees him – doesn't need too big a leap to equate that with stories of tricking a leprechaun, say, out of his crock of gold. These stories carry the cumulative received wisdom of millennia.

When we talk of *giants*, on the other hand, I think the time frame's rather smaller. We're talking about big, strange and impossibly old people, who fly into unpredictable rages and cow us with arbitrary rules we can't quite work out, who might not be ogres as such, but still hold all proper people – i.e. *us* – in thrall by way of their sheer size and strength. It's interesting that these stories, when we develop sufficient intelligence as a child to understand the words, have the inbuilt notion that giants lived in the past and that their age has long since gone. It's because, of course, when we talk about giants and ogres and trolls, what we're *really* talking about is us when we were very, very small and our parents were impossibly big . . .

. . . I didn't desert from the Military Academy out of fear or cowardice, and I certainly wasn't a traitor – however they might like to bandy phrases like 'face of the enemy' and 'in time of war' around. Much as I'd like to, I can't say I deserted out of some sense of higher nobility either – some sense that the War we were prosecuting was somehow immoral or wrong and that I had to take a stand against it. We were fighting a race that razed planets for the simple reason that they could, and just killed everyone who was not them or *of* them for the simple reason that they were not. You couldn't reason with them: you could only fight or die. It was us or them.

I deserted for the simple reason that I was fundamentally incompatible with military life. Through the training and indoctrination I saw precisely what they were doing to us, and why they were doing it, and it jarred on me, like biting on a bit of foil or taking a mouthful of wine so corked it's all but pure acetic acid. Now, that might not sound like much – but that's because if you bite on the foil or take the mouthful you instantly spit it out by pure reflex. Imagine, though, that you were forced to keep on biting or keep on swallowing and there was no way you could ever stop, for minutes, and hours, and days and weeks, and months . . .

I couldn't live like that. There was no way that I could make myself. So I didn't and I got out the first instant it was possible. Simple reflex, simple as that.

Rebecca didn't agree. When she came to me in my bunk and we talked, she told me that she'd stick it out, laughing inside at some of the nonsense, but ready to stand up and be counted for something that was so *right* to her that believing in it didn't even enter the equation. It was around that time I truly realized how different we really were, in so many things . . .

. . . never really notice how debilitating it is to go through life with a Big Secret, something you must never, ever tell on pain of, well, pain. Seven for a secret, never to be told. Something of which you must be constantly aware, so that you don't let it slip out. It becomes the gorgon of your thoughts.

Someone – I forget precisely who – who liked to think he was carrying on the Discordian tradition, once told me of one of the processes he used in his own personal self-imposed religion – the idea of it being that he got all the benefits of being a spiritual being without having to associate with those people who got organized and burnt things because they didn't quite conform to some set of *other*-imposed rules. What you did, he said, was put some arbitrary Article of Faith in your head. It didn't have to be a major thing, just something that stayed in your mind whatever you did, informing your impulses and actions in the world. You didn't have to even follow it. The point was that, like the injunction for a Muslim not to eat pork, which over the centuries after actual pigs as such became extinct has evolved into something almost entirely different, it would always be *there* . . .

In my friend's case, he chose 'I will not eat green food.' As with most of the males of the species, eating up his greens was something he would cross the street to avoid in any case, so he thought that it would make no difference at all to his day-to-day life. And then, over weeks and months, he started to notice just how many other foods were green, like lime-flavoured sweets and avocados, and just how many of the basic meals he ate, like burgers from a burger bar, *contained* green things . . .

. . . after my mother died, there was nobody to look after me. My father had long since gone – I didn't even have a memory of him. Oh, there were family pictures and pictures in the news, most of them in the stories about how he had turned his ship on its tail and run, but I could never feel a connection. I was so young when they were both gone – I look at the families I happen to know, how they squabble or fight or get along, and I wonder about that almost telepathic link they seem to share, the way that they seem to simply *get* what some other of them has just said, and I wonder if I'm just imposing that impression upon them. Am I just so desperate to feel some sense of connection myself?

Refugee ships, running from dead worlds. Does it always come down to that? Maybe I read too much into it for the simple reason that I first knew Rebecca then, as a child, on the ship that took me away from the dead planet that was Beta Caprisis . . .

Rebecca's always had a soft spot for the Bastard Don John. When he says, 'I cannot hide what I am' – so she says – he's effectively sticking a couple of fingers up at the saccharine piety of Leonato's court, and the subsequent events are more the result of the hypocrisy of others than of his own quite frankly villainous involvement.

Like that nifty Beatrice/Benedick subplot, so Rebecca says, it's as relevant now as then. We're all of us forced by circumstance into roles we don't want, must walk the walk and talk the talk until we collapse under the weight of it all – the only way out, if you have the strength for it, being to take what is essentially a villainous stance . . .

– Random extracts from the journal of Bernice Summerfield, recovered from the ruins of St Oscar's University, Dellah

CHAPTER 12

The story seemed simple enough. Bernice Summerfield had escaped the upheavals on Dellah and any subsequent incarceration on Thanaxos – either through her contacts or the simple fact that she had ended up on some other planet, somewhere else. She had then, for reasons I couldn't as yet fathom, organized a ship and come back. She might have slipped past the planetary defences in the confusion before the Blockade locked in, or maybe the ship had been cloaked in some way. And then she'd waited, passing the time by writing in her journal.

So what had she been waiting for? And why, when whatever she was waiting for happened – or it didn't, and she gave up – did she leave the journal behind?

The journal itself had quite obviously been written out over the course of weeks if not months. I got the impression that it had been edited down from other, far more circumstantial material, so as to collate together certain thoughts, reactions and ideas in general that she'd wanted to preserve as important in some way. On the whole, though, I could have done with all the circumstantiality of whatever Summerfield used for a *diary*, rather than interminable musings upon the nature of art, philosophy, personal and familial relationships and how they were related to the antics of the baboons in the Kalahari.

As I skimmed through the entries, trying to get some sense of Summerfield's actual life, I came across a number of names I was familiar with from the files – and one new name that stood out by sheer repetition. This Rebecca seemed to have run through her life like a golden thread, being there at every key point – or, if not, Summerfield's thoughts were never far way from her, turning to her like the needle of a compass. Their relationship seemed stormy at best, and they had split up more times than I could count, but she had loved her since she was a child, and they always seemed to find some way to get back together in the end.

I found myself feeling a bit jealous. I recalled some of the thoughts I'd had back in the detention complex that had kept me going, happy little daydreams of going up to an idealized Bernice Summerfield, showing her what she was missing with that clown Jason Kane from the New Frontier Adventures by the simple fact that I existed, promptly sweeping her up and heading off into the sunset.

This was different. Summerfield's relationship with her girl was such a real and complicated and long-term loving thing that I wasn't in with a chance, and wouldn't have tried for one if I was. Maybe 'envy' is a better word for it than 'jealousy' – that little weaselly feeling you sometimes get that two people are being in love with each other and incredibly happy just to spite *you*, when they are of course completely unaware of your existence.

Of course, on the plus side, it was lucky that I'd found out she was that way inclined before I met her, if I ever did, so I wouldn't make a complete and utter fool of myself by hitting on someone who was, fundamentally, not interested. I reminded myself sternly, yet again, never to believe one word of anything I'd ever read in the New Frontier Adventures.

The main thing was that I had another solid lead.

Summerfield was still alive, and if she was alive then she'd be with her girl – or, if they'd gone through yet another break-up, they'd be back together at some point. From the looks of it, it was a cycle of love and irritated argument rather than any violent or abusive pattern that either of them would ever truly want to break. It was just a matter of locating this Rebecca. From just that name. And from the complete lack of physical description that people always fail to give for those they love, in the same way that you don't write lovingly precise descriptions of your right arm . . .

I skipped to the back of the journal. There were fifty-odd blank pages left, but the text ended with a finality that told me that, so far as Summerfield was concerned, the work was complete. It dealt with those last events on Dellah but, as with all else in the journal, it was more concerned with what she thought about it than what had actually happened. I did my level best to read between the lines:

> . . . in any case, I know that I've had enough. I've had enough of playing games and never being told the rules, I've had enough of worlds that die and leave you crawling, sobbing, in the wreckage. And I know what I must do. I'm going to take the Mary-Sue and walk away. I've had enough.
>
> Rebecca is with me almost constantly now, taking care of me while I recover. It's a strange sort of comfort. She was unapologetic when she came back – as she shouldn't be after the way I treated her – but she was gentle and concerned. She was worried about me. She couldn't leave me in that state. She just wanted to help.
>
> When she came back to me, it was like the other times. I'd long forgiven her for all the times she hurt me, the things she'd said and done that split us last

time; I missed her so much that it was like a hook twisting in my heart – but I was terrified that I simply wouldn't feel the love again, as though a switch had been thrown, a connection broken, something in me dead beyond all resurrection . . .

And there it was, right in front of me. It was nice to see that Bernice and Rebecca were back in love again and all, but 'Rebecca' wasn't the name that leapt off the page and hit me like it was written in flashing neon light.

Sometimes, you can be waiting by the doors for hours, periodically checking the windows just in case – and the buggers come out through the ventilation shaft behind you. I looked at that name – which wasn't precisely a *name*, if you get what I mean – and all of a sudden a number of things became clear. I might or might not have exclaimed something, the eyes might or might not have popped out on extensible stalks, I may or may not have stuck a pontifical finger in the air with a hearty 'By Jove, I think I've got it!' – but you get the general idea.

I tucked the Journal of Bernice Summerfield under my jacket and wandered out into the sunlight. The shadows of the terracotta ruins were longer now and the light had a reddish tinge. The afternoon was wearing on. I found Prince Jimbo sitting more or less where I had left him, staring vacantly into space as though his mind had simply been switched off.

'Come on, Jimbo.' I nudged him with my boot. 'We're going back now.'

He looked up at me with a blank expression. 'Yes,' he said. 'We will return to the palace, now.'

The problem with sudden flashes of inspiration is that they can blind you to all else. At the time, what with other things on my mind, and a determination not to give the little idiot any more attention than I had to, I missed a number of important things. The sense of vacancy about him I put down to his basic doltishness, just another aspect of the stunted mind that had him prattling about everything that crossed it, now dormant because, here in the ruins, there was nothing to set it going. I noted in passing that his shoes were tied correctly now, and just assumed that he had hit upon it by a couple of hours of trial and error.

It's on such suppositions, incidentally, that the good intentions that pave the road to Hell are laid.

Some hours later I was back in the palace; Prince Jimbo was tucked up safely in his guarded room and I was in mine, showering off the grit and stink of travel.

Sela came in and dropped her camera. It might have seemed odd, what with the recent fundamentalist spin given to Dellahan society, that two unmarried people were allowed to share a bedchamber, but it didn't seem to be an issue. Possibly it was the result of that strange quality of being unnoticeable that appeared to affect me. Personally, though, I think it was the fact that, by their lights, it demonstrated the loose morals of Unbeliever dogs, and they allowed it to occur for the precise reason that they could then point it out and get all judgemental.

'Good day at work?' I asked when she had discarded her clothes and we were scrubbing each other off.

'If you mean I got the job done, sure,' she said sourly. 'Eight hours of covering this rabble-rousing hoopla, not counting coffee breaks and lunch. They wouldn't let me shoot anywhere else. I mean *Jeez*!' She spat down into the shower drain. 'My crew could have handled everything that's going on their own. They could just have pointed an autocam at the stage for all the direct input I'm allowed.' She stomped from the shower and towelled herself off with angry vigour on the luxurious towels provided, each with the Sultan's crest stitched into a corner.

'How long have we got before we can get out of here?' she asked me. 'You have the inside track.'

'Another day and then back to Thanaxos,' I said. 'It's a good idea, apparently, to get out before the ritual hospitality expires.'

'It can't run out soon enough as far as I'm concerned,' said Sela.

We slept.

In the depths of the night, I woke up in a cold sweat. Sela tossed and turned beside me, muttering some fitful kind of dream-litany in her sleep. I decided it would be better if I let her dreams run their own course and didn't wake her. I sat in the bed and tried not to shake, trying to pin down the nightmare that had woken me:

A sense of being utterly alone, hanging in some gulf of sense deprivation but with voices jabbering at me – my eardrums vibrating not from sound waves carried by the air, but by the fact that the voices were *making* them vibrate, firing off the sections of my brain that processed sound and language, giving me the physical sensations of hearing them in a way roughly analogous to the way that a speaker diaphragm can be used as a microphone, the signal going precisely the opposite way.

The voices had jabbered in chorus, discrete threads of intonation winding through their polyphonic mass – no, not threads exactly: more like tentacles – tentacles squirming round my mind and probing, trying to find a break in the defences, looking for a way in past the wall . . .

I had it, then. It was just a flashback to the time when I was a kid and in the EMG think tank. I get them, occasionally. My mind tends to shy away from them, and it takes some time to consciously work them out. Once I had, I could put them away from me and use a couple of autohypnotic techniques to seal them off. I shut my mind and visualized a translucent tetrahedron of jade, floating before me. I wrapped the memories inside it and made it spin, and watched it as I drifted off to sleep . . .

And woke. It was early morning, brilliant white light casting those hard-edged perspective rays you get in pictures of God behind a bank of cumulonimbus, through the muslin over the windows and the canopy over the bed.

Sela wasn't there. She was in the shower room, having just showered off the sweat of the night – the Tashwari heat made three or four showers a day almost mandatory, if you were expecting to move in polite society. I reached out and touched her shoulder – and felt a little strange. It wasn't much, just a kind of emotional equivalent of the crack when you touch earthed metal and discharge the static electricity from your body. It's just that sense you get, on touching someone with whom you've been intimate, that some connection has been dropped or broken.

She turned to face me, and I saw it in her eyes before she even spoke.

'Listen . . .' she said. 'I've been thinking, and I think we should cool it for a while. You know that what we're doing goes against the moral tenets of the All-High Gods . . .'

This was sufficiently unlike the Sela I knew – a Sela who'd have a bunk-up on the observation deck of the Luna-Titan ferry if the mood took her – that I raised an eyebrow in surprise.

Sela noticed. 'I mean, the locals here get hung up on things like this, and it's not making either of our jobs easier. Why don't we just leave it till we're back on Thanaxos and then take it from there?'

'Sure.' I shrugged as though it didn't matter. 'Let's take it from there.'

The sudden change in Sela preyed on my mind all through

the long hours of shepherding Prince Jimbo through the day, as the diplomatic ceremonies wore to a close and we embarked upon the Royal Yacht for the journey home. For a wonder, he was remarkably easy to deal with, that switched-off blankness he had demonstrated in the ruins of St Oscar's carrying through and replacing his more ordinary drooling idiocy. He went where I told him to and then just stood or sat there quietly. I decided not to push it by attempting to force some further response, and counted my blessings.

As for Sela, well, people have got sick of me and dumped me before. It was just possible, I supposed, that she had been villainously brainwashed and was under some nefarious and evil control – but that seemed a bit of a long run for the short slide of stopping her despoiling the sanctity of the Sultan's palace with acts lacking in propriety. I shouldn't let my suspicions run away with me and build up vast and complicated constructs of conspiracy, just to account for and rationalize away the fact that someone had gone off me and I'd been dumped. I didn't mention it in the slightly but distinctively different mission reports I prepared for the various editions of Volan – what would be the point?

The farcically haranguing and denunciative rigours of the diplomatic mission had taken their toll upon the various Thanaxon envoys. They slumped in their seats on the journey back in a defeated and slightly dazed manner that reminded me a little of Prince Jimbo's vacuousness. After a couple of days of being shouted at for being Unbelieving heathen dogs, I couldn't blame them. The Royal Yacht grounded, I delivered Prince Jimbo into the care of the palace guard, fired off my brace of reports, watched my clearing account until the fund transfer from the Thanaxon Council was confirmed and then headed off to the private landing fields.

One of the first things I'd done upon escaping the detention complex was to have the *Star of Afrique* released from impoundment. She waited, now, under a merchant-freighter cover name that was clean down the line, her lift and propulsion systems recharged and ready to go. Thanaxon airspace security had been tightened up in the last weeks, as a prelude to the coming war, but I had taken the opportunity of a spare moment to download the overriding protocols from the Royal Yacht. I had little trouble getting out.

The 'name' I'd chanced upon in Summerfield's journal had been Mary-Sue. Now that might not seem like much to *you*, but, believe me, it was the equivalent of intercepting a textmail message and reading, 'we explode the thermonuclear device under the President's bed tonight'. In the past, doing a Mary-Sue was a term used by critics to denote the act of the author's putting him- or herself into a work of fiction, like as not to get all hot and bothered at the idea of copping off with the lead character.

Nowadays, it means something different. A Mary-Sue is a mindwipe-and-rebuild process, used by the more heavy-duty policing, covert-observation and espionage services to give an operative a deep and unshakable cover – total conversion into a distinct new person, complete and whole, complete with memories, personality and an airtight life on file. If the person who had once been Bernice Summerfield had gone through a Mary-Sue, she was involved in something so heavy that this had been the only way to survive it – and I wanted to talk to her about it more than ever.

A Mary-Sue is almost impossible to acquire, outside of the seriously Big Boys. Even with my Stratum Seven status, there was only one place such a thing could be arranged. I cleared the Thanaxon atmosphere, reorientated the *Star of Afrique* on its axis, and laid in a course for the Proximan Chain.

Background Insert (Personal File):

Scenes from an Ordinary Childhood III

Moments of transition: the feel of plunging headlong through the void, the half-glimpsed flashes of reddish, slimy, organic-looking membrane walls, lit by clusters of sore-like polyps that seemed to be infecting them and giving off a sickly, phosphorescent glow. The slippery feeling against me as my fall brought me in brief contact with the walls before reaction bounced me off . . .

An explosion of static across my entire field of vision, the sound of white noise in my ears . . .

An endless time with no sight, or sound, or sensation at all – not simple darkness, because darkness at the very least needs some possibility of light with which to stand in contrast. No sound at all, not even the never-noticed pulse of the blood, the sounds we live in all our lives and never hear, and which I only so much as barely intimated, here and now, now that it was gone. No sensation, none at all – I could not even feel the secondary senses, the internal gauges of position and orientation through which one can develop strategies to deal with prolonged terms of sensory deprivation. Nothing but the blankness. I existed as a kind of singularity of identity, alive in some sense and aware – but without thought process or memory, and there was nothing for me to be aware *of* . . .

I have no idea of how long I existed in that state. Could have been minutes, could have been weeks. Could have been years.

Then the static was back, and everything changed. It was like a monitor being switched on in front of your face, or a full-sense VR rig running with the gain to high and plugged straight into a sequence that was already running. Ragged, blazing lights tore across my vision and a shriek split through my ears. My skin burnt with agony, something exploded in my guts and I screamed, soundlessly and unable to make the muscles work in my mouth.

My senses spun with synaesthesia, then settled down a bit. The forms resolved themselves in front of my eyes: a grainy, strobing face that filled my entire sight. The colour register was off and the image was distorted, so that the eyes seemed huge and the lower face and mouth Dopplered off in a manner reminiscent of those old pre-space-flight sketches of the Grey aliens, who abducted people and did nasty things with probes. Even so distorted, I got the distinct impression that this was not a particularly nice face – not the face of a particularly nice man at all.

The diminutively shrunken mouth worked. A fraction of a second later, the voice sounded in my ears – a kind of tinny, modulated buzz like you get when you plug a sound system up on maximum gain through a speaker without amplification.

'*Test subject, oh one seven three four six slash, ah, four seven three point one point two*,' the tinny little voice said. '*Initialization routines complete. Resetting input preferences* . . .' The sound of breathing and a little absent-minded grunt filled my ears with the force of a thunderclap directly overhead in the middle of a gale – then the noise-levels settled to something approaching normality.

'Hello, there!' said the face in front of me, the voice and the mouth now more or less in sync. 'Don't try to speak, yet – it wouldn't do you any good. We've yet to bring your response mode on line and fine-tune it.

'Now, I expect you're wondering what's happened to you. You things always seem to want to know. Well, the bad news, I'm afraid, is that you're dead. You died resisting arrest by EMG ground-force operatives, seven years ago, of – let me see – severe gunshot trauma to the abdomen and chest. I understand that the result was not a pretty sight.'

The distorted face warped even further as it beamed. 'The good news is that the head – and, more to the point, the *brain* – was preserved intact. You've been kept on cryogenic ice since then, here in the good old Festival Hall facility . . .

'Dear me, look at those telltales – I do believe your synaptic mesh is positively *spiking*. Just let me . . . There we are . . .

'There's nothing to worry about. You're not some disembodied head hooked to the power grid or anything like that – that would be completely and utterly ridiculous, and not to mention in entirely questionable taste. Strictly speaking, you're not a head at all. Your *head's* already sliced up and thrown away like so much leftover wafer-thin ham. Do you remember when you could get such a thing as wafer-thin sliced ham? I do.'

The face smacked its lips reminiscently, and resumed: 'Strictly speaking, you're in what we call the Think Tank. The Emergency Military Government has found applications for the process in what might be called Information Gathering, of course, but that's neither here nor there – you are, whatever else, participating in the greatest advance in artificial-intelligence research since the construction of the very first transputronically based machine network. Think of that!

'For far too long,' the voice of the face continued, obviously burning to share some long-held personal enthusiasm, 'the development of true artificial intelligence has been hamstrung by the mechanistic approach of Turing and his ilk.' The voice of the face contrived to give the impression that it wished it were physically possible to spit out the word 'ilk'. 'He and others mapped their theories and their rather squalid little personal neuroses on to the world rather than vice versa. They persisted in seeing human intelligence – intelligence *itself*, as we know it – as algorithmic, when it is, in fact, holistic.

'The refinement of holographic technology in the world outside, the ability for a holographic matrix to *evolve* in real time, has given us an entirely new approach – the way to go is the generation or replication of a synaptic structure in its entirety, as opposed to merely emulating that structure's apparent function by way of some imposed decision-tree nonsense of a step system . . .'

The voice of the face paused, proudly. I got the distinct impression that whoever the voice and face ultimately belonged to was simply reeling off ideas parrot-fashion, with no real idea of what it actually meant.

'The Think Tank is basically a real-time holo-projector,' it continued smugly, 'of such a high resolution that it operates upon the subatomic level – the level, it seems, upon which true consciousness operates. The brain of a subject – you yourself, of course, in this case – is scanned by high-powered lasers and mapped into the Tank as a stable system of connections. The process destroys the brain itself, naturally, but you can't make an omelette without breaking eggs, can you? Or make progress without breaking skulls.

'A stable structure is of no use at all, however. It doesn't *move*. The process of human thought is merely the by-product of the incremental collapse of the brain under entropy. So we destabilize the artificial construct, simulate the decay of an actual brain. The resulting output is transferred by some rather sophisticated imaging techniques into a real-time simulacrum, precisely mimicking the thoughts and responses, even the memories and personality of a living human brain – and that, of course, is *you*.

'The only drawback is that the unstable construct is subject to accelerated decay. At the moment, I'm afraid, you have a life expectancy of around seven hours. So I think I have to turn you over to the more, ah, practical-minded powers that be before you become completely unusable. I'll moderate your impulses so you don't act inappropriately, make sure you tell them what they need to know, never fear . . .'

For hours another face asked me questions: yes-and-no answers read off a list. Did I have regular contacts, when I was alive, who supplied me with arms? Was it a person with this name? What about this name? Had I met people who might have somehow broken the Perimeter and come in from the outside world? That sort of thing.

I couldn't have lied if I'd wanted to – or told the truth, for that matter. In my virtual state I could *feel* that I had lips and a mouth, but nothing I did seemed to make them work to answer yes, no or none of the above. I assume they just monitored my virtual thought processes to see how I responded, in the same way as in some kind of polygraph test. My only comfort was that any information they might glean was at least seven years out of date – if I could believe the voice of the first face I'd seen – and a lot can change in seven years.

Throughout it all I hunted round what I assumed to be still, in some sense, my own mind with a kind of desperate terror – trying to find the sort of damage that I assumed would be the result of its destroying itself from the inside. I couldn't seem to find any – but that wasn't exactly reassuring. If there were blank holes eaten in my mind, then how the hell could I think of them in the *first* place and realize that they were blank?

After a seemingly endless time the questions stopped and the other face went away. I looked for a while at a hazy collection of forms that might or might not have been a wall, something that might or might not have been a notice board on the right periphery of my vision, smaller, vaguely oblong shapes on it that may or may not have been tacked-up notices that I would never be able to read.

The original face – the face of the guy I'd first seen and who seemed to be into casual torture of the helpless little putative AI experimental construct – hove into view again, and regarded me, so far as my grainy vision could guess, critically. It didn't say anything.

The burst of static and white noise and then, again, the blankness.

I opened my eyes.

That was the first surprise – the fact that I had eyes to open. The second surprise was how utterly *well* I felt. I mean, I don't mean I felt well after being some kind of disembodied and prototypical AI construct – if I could believe the Voice and it hadn't all been just some incredibly complicated interrogation technique. I mean that I had never felt this sense of physical strength and lack of pain in my life – and certainly not for the years of chronic malnutrition, lice and hard knocks of the Birmingham EMG Zone.

I was flat on my back, lying on something almost impossibly smooth-feeling and soft, in a cool white room. The air tasted weird, until I realized that it just tasted fresh. Somewhere I heard the distant sound of air conditioners.

A face loomed over me. Female, quite possibly the most beautiful face – and certainly the most healthy-looking – I'd ever seen. There was a vague sense of disorientation about it, though – look, given the tenor of my times, I was slightly less of what used to be called racist than otherwise, and the self-enclosed, blockaded life within the city meant that what in my day was called mixed race, and in these days is called hybridity, wasn't much of an issue. But even so, the face of the woman just seemed *wrong*. Little things happening at the edges of her eyes and mouth, a skin tone that had a slightly greenish tinge – it wasn't that she was some saurian monster with scales and claws or anything. She just seemed somehow fundamentally *wrong* . . .

Panic reflex cut in. I tried to lurch away, found that my forearms and shins were restrained – and then I saw just what, precisely, these forearm-and-shin-restraining restraints were restraining. '*Jesus fucking Christ!*'

You have to remember that I came from a time when body-swapping or even body-*bepple* wasn't even so much as a workable concept. There was a small minority of people in my time who were transsexual, trapped in a meat machine that was entirely wrong for them, and had the sheer guts and courage to undergo extremely primitive surgery to correct their bodies into a form that was approximately right for the person inside. The point is, to be a candidate for such procedures, you went through years of psycho-testing beforehand and intensive psychotherapy after.

It wasn't just the fact of sexual reassignment that made this necessary: it was the simple, fundamental shock of waking from the anaesthetic to find yourself inhabiting a completely different body. Similar counselling was needed for amputees or those with spinal injuries – no spare body parts in tanks or nerve-regeneration grafts in those days. Embodiment was so much of what we were that finding our bodies suddenly and irrevocably *changed* was literally unthinkable. Oh, sure there were wish-fulfilment fantasies of saying a magic word, or being shot to a low-gravity planet where you're really, really strong in comparison –

but these were of the nature of the happy little thoughts you have to help you to get to sleep. Of copping off with a girl you saw that day and fancied, of smacking the face of somebody who irritated you. If it really happened it would flat-out kill you with its psychic blow.

All in all, and all things considered (and due in large part, I later learnt, to a couple of months of subliminal conditioning before I was even woken up), I'm rather proud that my reaction was as calm and restrained as it was.

'Listen!' the rather nice but fundamentally wrong woman cried as I struggled in vain against the straps. 'Just listen, please! We're here to help you through this. Please, try to be still and I'll try to explain . . .'

CHAPTER 13

The Habitats of the Proximan Chain are a sort of three-way hybrid of the various ideas of space stations, colonies and planetary settlements. That is, the physical space they occupy is spread out over those locations, but they're linked by a series of mass-transit pads, taking you from the one to the other instantly, so that the end result is a single and coherent environment.

'Coherent', though, is probably not the right word. I've mentioned how places can be low- or high-tech – but the Proximan Chain takes the 'high' in 'high technology' to the extreme. It's a kind of playground for the grey-market people involved in anything from body-swap, mind-sculpting, AI-envelope-pushing, tailored pharmaceuticals, weaponry development and anything else with an acronym or a hyphen you can name.

I love it, frankly, in the same way I love my arms or my eyes – it's my natural environment, simple as that. I've talked about the way that things get around in other places, but here, in the Proximan Chain, you can't make a move without *everybody* knowing – if they happen to feel like pulling it out of the informational chaos of what everybody *else* is doing as well – and you *know* that, deep in your bones and in your implants.

The feeling of hooking yourself in and moving through

is impossible to describe if you don't know it, any more than a mediaeval peasant could describe all the feelings he got walking through a field and being aware of all the plants in it, knowing that each one was special and had any number of uses and aspects. It would take an hour to list the specifics of experiencing a minute of it. It was, quite simply, *home*.

'Put out a trawl for anything useful, Box,' I said, as I came down the ramps from the docking complex. 'I'm looking for refs on a Bernice Summerfield, out of Dellah, possibly going under the name of Berni.' What the hell. The New Frontier Adventures might pay off at some point, if only by the law of averages.

'Time frame?' Box asked.

'Stuff from the last four months. See if anybody's got a physical lock on her and wants to share. Weed out all the spam, New Frontier Adventures shit and word-search wannafuck personals and just tell me what you think I want to hear. Your fuzzy-logic routines should have more than enough parameters by now to give you an idea of what I'm after.'

'Pretty much,' said Box. 'Just be nice when I come up with weird stuff and you knock me back on it. This Bernice Summerfield paradigm's getting rather more complex than most.'

'Don't I just know it, Box,' I said.

The Habitats are a place where you don't need maps – a place where *I* don't need them, at least. You know where you want to go and you just drift through them, through the crowd, and sooner or later you just find yourself there. I breathed in that mix of esters, pheromones, secondary ketones, that aren't so much a fixed and constantly *distinctive* smell as the culmination of diversity. Everybody, every species and racial subset of those species, comes here at some point and leaves a trace. It's that special kind of sensory overload that you get here, and nowhere else. It's like the taste and feel of tobacco smoke in the lungs: there's nothing quite like it and you miss it when it's gone.

I wandered through the catwalk streets just breathing it in, taking in the sights in an absent way: an animated bundle of splintery sticks that was in fact a Drolag from the Cool Stars, opening up his meat locker – sculpted from real meat – to display a collection of *hoki* crystals to some interested human customer; the Spindlekings dancing through the crowd, moving so fast when they moved, and staying so still when they stopped that they seemed like statues appearing and disappearing at random; an Oroborous Worm, sedately rolling along a walkway as it ate itself . . . It's nice to be reminded sometimes that humanity isn't, in the end, a kind of galactic species-default setting, and of how insular the human way of looking at things can sometimes be.

I picked up a *hoki* crystal from the Drolag and carried on, the smooth-plane facets in my palm making my nerves sing in a way that's, apparently, cumulatively harmful, but no more harmful on a day-to-day basis than a double Scotch.

'I've got a possibility,' said Box

'Is it a good possibility?' I said.

'It's a pretty good possibility. No real names, just a mail drop and the location for a meet. Dead Dog in the Water Preproductions. Learn something to your advantage, so they say, and they're naming a price. Twenty-five per cent up front.'

'So pay it,' I said. 'We're on expenses.'

Box transferred the funds and reeled off a location – you'd never find it now if you went to the Proximan Chain. The addresses in the Proximan Chain tend to move around. I flagged down a traveller as it sculled through the thoroughfare by way of an even hundred little oar-like appendages between its flotation tanks, hung on to the straps it had thoughtfully bolted to its carapace and, when its ear-and-eye appendage swung back to regard me enquiringly, gave it the address.

My destination wasn't exactly prepossessing. It was the kind of low-rent storage-and-repair garage for personal fliers, off to one side of a citadel in one of the planetary-based habitat areas, that you just knew was the front for a busy little chop shop.

It was night-time. The doorway was open invitingly, revealing the brightly lit workshop space beyond, so I walked round the structure until I found a side hatch. It was padlocked, so I pulled out my Allen key and little bit of wire and went to work. Holomovies notwithstanding, it takes a bit of time to pick a lock – but what the hell. I had the time. The hatch swung open smoothly, on oiled hinge springs, to show utter blackness within. The hatch obviously led into a room blocked off from the workshop space. It was too dark even for my slightly enhanced eyes and optic nerves to pull out shapes and forms. I hung back to avoid presenting a target profile and considered my options.

In the dark, what with the ambient street light from the hatch, I'd have a slight but possibly vital advantage over whoever might be waiting in there for me – if they weren't wearing snoopers.

As it happened, snoopers weren't the problem. I went through the hatch doing all the right things – and felt the muzzle of a blaster pressing firmly into the nape of my neck.

'Hang loose,' said a cheerful, female voice. 'Take ya head off if you don't.'

Fluorescent neon flickered on. I was in a smallish office, a battered panel door blocking the path to what was presumably the workshop. Racks of old and dirty-looking mechanical parts ran along one wall; another wall was covered with a blizzard of old tacked-up invoice forms, manifests and a calendar intended for the Sloathe market, and which was probably highly erotic, assuming that your tastes ran to amorphous slimy lumps with tubes and suckers.

There was an ancient, roll-top desk that looked like it had actually originated from Earth. Lounging by it with a kind of easy nonchalance was the figure of a man. Mid-thirties, with the lean kind of muscularity that comes from putting muscles to their daily use, brown-skinned with that distinctive tone that spoke of expensively microcustomized gene-modification so that the skin could stand long periods under high-UV and high-radiation suns. Baggy trousers of green-stained suede, tucked into calf-high lace-up combat boots; a vest that showed the traces of primitive childhood gang tattoos on his shoulders and arms.

His hair was cut in the kind of ragged mop worn by people who don't care much about their hair and just want to keep it out of their eyes. A month-old shot at bleaching it was growing out. His face was one of those you just see every day, on the people who walk by as part of the mobile scenery – unremarkable, save for the fierce and bright, if somewhat transient and unpredictable, intelligence behind the eyes. The man grinned with a kind of easy nastiness reminiscent of the tone of voice of the girl with a gun to my head. 'Wotcha, cock.'

There were any number of witty responses to this, but I wasn't in the mood. I debated with myself whether or not it was worth trying to catch a glimpse of the woman behind me, and decided against it. I knew where she was, and what she actually looked like while she was there was beside the point.

'I think this is the point,' I said to the grinning man, 'when you say I don't have to worry, you mean me no harm, and you tell your friend to put the gun away.'

'I don't think so, matey.' A look of barely suppressed rage crossed his face. 'My name's Jason Kane. And I want to know what a Stratum Seven mechanic out of Pseudopod

Enterprises is doing, nosing around and looking for my wife.'

I think I might have stared at the guy, startled. Once again, the assumptions I had subconsciously made, from reading about real people in the New Frontier Adventures, had turned around and bit me on the arse, snapping me back to reality with an almost physical jerk. Whatever this guy was, he certainly wasn't some amiable, muscle-bound lunkhead who needed to be told by Bernice Summerfield, or anyone else, what to do.

The woman took advantage of my moment of surprise to shove me forward with the flat of her hand, catching me off guard so that I lost my equilibrium and stumbled. This was nice in that the gun was not now pressed directly to my neck, but *not* so nice for the same reason: there are a hell of a lot more things you can do to counter a projectile weapon when you actually have close contact with it. I heard the hatch behind me shut with a clang and then she walked round me to join the man, still covering me with the gun. I was rather glad I hadn't seen it before – I have a sort of allergy to plasma-based handguns so fuckoff huge that you could drive a hov-truck up the ejection snout and park.

She was wearing something skin-tight, black and shiny under a voluminous, full-length overcoat, and had a widow's peak of cropped, jet-black hair and a foxy-looking face half buried in its turned-up collar. A street-kid-grown-up face, interesting rather than classically beautiful – and, classical beauty being as overrated as it is, I'd go for interesting every day of the week and twice on Sundays.

She scowled at me. 'I've got a girlfriend and I don't like you. I know what you're thinking – I mean I *really* know what you're thinking – and I don't look even remotely similar under the coat.'

Just my luck. I think I've mentioned that the old sci-fi

idea of telepathy is physically impossible – and this woman was one of the telepaths we haven't got. Something like the implantation Volan and his sort use for business negotiations – but jacked completely off the scale. These people are packed with superconductive sensor systems, running parallel to the major ganglia, which can be set to resonate along with an approximation of a target's automemic neural construct. With the proper training and a certain degree of personal insight, they become what might not technically count as mind-readers, but are so close that you might as well call them that and give up.

On the one hand this made me feel better about myself – I'd been doubting my own skills for a moment, thinking how I must have slipped one hell of a lot if you could get the drop on me so easily. I hadn't missed noticing her when I came through the hatch because of any lapse, though, and neither had she been preternaturally stealthy and quiet. She'd made moves and noises – but she'd made them at the precise point that she knew my attention was elsewhere. On the other hand, I felt obscurely, going about things in that way wasn't quite playing by the rules.

'Hey.' The woman winked at me. 'Whatever gets the job done.'

'You still haven't answered my question,' said Jason Kane. 'What do you want with Benny?'

'So it's *Benny*, is it?' I said, more or less to give myself time to think. 'I thought it was Berni or something.'

'Not if you want to live. That's not a threat, though. She just hates it.' Kane gestured towards the woman's gun. '*That's* a threat. So cut the who-me crap and spill.'

'I just want to talk to her,' I said. 'She's involved with my case and I want to know what she knows.'

'So making sure she's not in a position to tell anybody else *isn't* part of it?' said Kane – and I didn't need to be any kind of mind-reader to know what he was thinking.

'It's not that sort of job,' I said.

'He's telling the truth,' said the woman to Kane, in that sort of clinically chatty way some techs have of passing on the data from their readouts. 'I mean, he'd do her if he had to, but he wouldn't like it, and he doesn't think the situation's anywhere close to that.'

'Yeah, well.' Jason Kane wandered from the desk and came to get a closer look at me, stopping just short of the point where, if I tried to make a lunge-and-grab, it would do any good. It seemed that he just knew instinctively at which point to stop, rather than out of any fear or caution that I might have been able to turn against him. 'Much as I trust your judgement, Mira, this guy's about as shifty as they come. The moment you came sniffing round our patch –' this to me '– we put together seven sorts of dossier on you from Sunday.'

'So what's your line of business in this "our patch"?' I asked.

'You'll never know. Suffice it to say that we know stuff from the people that even the people *you* don't know don't know about. What's this total shit about being a *time*-traveller?'

'What would you call it?' I said, a little indignantly. As I've mentioned before, my temporal status is one of the things that, while it doesn't prey on my mind the livelong day to the detriment of all else, it's like a burr in the brain. It gigs me when I brush against it. 'One minute I'm lying in a twenty-first-century pool of gut-shot blood and dying, the next I'm waking up with a freshly cloned body in a Catan Nebula medical centre. What would *you* call it.'

'I wouldn't call it the real thing, sunshine,' Kane growled. 'Some of us have *done* the real thing.' He scowled at me with a kind of vague contempt. 'You know what the Catan Nebula's famous for, right? They breed up artificial humans and load them up with synthetic personality constructs and memories . . .'

'Of *course* I know that!' I said.

'Hey, there's no need to shout,' said Jason Kane.

'Of course I know that,' I said. 'And just *what* do you think the constructs and memories are synthesized *from*? They needed a model, and it was the rediscovery of a cache of EMG engram records – what they used to call Think Tanks – half a century ago on Earth that formed the basis for the entire process. They've been trying for years to reintegrate those original engrams properly – and I'm about the only one with which they had any real success. The process involved destroying the engram itself, in the same way that my original brain was destroyed to make it in the first place. They can't make any more of me. I'm the culmination, a complete and distinct individual and basically as human as you are.'

I tried to keep my voice level and calm throughout this little speech. I knew it was true. After I'd worked off my manufacturing indentures – bought my body and my life back, in effect – I did a little high-level checking, and the story matched up all the way down the line. But then again, like so much else in life, you can never be entirely sure . . .

Jason Kane snorted. 'That's the sort of rationalization people like you are always coming out with.'

'I've never seen an artificial quite so complex, for what it's worth,' said Mira, instantly earning herself a little note in my good books. 'It's as close to *human* as I can't make the odds. Either there's been some whole new order of breakthrough in the nebula, or he's maybe telling the truth . . .'

I shrugged it off. 'And plus I've got a physiology and a biological life expectancy that would make you sick. Not that bad a deal. And, even if it wasn't true, what would you expect me to do? Go around going click-click-whirr and pretending to be a robot? In the end they're still *my* memories and it's still *my* life, so what's the difference?'

The difference didn't seem enough for Jason Kane to think it worth pursuing. 'OK,' he said. 'You want to meet Benny so's you can sit down and have a nice little chat, all friendly and *individual*, like. So do we. She's sort of known for dropping out of sight, for months at a time, and coming back with the sort of stories that would make your toes curl – but she's never been out of contact for this long and we're getting worried.' He smiled at me rather humourlessly. 'Tell you what, why don't you tell us what you have? And if we feel like it we'll share.'

I thought about it. Sometimes in this life you've got to give a little to get a little more back. 'What about the confidential details?'

He grinned with some genuine humour this time. 'Hey, don't worry about it. You don't have to land your bosses in it or anything. Besides, we already backtracked your employment record for a couple of years before we lost interest, anyway.'

I told them of the leads I'd followed, glossing over the time in detention with a few quick sentences (though I noticed Mira's mouth tighten a little sympathetically). When I got to the point where I had found the journal in the ruins of St Oscar's, Kane's eyes widened a little.

'Can I see it?' he said.

I nodded my head towards the holdall I'd been carrying since entering the Habitats. 'It's in here. I have to tell you that when I open it up you're going to see quite a large number of weapons in there.'

'So give the bag to me,' he said impatiently.

'You'd also find a couple of rather nasty security devices. Active security devices as opposed to passive. Take your arm off if you don't have the right DNA.'

Kane nodded thoughtfully. 'OK,' he said at last. 'Do it slow and easy.'

I stuck my hand in the bag, doing it slow and easy, and

pulled out the Journal of Bernice Summerfield, then handed it to him. It might or might not have been possible for me to make a move as he took it – but the dynamic seemed wrong for that, now. At this point I'd get further with these people talking to me, if not actually trusting me. In turn, I was almost completely sure that Mira wasn't going to shoot me out of hand, just so long as I played nice. Almost completely sure.

Kane flipped through the pages of the Journal in the manner of one who handles books badly, tearing through them literally and figuratively, more concerned with the words than the form. As he did so, his expression darkened from the puzzled to the suspicious to the out-and-out incredulous.

'What the hell is this shit?' he said. 'Who's this *Rebecca*? I was on the Squaxis border, and I know for a fact there wasn't a Rebecca there – and I know for a fact that in the Dagellan Cluster it was *me* . . .' He flipped back and forth through the pages, muttering bad-temperedly at the intransigence of those who go around changing historical fact without any kind of thought.

Abruptly, towards the start of the Journal, he stared for almost a full ten seconds at an entry, and his face seemed to collapse in upon itself. It wasn't so much that he was upset, it seemed, but that his mind had hit upon something so painful that it was too busy coping to remember to look after the muscles of his face. Off to one side, Mira shot him a glance of fearful concern.

'Oh dear God,' he said at last. 'I think I know who this Rebecca is. And I think I know where Benny is.'

ATTACHMENT (SUPPLEMENTARY):

To: brown@135474.346.12.ccserv.dnet.com
From: pubterm@lunet.com
Organization: Archive News Services Bibliotheca
Subject: FYE

Dear Mr Brown

Here is the article as per your request.

----BEGIN----

In the name of the All-High Gods, the carbuncles upon the heels of whom mere mortal life is unworthy to scrape

ALL HAIL THE TEACHINGS OF PRINCE G'JIMO UPON HIS RETURN FROM THE NEW REVOLUTIONARY PARADISE OF DELLAH, AND FOR HIS TEACHINGS WHICH SHALL GUIDE THE HEATHEN UNBELIEVERS OF THANAXOS TOWARDS THE REVOLUTIONARY LIGHT!

(Op-Ed by ex-DataDay outworld correspondent, Sela Dane)

Oh Ye Believers

Glory to those Believers working assiduously towards the day when the light of revolution under the All-High Gods shall sweep the galactic firmament clear of all filth and evil conduct, damnation in the very bile of Hell for those Unbelievers, in whose employ I was, to my everlasting shame, until this very week, and who now – terrified of the Truth of Light and the True Faith, as only worms should be – consign my words to their public-access channel.

I have no fear, however, that the Truth shall not reach the Believer in all its bright, unvanquished light. The hands of the All-High Gods shall guide his way that he might spread their word to further ignite the Faith of all who hear.

Since my return from the Revolutionary paradise of New Dellah, I have been sickened by the most foul and obscene depravity of conduct I see about myself. I see the heathen dogs of Unbelievers making light of the True Faith as evidenced by the good Believers of that now-glorious planet from which I have returned. They are dogs, and lie in filth like dogs, and when the Light of the True Faith shines upon them they shall burn and die like dogs.

For all of this, there is hope. There is news so Great and Good that I, a mortal of the weaker sex, whose lips are not fit to kiss the lowliest garment of the All-High Gods, barely dare to speak it.

A Prophet has returned this day from New Dellah, returned to Thanaxos to make his Word known and to bring Light and Peace under the All-High Gods for all eternity. It is the Prophet G'jimo, the Prince Regent of the Thanaxon House Royal, within which now all Unbelievers must needs now tremble at his Name and we must now perforce call Lord.

His word is the Word of the All-High Gods and his pronouncements shall soon bathe his word in Holy Light.

This Melkinday. Royal Festival Park. Tickets retailing at 15 Royal Crowns. 9 RC Concessions.

In the Name of the All-High Gods and their Thanaxon Prophet, G'jimo, who in his Worldly Guise as Regent is become our Lord.

– transcript of DataDay broadcast filtered for text transmission by Archive News Services Bibliotheca

----END----

To: brown@135474.346.12.ccserv.dnet.com
From: winwinwin@yourfriend.com
Organization: [type your organization here]
Subject: WINWIN WIN THE LOTTRY!!!!!!!!

WIN ONTHE LOTTRY WITH THESE NUMBERS!!!!!
SEND 10 CREDS AND WELL SHOW YOU HOW!!!!!!

25, 48, 46, 18, 27, 83, 140, 52, 5, 15, 135, 13, 27, 12, 111, 93, 4, 157, 79, 24, 96, 11, 16, 8, 68, 96, 57, 5, 81, 18, 21.

JUST SEND US 10 CREDS AND WIN WIN WIN THE LOTTRY!!!!!!!

[to remove your name from this mailing list, type 'remove' in the header line and hit 'send']

CHAPTER 14

The *Star of Afrique* ploughed the – ahem – ghusty depths of space on overdrive, hopscotching through various jump-nexuses with barely an on-the-fly recharge. It might seem slightly weird, after weeks and months of searching, to rush like this – whatever might have happened having possibly already done so and so forth – but how would you feel if, once knowing where the object of your search was, you took your time, ambled along when you felt like it, and found that the worst had happened bare minutes before you actually arrived?

It might seem even weirder, on the surface, that Jason Kane and Mira let me tag along – but only on the surface. For one thing, I had a fast ship on short notice. And for another, they might not trust me, but they didn't actively *distrust* me enough to shoot me on the spot. They knew that if they left me I'd be coming after them in any case, and they wanted me where they could keep their eye on me.

After I had given the Journal to Kane, they had taken me out of the office and into the workshop where, on a hydraulic ramp, sat a big red hov-car reminiscent of a mid-twentieth-century convertible. I had nasty thoughts of being taken for a short ride but a happy one in the boot, but Mira had put her gun back in her pocket. The fact that she kept her hand in the same pocket thereafter stopped me from being *too* reassured: I only hope she was aware of the recent development known as a safety catch.

The car was lowered and Mira took me into the back to keep an eye on me. Kane had swung himself into the front, racked down the control bar, and off we went – at such speed going into the corners that I felt as if the bottom might fall out of my world, if not in fact vice versa.

As the lights of the various Habitats flashed past, Kane had pulled a small comms pack from the heavy, battered flak jacket he had pulled on before leaving.

'Kimo Ani?' he said into it. 'It's me. Small job for you. I'll be there in five – No, I'm on an open linc. Tell you about it when we get there . . .'

In the promised five of whatever it was, we had pulled up outside the sort of dive that would merit a lot of further investigation – if this were the holomovies. An expensively seedy-looking subterranean nightclub dive, in a Habitat where it was *always* night, the ramp leading down into it flanked by animatronics of rather fetching young ladies in top hats sitting on chairs the wrong way round, and a tethered and illuminated pink polyurethane blimp in the shape of a pig in a suspender belt.

Strolling out of this, at the precise moment we arrived, was a thin man of indeterminate age, with that greyish, ravaged, teak-hard look of a user who has taken everything that the pharmaceutical industries can throw at him for years, and possibly even centuries. He was whip-sharp in a black tuxedo, the collar and bow tie hanging open from his neck. Obviously this was Kimo Ani. He had appeared to be wearing dead-black wraparound shades, until he pulled them off with an audible and multiple click, and I saw the spikelike contacts that had been plugged into his engineered eye sockets, feeding the signals from the microcams in the shades to his brain.

Kimo Ani had plugged a couple of customized datastream units into his sockets, then lounged in the shotgun seat while Kane fed him the search parameters.

'We're looking for a guy who does Mary-Sues. Doesn't matter if he's ethically iffy – just so long as he does them well. I can't see Benny going to some cowboy outfit. Check anything that looks like a confidential file, 'cause he's gotta know what the old life was before he builds a new one. He might just have left some traces lying around. Use the data on Benny you already have for a match. Keywords: Bernice and Benny, obviously . . .' Kane looked at me and frowned. 'Maybe even Berni. Usual phonetic variations. Joker-word: Rebecca.'

We had then just driven around for a while, while Kimo Ani lounged there silently and apparently asleep. We went through places in the Habitats I knew like the back of my hand. It wasn't particularly odd that, whatever Kane and Mira and their Dead Dog in the Water were involved in, I had never come across 'em, or had never so much as been aware of their existence. There are so many outfits and factions, rival concerns and scams running parallel to each other in the Proximan Chain that it's impossible to know of even a fraction of them.

After maybe half an hour, Kimo Ani said, 'I've got a name.' And Jason Kane nearly got us sideswiped by three cargo pods and a motorized rickshaw turning the car around.

The name Kimo Ani had got was that of Dr [name withdrawn from manuscript]. Dr [name withdrawn from manuscript] gave off all-but terminal vibes of being a *bootleg* medic, even in a place as law-and-order-free as the Habitats. In his grubby consulting offices, perched and hunched behind his desk and looking like a kind of humanoid cross between a rat and a guinea pig with his elongated and yellowed incisors, he had been quite naturally reluctant to break his oaths of confidentiality.

'Fair enough,' Kane had said. 'I've never been an unreasonable man, who'd work some poor sod over with a pair of pliers, douse him in heating oil and then torch him and his house just because the guy crossed me. My associate –' he gestured in the direction of me '– on the other hand, is.'

I did a kind of method-acting thing, where I imagined what I'd feel like if Dr [name withdrawn from manuscript] were on my better-dead list, and smiled at him. I honestly have no idea why doing that appears to work.

'Toast your teacakes as soon as look at you, probably,' said Jason Kane.

Dr [name withdrawn from manuscript] suddenly allowed that, just in this special and particular case, given Kane's obviously quite genuine concern for his friend Summerfield, his oaths of confidentiality might be relaxed.

Kane had then turned to me. 'Look, I'm not going to hold out on you much – but this is my *wife* we're talking about.' I got the distinct impression that, even if they weren't still married, there was some connection that was so deep as to make the *wife* more than an unconscious refusal to admit that they weren't. 'Stuff like this can give you power over people, and, while I wouldn't trust myself with a hammer and a piggy bank, I want to be the only one who hears what the guy's got to say. Don't worry,' he continued, turning back to Dr [name withdrawn from manuscript]. 'One thing I'll be *sure* to tell him is if you don't give me what I need.'

I remained in the waiting room, with Mira keeping watch on me. I strained my aural enhancements to breaking point trying to pick out something useful in the offices beyond, but the door was soundproofed solid.

After five minutes Kane had come out, frowning and seemingly a little worried.

'Any luck?' Mira said.

looking with a kind of polite, bemused smile from one face to another. *Well*, this little tea party didn't seem to be going quite as smoothly as she'd expected . . .

What with everybody being thus disposed, I was the only one who noticed a metallic flash up in the flat-grey sky – just before the voice of Kimo Ani patched itself through on Box's comms systems: 'We've got a bogey. Nasty-looking bogey, heading right for us.'

The metallic flash resolved itself into a smallish courier-class pursuit ship: little more than cockpits, quarters and provisions stores for two, bolted on to a drive core and a thruster array for manoeuvring. It seemed to be coming for us, as Kimo Ani had said, its descent somewhere on the other side of recklessness. Atmospheric friction burn left a trail behind them and the leading edge of its nose seemed to be actually *glowing* . . .

Now I'm going to break in here and spoil the world-shattering surprise that the people who were *in* this ship meant us harm. I'm sorry and all, but it has to be done – things got a bit hectic after the ship landed, and I'd far rather talk about these things here than have everybody sit down in the middle of some jolly exciting action, and wait while I have a chat. 'Jolly' and 'exciting' are relative terms, of course: those expecting a spectacular and pyrotechnic firefight, with all guns blazing and lots of people being flung around dynamically by artfully detonated, low-yield, powder-packed incendiaries are going to be sorely disappointed. I just mean the situation transformed itself into something slightly more potentially dangerous than popping down to the shops. Then again, it depends on which particular shops.

Anyhow, because of the holomovies, the New Frontier Adventures and their ilk, people seem to have the idea that starships zoom around firing blasters at all and sundry in a blaze of stuttering photons and discharging singularity mines left right and centre. In fact, they carry nothing of the kind – I mentioned before that the process of pursuing or defending against space piracy is one of hand-to-hand combat inside, after the space pirate's ship itself has clamped on. The only spacegoing weapons that are armed, in this sense, are the ones that *are* weapons in and of themselves – kilometre-long rail guns, with a minimal control gantry and thrusters, and which have to be manoeuvred into position by tugs. Planetcrackers, which are basically five-mile-wide bombs with drives, and which have pressurized human-type conduits left over from their construction, and a control bridge to use for positioning them over the planets they're going to crack. Orbital strafers, the only function of which is to orbitally strafe. Stuff like that. The point being that if a ship has some integral weapons package, then there's simply no room for it to be anything else. Freighters, corvettes and the courier-classes by their very nature don't pack armament.

All of which is to explain why the approaching ship, meaning us harm, didn't simply fire upon us or drop a pony bomb on us from the air. Even so, had I been piloting it with evil and nasty intent, I could have thought of a number of things to do, working with what I had. I could have landed the damned thing on top of us, or put it down between us and the *Star of Afrique*. I certainly wouldn't have done what the ship in fact now did – which was to set down at a point roughly equidistant from both us and our ship, forming the third point in a positional equilateral triangle.

The new ship sat there for a while, turning whatever was suspended in the air around it into a kind of greasy steam with the heat of its atmospheric entry. Even at this distance, I fancied I could hear the pings and crackling of its cooling polyceramic sheath. After a while, someone shot the hatch and two figures came out, dressed in actual armoured vacuum suits rather than the radiation protection we had opted for. Each carried one of those lightweight but bulky and heavy-duty cases that one just knows don't contain happy little treats and party favours.

Kane had got the dazed Bernice Summerfield to her feet and was attempting the impossible juggling feat of chivvying her along without losing his temper and struggling with a now awake and annoyed cat, which he had picked up by the scruff of the neck. Mira had pulled her overlarge blaster and was watching the activity of the people from the other ship with an expression of alarm.

'They're setting something up,' she said.

'Tell me about it, why don't you?' I said as a patch of glassy plain between us and them exploded into crystal powder, the sound of the weapon's discharge coming a bare fraction of a second behind.

I think it was the chance to finally do something positive again, after feeling a bit like a spare prick for a while, that had me taking charge of things. I mean, I got on with these people OK, and they seemed OK as people, but that's not the same as really knowing or trusting them, or they me. On the other hand, we were all in the same boat – and here and now, if I was going to throw my lot in all the way with one faction or another, there was hardly any choice.

'Get her back to the ship,' I snapped at Kane. Then I overrode him totally as he opened his surprised mouth to say something that at any other time might have been pertinent for me to take on board. But here and now that would just have us farting around and arguing until we died. 'Just shut the *fuck* up and do it. Don't worry about being a target. Bad guys will be taken care of.'

Another detonation courtesy of the other team. They'd get the range less than ten seconds from now. I thumped Mira on the arm, not hard enough to hurt, but hard enough to get her full attention. 'You and me are going for them,' I told her as she spun to face me indignantly. 'You dodge left when I dodge right, you get me? Good. Let's go!'

I broke from our position from a standing start, dodging initially away from but inclining ultimately towards the new arrivals, not bothering to check to see if Mira was doing the same. That's a part and parcel of the way to snap orders and have them obeyed that I can't convey in cold print – it's a combination of the tone of voice, the rhythm in which you rap said orders out, the fact that you *never* apologize or explain, or give 'em time to argue, 'cause, if you hang around dithering and discussing in those times right on the edge, then you're dead. You're telling people how the world is going to *be*, and the fact that it could, hypothetically, be any number of other things doesn't enter into it.

All the same, I was glad to hear the sounds and catch the peripheral flashes of movement that told me Mira had followed my lead. Maybe Kane had got his finger out by now, and was hustling Summerfield towards the *Star of Afrique*. Maybe he was even bothering to take the cat. It was his lookout either way. My unilaterally imposed strategy was in place and we were committed to it.

And it was *strategy*. It wasn't actual *combat* in the sense that we could now respond and react. Instead of a static group target, we now had three separate targets, all of them moving. The Kane–Summerfield axis might have been the easy one, but Mira and I were the actively and erratically *threatening* ones. The optimum result was that it would disrupt and confuse our attackers' own strategy, but, even if it didn't, at this point there was nothing that could be done about it.

I didn't let myself feel fear or excitement or anything else that might have me break momentum – concentrating my entire being on closing the gap between me and our attackers. It's moments like these that seem an eternity when you're actually going through them, but less than the blink of an eye when you look back.

I was coming up on their position fast. The distinctive form-and-posture patterns of the two were familiar – one big male, a smaller female – but there was absolutely no use in that here and now. They were crouched by a big precision-aiming blaster on a stand, reminiscent of an ancient Vickers gun and used for precision-placing over distance – and were just starting to realize that it wasn't much good for fast-moving targets coming rapidly up close.

Having gone into the details of our actions, I might have given the impression that they took far longer than they really did. In real-time terms, it was maybe five or six seconds since Mira and I had begun our mad advance – just long enough to catch the tail end of our opponents' surprise, the lag of action that comes from having to improvise and re-evaluate on the fly (if you want to *do* something, you just do it; reactions take a little longer) and of having to switch from one kind of weapon to another. Whatever else they are, power weapons tend to be relatively heavy and cumbersome items of machinery; it takes a little bit of time to fiddle around with them and heft them around by sheer physical law – and, in a case like this, fractions of a second either way can make the difference between life and death.

In any event, that said, none of it would have meant a rat's squit – and me, and Mira, and quite possibly Summerfield and Kane, would have been left lying on the ground with smoking holes in us – had not our attackers made the mistake of wearing armoured suits that were really not meant to operate under gravity. Even the space-station riggers who wear them all the time, in free fall, take a couple of seconds to so much as pick up a spanner.

Under gravity – and if you're unused to wearing them – they slow down the speed of human action immensely. Thinking about it later and consciously, I decided that this had been the impulse behind our, quote, mad dash, unquote, in the first place. By the time I'd closed the distance, this couple of clowns had barely lurched up from their long-range weapon to track a couple of clumsily held sidearms in my general direction.

I was subconsciously aware, without quite seeing, that Mira was off to one side and keeping up. 'I take the big guy and you take the girl,' I called to her, and hoping like hell that my awareness of her was actually *true* and not wishful thinking.

'Story of my life!' she panted, from more or less where I'd expected her to be, which was a bit of a relief.

The big man's sidearm discharged as I barrelled into him. I have no idea where the charge ultimately went; maybe it went into the air. The blowback burnt me across the chest rather nastily and half-blinded me for an instant. My transferred momentum toppled the guy over and on to his back with a crash. I landed on top of him and windmilled my arms around to slap away anything that came near them, on general principles, until I could see again.

Off to one side I heard a similar crash and the sounds of Mira's struggling.

My sight cleared and I found myself looking at my own pale and rather desperately terrified-looking face, reflected back at me from the mirrored surface of my opponent's helmet visor. The guy himself was struggling, but feebly, weighed down by the suit. He made absolutely no sound, the suit being air-sealed. He probably talked to his little friend via two-way.

I bounced off his chest and backed slowly off as he struggled and jerked with the clanks, clicks and hisses of various servomechanisms. As I'd suspected – from just after hitting him if not the start – toppled on to his back like this he could no more get up than could an upturned Bolobarbiquan turtle. I glanced over to where Mira was standing, looking down at the suited woman, having discovered pretty much the same thing.

‘What do we do with them now?’ she said.

I turned to look at their ship and jerked a thumb towards the open hatch. ‘We’ll take that away from them for a start. Just leave ’em here, I suppose.’

The struggling of the suited figures became noticeably more frantic. I hefted their long-range gun off its rack, broke it down and wedged a couple of components either side of the man. That’d stop him from making it any time soon, if at all.

Off in the distance, I saw the figures of Kane and Summerfield standing by the *Star of Afrique*. I pointed to our attackers’ ship and pantomimed speaking to someone on a comms rig.

A thought occurred to me. ‘Any chance you can scan these creeps and pull out their names?’ I asked Mira.

She nodded dubiously. ‘I could do that. I’d have to pulse-pump through their suits to get anything useful, though. Do too much and it could seriously scramble their brains, what with the harmonics from all this metal and stuff.’

I looked down at our attackers and shrugged. ‘The poor dears. My heart bleeds. You going to do it or what?’

CHAPTER 15

Our attackers' ship was of the sort you can charter on the cheap from just about anywhere. There was nothing inside it worth learning, save that, in the cramped living space, one of the occupants had been obsessively neat and the other hadn't given a damn. This had led to one half of the compartment being neat and clean, the other piled with dirty clothes and trash with an almost perfectly straight dividing line between. This told me something about the relationship between the two people who shared it, but nothing of any actual use. Strangely, and going against the more common arrangement for cohabiting humans of different genders the galaxy over, it was the female side that seemed to be the messy one, and the male side the neat.

Once we were in orbit, the *Star of Afrique* docked with us, and Mira and I transferred back – me lugging the pair of sidearms I'd taken from our attackers on the planet below, and nothing else. I suppose we could have stripped the ship down and sold it for parts or something, but it simply wasn't worth the bother. I'd made sure from the control systems that it couldn't be called down again to land on remote, so we just cut it adrift.

Jason Kane laid in a course back the way we had come, set the automatic protocols and then went back aft to the sleeping quarters where he had taken Summerfield. The

Mary-Sue restructuring from Dr [name withdrawn from manuscript] had not, apparently, been a complete wipe-and-burn. Summerfield's memories and personality had simply been repressed and overlaid with the new one, this latter set to self-destruct over the course of a few months in any case, and he had high hopes of speeding the process along with certain keywords and mental triggers that Dr [name withdrawn from manuscript] had given him. Out of gratitude for my recent help, he promised to let me question her about my own concerns the moment he was sure I could do it without damage.

Mira went off to do something or other – I have no idea what – and Kimo Ani stayed hooked to various ship's systems. He seemed to be happy enough just doing that thing where you play around with a transputer rig sometimes, for no other particular reason than for the fun of it; fiddling with the interplay of its configurations to get the most out of it as if you were playing with a puzzle box – but on a level that someone without Kimo Ani's various enhancements and implants could barely comprehend. He didn't seem inclined to talk, and so I was once again, for the moment, at a bit of a loose end.

I passed the time by hooking Box up to the comms rig and the GalNet data stream, and running down the names Mira had pumped out from our attackers. As I'd suspected, it had been the pair who had shot at me on Luna and whom I'd seen in the hotel on Thanaxos. The ID stills I pulled from their personal records tied in with the glimpses I'd caught, and I now fixed their actual faces and specs in my mind. They might or might not get off the planetary ruin that was Beta Caprisis, but I wanted to be ready for them if they did.

The woman was one Mara Lutace Grabor. The recent stills of her showed a physically beautiful face, but with the kind of cold and dead-eyed stare that gave the mind a little shiver when you looked at it. They were the sort of eyes that, if she couldn't get at you, spoke of some past trauma that might explain her to you – but if you came upon them when she *could* get to you, and had access to a knife or suchlike, you'd back off slowly and then run a mile.

Grabor had come out of the Squaxis Sulan colonies, born there rather than deported. They were the modern-day equivalent of a Botany Bay for their galactic sector, their economy based around heavy-metal mining and refining by way of convict-slave labour. The place was a hellhole and I suppose, in one sense, she got out in the only way she could. She hooked up with an escapee, and for two years they terrorized the surrounding systems in a crime spree reminiscent of Bonnie and Clyde without the restraint.

When the local authorities finally tracked them down, she'd set up her lover to take the fall and got out. Sporadic reappearances, some for what you might call criminal activity but most involving dirty working for various low-rent concerns. The people who don't care how sloppy the work is if it gets halfway done, and don't care how many people die. Whereabouts currently, so far as anyone was going to admit on GalNet, unknown.

The man was one Simonon Leviticus Sleed. The stills showed a face that looked as if it was going through the throes of terminal constipation and a short, severe haircut dragged firmly back against the grain, thus looking far more *wrong* than if it had been just allowed to grow how it liked. Like Grabor, he was one of those people you could say were born into a certain life rather than just drifting in or jumping into it spectacularly.

In Sleed's case, this life was that of the White Fire, that repository of militantly active bigotry that seems to turn up right across the human spaces of the galaxy. White Fire has no overall galactic cohesion or political ethos, of course, being merely just a kind of easily recognized, *samizdat* franchise trademark, serving as a kind of handy tag for morons, thugs and whackos to swarm around wherever somebody feels that somebody else deserves a good kicking or worse.

Sleed was born into an offshoot of these charmers in a fortified commune on Squaxis Prime. This particular White Fire subsect variety had fixed upon the idea of natural selection as a way of Improving the Human Race and, naturally, had twisted it out of almost all recognition. They sent out squads of paramilitary troops to deal it out at the sharp end, taking groups of people hostage and then picking off those who, by their lights, didn't measure up. An interesting aspect of that was that they tended to utilize a series of complicated AI-based weapons designed to home in upon specifics of so-called inferiority. This had tended to backfire rather more than otherwise, what with the fact of being used by a paramilitary squad drawn from thugs and morons and whackos.

Sleed had been on one such hostage-taking operation when the Squaxis local authorities did something broadly similar of their own but on a larger scale, by laying siege to the White Fire commune and eventually obliterating it – more or less by misfired accident – by way of a small tactical nuclear device. The support of his particular White Fire subsect now gone, Sleed was forced to eke a living doing whatever jobs he could . . .

All in all, the files on this pair seemed to confirm what I'd suspected from the start. A couple of jokers, doing what could be broadly considered the same line of work as myself, but on a level so far down the food chain that they were like bugs. This made the fact that they seemed to have got as far as they did, for as long as they did, all the more worrying. Someone was running them, and was giving them access to some high-level, heavy-duty resources – and seemed utterly unconcerned that these people didn't have the first clue about how these resources should be handled. It was like giving a loaded handgun to a young and stupid but particularly evil and nasty-minded child. When the gun went off it could blow anybody away.

Maybe it was a double-bluff and there were checks and balances in place on the pair. And that was worrying in itself, because, if there *were*, then they were so good that I couldn't so much as spot them. Or maybe it was this putative *controller* who was really the hypothetical kid with a loaded gun – didn't know what the hell he, she or it was doing with all that potentially lethal power, and simply didn't care. That was even worse . . .

My somewhat gloomy reverie was cut short by a chime from the *Star of Afrique*'s internal comms. It was Jason Kane.

'Benny's feeling a bit more like herself,' he said. 'She wants to talk to you about Dellah and Thanaxos. She says it might just be important.'

Bernice Summerfield looked entirely different from the wasted form I'd seen on Beta Caprisis. Physically, she seemed more or less the same, because the various glucotics, nutrients and anti-radiation compounds being plugged into her from the medical stores had not yet had the time to do their work. That personality and intelligence that had so informed the stills I'd seen of her, months before, was back with a vengeance, like a light going on behind her eyes. She sat up weakly on the bunk and regarded me through them.

'I hear you've been looking for me,' she said drily – I mean *sardonically* dry, as opposed to a dry croak, though there was still an element of that, too. 'Should I be afraid?'

Something about her elicited candour. 'You know,' I admitted, 'it's been so long since I thought about it that I'm not sure. I don't think so. Besides . . .' I glanced to where Jason Kane was hovering protectively. 'I think your husband's maybe good enough to stop me if I try anything. He's got the incentive, after all.'

Summerfield turned to Kane and raised an eyebrow, then turned back to me. 'He's not my husband.'

'That's not what I've heard,' I said.

'Well, if you think about it, Benny, we never really got a divorce,' said Kane.

'Well if you want to think of it *that* way, sweetie,' Bernice said to him, archly, 'we never really got married in the first place either. Long-dead religious ceremony and there's absolutely no record of it anywhere. What do you think?'

'I think I could take your proper diaries to any court of law and put you in the poorhouse with the alimony,' said Kane. 'Once they work their way through all those bloody Post-it notes.'

I'd reflected upon the rather complex nature of Kane's relationship with Mira before – but, watching these two together, even just amiably digging at each other like this, that now seemed about as simple as I feel myself, most of the time. There was a sense of so many things moving under the surface – some of which might be so nasty as to pull you under and rip your arm off, if you weren't careful – that I could imagine them taking years to fathom. In the sort of relationship that could last for years. Here and now, though, I didn't have that sort of relationship and I didn't have the time.

The mention of Summerfield's *diaries* reminded me of the Journal I'd found, the one that had led us, via Kane's leap of intuition, to where we were at this point.

'Did you just want to get out?' I asked her. 'Did you do the Mary-Sue so you could get away from it all, stop thinking about the stuff that happened on Dellah for a while?'

Summerfield frowned. 'I hadn't thought of it in those terms, actually. Now I come to think about it, that might have been a part of it, unconsciously. That wasn't what I thought at the time – and what I *thought* at the time was quite bad enough, believe me.' She looked up at me with a complete and utter seriousness, made all the more poignant by the fact that, in her basic person, she didn't allow herself to be completely and utterly serious if she could help it.

'Jason's told me what you saw on Dellah,' she said. 'At that diplomatic conference thing. The thing is, I think, to a large extent, what you saw on Dellah was what They wanted you to see.'

You could hear the capitalization as if it were cut into a stone slab.

'Who's this They?' I asked her, with the nasty suspicion that I already knew. 'Are we talking about the All-High Gods or something? Like they really exist?'

She nodded, slowly. 'They weren't called the All-High anything, exactly, last time around, but I suppose it's as good a name as any for these . . . entities.' She shrugged to herself and smiled, her innate humour bursting through the seriousness, momentarily. 'If that's what they're calling themselves now, I suppose we'll have to live with it.'

She became serious again. 'These All-High Gods of yours are incredibly dangerous. They do things to the minds of those around them, twist them into a state of unquestioning belief. I think they *feed* off that belief . . .'

I remembered the obviously recent changes I'd seen in Dellahan society – even without having seen the state of it before, I realized that it was as though *something*, whatever it was, was changing whatever it had been before into a kind of global Belief Machine.

'. . . then there are cases of active, absolute *possession*,' Bernice Summerfield was saying. 'I think I was slated for one of those. After I escaped the first time I felt this – I don't know what to call it – this overwhelming urge, like a fist around my soul, hauling me back. I could just about control it, but it preyed on my mind and invaded my dreams . . .'

'So why go back?' I asked. 'If you could fight it then why go back?'

Bernice grinned – that sudden flash of humour again. 'You'll think me silly when I tell you. There was something I just couldn't leave behind. Something I had to find and save whatever else happened . . .'

'She went back for her fucking *cat*,' said Jason, obviously not a cat person – something I can get behind, personally, one hundred per cent. 'Can you fucking believe it? I fucking can't.'

'Well, leaving the multiple expletives aside for the moment,' said Bernice, coldly, 'it was something that I had to do. I took precautions, and left that Journal behind so I could be found in case something went wrong. Anybody reading it would know from the start, if they knew me, that something was *wrong* with it and wonder why . . .'

The businesslike way she said this had me thinking again that, despite protestations to the contrary, there had still been certain things about the Journal, on the personal and emotional level, that she refused to admit. There was something just that little bit too studied in the way that she dismissed it.

'For a number of reasons,' she was saying, 'I knew people who could organize me a ship, and provide me with the technology sufficient for getting through the Dellahan planetary security completely unnoticed. Then I just wandered around until I found Wolsey . . .'

'The fucking cat,' Jason cut in again.

'Quite,' said Bernice icily. 'The poor thing had been living on the local equivalent of rats, a kind of six-legged iguana that doesn't do much for the feline digestive system. He was skin and bone by the time I found him.' Bernice frowned, thoughtfully. 'By the time I found him, I wasn't in a very good state myself. *Something* seemed to be moving through the ruins of St Oscar's – I don't know if it was one of those things you now know as the All-High Gods, something related or even something else. Something the Advanced Research people let out and forgot to tell us about, maybe. On the whole, though, it seems to fit with the things known as the All-High Gods. All I *truly* know is I could feel it probing at my mind, tearing at it, trying to find a way inside . . .'

Her face cleared a little and she smiled. 'Fortunately, finding Wolsey was the trigger for the Mary-Sue procedure I'd had done. I found him and went dormant. That broke the connection with whatever it was. The new personality – the new *person*, I suppose – had been constructed with certain overriding impulse-complexes. She just picked him up, walked back to the ship, blasted off and headed for Beta Caprisis on overdrive.' Bernice scowled. 'I wish I'd remembered to specify a person with the ability to *land* a ship properly, when she got there.'

She paused, waiting for some reaction. Personally, I was kicking myself mentally for not realising she'd had the Mary-Sue done *before* returning to Dellah. All the clues had been there.

'Still seems like a lot of trouble to go to just for a cat,' I said at last.

'Too bloody right,' said Jason.

'Well, the trouble's not over yet,' Bernice said, with that cool and pointed contempt that cat-lovers have for those who loathe the little bastards the whole universe over. 'What with *you* –' this while pointing to me '– taking an entirely unjustified interest in me and my doings, it appears that the Dellahan situation has taken to a bit of planet hopping, and not to mention species jumping, on the quiet.'

This, if it were so, was news to me. 'What are you talking about?' I said uneasily.

'Show him, Jason,' said Bernice.

'Mira pulled this off the news services.' Kane passed me a hardcopy flimsy. It appeared to be a text-converted print-out of a GalNet item. A piece by a suddenly *ex*-DataDay outworld correspondent, Sela Dane, dated a couple of days before.

I read it. Then I stared at it. Then I read it again.

'Oh shit . . .' I said in a small voice, as I finally realized how stupid, how short-sighted, and how wrong about almost absolutely everything I had been from the start.

'That's putting it mildly,' said Jason Kane.

'The thing I'm worried about,' said Bernice, rather calmly and clinically I thought, given the circumstances, 'is the question of biological imperatives – if we can truly apply a term like biology in this case. Why do organisms swarm?'

'To reproduce.' I rattled off the answer automatically, still too dazed to take in the full enormity of it. 'To breed.'

'That's right,' said Bernice Summerfield. 'They swarm to breed.'

CHAPTER 16

This new planet didn't have a name. It could just about support life, but not a lot, and as opposed to Beta Caprisis – where entirely too *many* interesting things had happened for it to be inhabited – this planet simply wasn't interesting enough. It had a galactographic classification, in a desultory sort of way, but for various reasons you're not going to get it out of *me*.

We had come here, at the insistence of Bernice Summerfield, as a small diversion en route to Thanaxos.

'Remind me again,' I prompted Bernice, as Jason took the *Star of Afrique* down on a spiral incline, heading for the location – rather like we had on Beta Caprisis – of the single point of organized life. 'What is it we're doing here, precisely?'

'Looking for a friend,' she said, a little vaguely. Though still very weak, she had insisted that she be on the bridge, with everybody else, for the landing. 'He's another survivor from Dellah.' She frowned a little worriedly. 'Then again, you might say he's a . . . casualty. Though not in the usual sense.' She turned to the acceleration couch in which Mira was lying. The telepath we didn't have had a strange look of concentration on her face.

'Did Kimo Ani modify your systems properly?' Bernice asked her. 'Can you broadcast the proper selective fields?'

'I think so,' Mira said. 'If you gave me the parameters, and if you all stay close. It's slippery, though. It's a bit like juggling with frozen balls.'

'And you're sure you can keep us covered?'

'Maybe.' Mira looked around with the kind of careful precision you get when you're thinking of the things around you and don't want to break the thought. 'You and Jason, Kimo Ani and myself.'

'What about *him*?' Kane gestured towards me from the conn.

'His mind doesn't fit the parameters. The constructs might be complex enough to be human, but the artificial nature of them puts them out of sync. I can't get a lock on them without losing everybody else.'

'For what it's worth,' said Benny, turning to me, 'I think that means the Entities we're talking about can't get a lock on you either. I think, from what you said, that stopped you from being converted back on Dellah.'

'Personally, I think we should just dump him somewhere,' said Kane. 'Just to be on the safe side. It's your call, though, Benny.'

'Yes,' said Bernice, shortly. 'It is.'

We grounded on a rocky plain, bare of almost anything but lichen – another similarity to the planet from which we'd just come, achieved by this planet from going in an opposite direction. A small pup tent had been pitched here as protection from the minimal elements, secured by way of crampons hammered into the rock, and outside it sat a cross-legged figure – yet another echo.

There the similarities ended, however. This figure was male, naturally slim of body but better fed than Bernice had been, and little more than a boy. His head was shaved, his features delicate in a way that, I suppose, a certain kind of man could go for big-time. When I go for men, personally, I tend to go for the masculine rather than the feminine –

otherwise what would be the point?

The boy wasn't particularly interesting in himself – what *was* interesting, to the extreme, was the collection of small and rudimentary sluglike creatures before him, and what they were doing.

The boy looked up as we approached, and, very carefully, smiled.

'Hello, Benny,' he said. His voice was even more careful than the smile. It was the voice of someone exercising complete and entire control, not so much for the sake of it in itself, but out of fear of what might happen if he lost it. 'What are you doing here?'

'We need your help, Emile,' said Bernice, gently. 'We need you to come with us.'

'I . . . can't,' Emile said. 'I just can't. I came here to try to deal with the thing inside me. To try to keep it where it can't do harm. It . . . just wants *control*, you see. That's all it wants. Control of everything. And there's just so much you can do to pognophores . . .' He gestured to the little sluglike things. These, presumably, were they.

'It can't control *us* for the moment,' Bernice said. 'See for yourself, Emile. Let it try.'

'I . . .' Abruptly, the face of the boy went blank. And then something surfaced in it, something *else*. I really don't know how better to describe it. It was inimical to life – perhaps all life – but it didn't seem monstrous as such: it seemed to have no connection with evil, or good for that matter. It was an Entity, truly, in the sense of being completely in and of itself. It was unknowable, on any human level – and as such it was somehow *worse* than if it had been merely evil: it was simply something *else*.

I felt a kind of intangible probing at my head, at the mind inside the brain inside the skull – I flashed upon the so-called dreams I'd had on Dellah, before the minor and, so it had seemed at the time, ultimately unimportant change in Sela.

'Oh little creatures,' said the Entity, speaking through the boy Emile's mind and mouth. 'Do you *really* think you can . . .?'

And, quite suddenly, Emile's face changed again. 'What . . .?' said the Entity. 'What . . .?' said Emile – and then the haggard and precisely careful expression that was himself surfaced again.

'You see?' said Bernice, speaking as gently as ever. 'It can't harm us, for a while at least. We need your help, Emile. Please come with us.'

As Emile walked with us to the *Star of Afrique*, I glanced back. The little pognophores, who had been doing complicated midair somersaults, and arranging themselves in the sluggy equivalent of human pyramids, were crawling aimlessly away.

SUPPLEMENTARY INSERT:

Summerfield gripped the controls of the *African Star* and swung it through a ninety-degree turn with a roar of megaton thrusters. The spiderlike alien fighter failed to make the turn, shot on ahead and crashed into an asteroid with a gout of flame.

'Scratch one problem,' Summerfield said grimly. She turned to Jason. 'Make sure our little friend doesn't try to escape.'

'Sure thing,' Jason said, looking with disgust at the trussed form of Moloch on the floor. His simple but essentially noble heart was sickened by the sight of the assassin, who had so recently tried to use Berni's own, stolen knives on her. It had only been the fact that Berni made her own blades, he thought, and that this killer had not the expertise to use their specially customized nature, that had saved her life.

Moloch glared up at him, the dark eyes in his unnaturally pale skin flashing with pure hatred.

'You'll never get away,' the brutal assassin spat. 'You might have won this round, but our plot to kill King G'jimo of Thanaxos continues unchanged. You'll never make it in time . . .'

Jason cursed the luck that had had him imprisoned, for a crime he did not commit, on the prison planet of

Caprisis Beta, forcing Berni Summerfield to cut short a long-deserved butterfly-hunting vacation and go there to effect his escape. Had it not been for that, he thought bitterly, they would not have found themselves two galaxies away from Thanaxos and the plot to kill the King. Even now, the demonic monster that these villains had summoned by their blood-soaked rituals on Dellah could be lurching through the streets towards the Royal Palace, feeding off those poor victims it encountered in the night and growing stronger all the time as it made towards its goal.

Only Berni Summerfield could stop it now, he thought. She alone in all the universe had reached the centre of the Temple of Tashwari, through any number of fiendishly designed death traps, had read the inscriptions written in the human blood of slaves and made it out again, despite the Temple's huge revolving granite balls.

Only Berni Summerfield, he knew, could say the words that would send the Dellahan monster back to the nether regions of the cosmos whence it came . . .

– extract from *The Dellahan Conspiracy*,
a True Adventure of the New Frontier

CHAPTER 17 (ENDGAME)

Now, right at the start of this I said how things fell apart spectacularly right at the end. That's not quite true. In another sense, they came together catastrophically, in a moment of transition and transformation that changed everything. Whether for good or for ill, in the end, it's impossible to say – the point being that in an instant they *changed*. It was like carefully putting together a lump of plutonium, gram by gram, over the course of months. At some point things hit a critical mass, and suddenly everything's happening in an instant and all at once. The rest of your life, for starters . . .

So much has been said of the events on Thanaxos at this point: the sense of religious monomania that seemed to be sweeping the planet, converting the extant sense of impending war into a *jihad* aimed not so much at the planet of Dellah now, but at absolutely everything and anything in the galaxy – the entire universe, for that matter – that was *not* Thanaxos and didn't Believe. So-called heretics were being burnt on the streets, people were committing ritual suicide left, right and centre, and off-worlders in their thousands were making hurried preparations to leave – a lot of them with the intention of leaving to spread the Word, whatever that word might subsequently prove to be.

The planet, in short, was dancing on the lip of the

catastrophe curve. The finger of history was poised on the button of the blender of Chaos, and gods (or whatever Entities might ultimately emerge) knew what would happen when the button was pressed.

Thanaxos as a planet was going through the incipient stages of the upheavals that had so changed Dellah. All it would take to tip things over the edge was a minor shove in the right direction.

So much has been said about it – but, as I've said from the start, this is a personal and subjective account. It might not be the whole truth and nothing but – and it's an odds-on bet that it won't be *yours* – but it's *my* truth, and all I can really talk about is what happened to me, and what I thought, and what I did. And, if that leaves gaping holes in the Big Picture, well, find somebody else and ask *them* to take up the slack. It's no skin off my nose; it's none of my business and I couldn't care less.

We gleaned the salient points noted above as we burst into Thanaxon airspace. What with Bernice working in conjunction with Kimo Ani, the various systems of the *Star of Afrique* were set to avoid any planetary defensive measure a relatively minor world like Thanaxos, in the great galactic scheme of things, could throw at us. I don't know the full specifics of what they did to the ship, and I wouldn't tell you if I did. The last thing such things need to be is commonly known. For one thing, their blanket use would lead to interstellar chaos before countermeasures are devised – and for another, once those countermeasures *are* devised, the people who might really need to use the techniques won't be able to.

Suffice it to say that we pancaked down on the lawn of the Thanaxon House Royal, with nary a glitch on the planetary defence sensors. The Royal Guard were another matter entirely, of course – it's hard to disguise the fact of a fuckoff-great space cruiser coming down from plain visual sight. I detonated a couple of neurasthenic smoke bombs that had been part of the *Star of Afrique*'s arsenal when she was a pirate ship, which I had missed in clearing her of suspicious items after stealing her, and which I had subsequently discovered in a hiding place so obvious that I'm too ashamed to so much as say where it was.

If you've been reading carefully enough, you'll probably be able to hazard a guess. The important point was that the first squad of guards to arrive on the scene stopped being a problem long enough for us to disembark – Bernice, Jason and Mira shepherding Emile – leaving Kimo Ani behind to deal with any reinforcements, by way of his implants hooked to servo-assisted weapons packages we had improvised.

The more ostentatiously splendid public areas of the house were still wide open to the populace, but we eschewed them in favour of the shabbier, workaday areas I had been in once before. We weren't interested in dealing with the flashy trappings – we were here to deal with the worm in the true heart of planetary power.

'How could things have got so bad so quickly?' I asked as we ran through the worn and peeling corridors. The violent confusion of the disrupted news reports was preying on my mind. 'It's only been a few days . . .'

'I saw something similar to it on Dellah,' Bernice said. 'It's like a ripple effect. The Faith spreads like wildfire, accelerating as it goes. I think that, in a sense, these Entities create the medium through which they can move and propagate . . .'

'And with luck,' said Jason, 'we can stop the actual *propagation* at its source.' He hefted the handgun he carried, one of those I'd lifted from Grabor and Sleed on Beta Caprisis. 'Are we clear on what we're doing?'

'I am prepared,' said Emile in his distant and tightly controlled voice.

The plan was relatively simple, if dangerous enough to put several varieties of willy up a braver man than I. We were to meet the Entity and its host, face to face, in its lair, relying upon Mira's enhanced and pulse-pumped psychic fields to protect us against those under its direct influence, making us unnoticeable to them in a way more or less similar to that which I'd come across on Dellah, when the native Dellahans in the Sultan's palace had looked through me and continued on their merry way without a second thought. The Entity inside Emile wanted control of all things for itself and, brought into contact with each other, these two opposing powers might at some stage, we hoped, cancel each other out.

That was what we *hoped*, of course – this specific part of the plan had had to be discussed outside of Emile's presence, to prevent the thing inside him catching wind of it, and so far as he knew he was along merely to help his friend Bernice and the rest of us out if he could. Personally, I wished that a way could have been found to ask him for his advice on the matter. I had a nasty feeling that we might be just participating in a dynamic that allowed a pair of the buggers to breed . . .

So far as the rest of the plan went, it was utterly simple, owing to the fact that it was utterly nonexistent. Whatever the presence of Emile's Thing did, one way or another, it would at the very least disrupt things and make a *change* – and from that point we would simply try to take advantage of it and attempt to improvise.

We burst into the Council chamber. Floating in the centre of the room, arms akimbo, an unearthly light blazing from his eyes and surrounded by the members of the Thanaxon Advisory Council to the House Royal, was the Prince Regent – Jimbo. The members of the Council stood stock-still, gazing at him with a kind of divine adoration that was effectively catatonia. Among them I saw Sela Dane, as slack-jawed and drooling as the rest. The sharp, designer combat-gear that had been her trademark hung off her, like grubby rags: she hadn't changed, or washed, or eaten in a week.

Prince Jimbo turned, slowly in the air, and regarded us with a knowing smile.

'Good evening,' said the Thing inside him. 'So glad you can come – especially my little brother, there. Do you expect to *fight* me, little brother? Do you expect to fight me for Dominion of this place?'

'I don't think so,' said Emile – but it wasn't Emile now: it was the Thing inside him. 'I expect to eat.'

'Ah yes?' said the Thing inside Prince Jimbo. 'And how do you expect to accomplish *that* in the face of Me, who have grown strong, have gorged myself upon the Belief of all these people till I am all near inviolate?' It chuckled. 'When I found this host, a mind so blank and empty that I couldn't see the end of it, I filled it *up*. I am bigger, little brother, than you can ever possibly imagine.'

'No,' said the Thing inside Emile, softly. 'You don't understand. It is not the satiation, or the size – it's the *hunger* that's the thing. This host of mine has tried to starve me for a long time now, and I am very, *very* hungry.'

Now, in other accounts I've read of the events on Thanaxos – and guess which ones are the worst – there now occurs a massive discharge and battle of energies, laying waste to all around them and lasting for up to a week.

In reality, in this universe at least, what happened was this: the lights simply went out of Prince Jimbo's eyes and he dropped like a stone. And light's came on in the eyes of Emile, and he began to rise . . .

'Oh, dear God,' cried Mira. 'He's taking on the power! I can't *hold* him, I can't . . .'

Bernice and Jason stood transfixed, as the protective mental field of Mira spun away from them. They stood helpless, their faces blank and slack as the thing that had been, and to some extent still was, Emile rose before them, reaching for them with hands that seemed part those of an angel taking supplication and part the claws of a devil.

It was at that point that I recalled something. It was something about the fact that I was, in some sense, when it came right down to it, an Artificial Personality – and the thing about Artificial Personalities was that these Things seemed to have no effect upon them.

It was a fraction of a second after that, that I turned and rabbit-punched the thing that had once been a Thing that was in some way still Emile in the face. The light died in his eyes and he hit the ground with a thump.

It was slightly later.

A rather bemused and shaken Council had emergency-convened and were sitting at their scuffed official table, looking at Bernice Summerfield, Jason Kane and me. Off to one side lay the still unconscious Emile, watched over by Mira with her full enhanced attention, ready and waiting to put a mental lock-hold on him if he so much as stirred.

Off to one side, the newly exorcized Prince Jimbo sat in a high-backed chair, returned to what for him approached normality, and beamed at all and sundry with imbecilic stupidity. I could have personally done with the Thing that had possessed him leaving behind some trace of an intelligence, or a personality, or indeed any kind of a clue.

We had filled the Council in on the basics of what had happened to them, and what we had done – basics of which they were largely aware on the subconscious levels that had remained awake and aware even when they had been in the thrall of the Entity that had so subsumed them. Enough, at least, so that they had accepted our story, in broad outline, without question. However, being a bit of a political body on the quiet, they were quite prepared to question, debate and demand satisfaction upon the minutiae – and now they all began to try to talk at once.

'Gentlemen and ladies, please!' The Minister for Off-world Affairs, the Thanaxon counterpart of Pseudopod's Volan, waved a silencing hand. 'I think that we may safely leave such trifles for later. For the moment, I suggest that we vote these remarkably courageous people our heartfelt thanks, both on behalf of ourselves and the nation itself, and turn our attention to setting to rights the deplorable state of affairs that these recent disruptions and upheavals have caused.' Receiving an apparent consensus, he glanced meaningfully towards Bernice, Jason and me with an air that informed us that, for the moment, our audience with the Administrative Council to the House Royal had ended.

'Not so fast, Volan,' I said.

The ersatz Volan paused in the act of returning to the Acts of State. 'Pardon me? I beg your pardon?'

I climbed from my chair and fixed him in the eyes. 'I have something to say that is not strictly relevant to the matter in hand, but is nevertheless interesting to you in a personal capacity.'

'Well if it's a matter of a personal nature,' said Volan, a little stuffily, 'it can surely wait until the Council is not in session. Now, as I was saying . . .'

'Oh it's of interest to the Council, too, all right.' I said. And oblivious to his attempts at interruption I began to prowl the room, making use of the fact that a moving object becomes the centre of attention and counting points off on my fingers.

'As you are well aware in your private capacity, Volan, I am currently in the employ of Pseudopod Enterprises. In the instant I was engaged for a consultation with them, an attempt was made upon my life by a pair of low-level little sods going by the names of Grabor and Sleed. As I've pursued my duties, in locations known directly only by me and a very few others, they've always been one step behind me. Now, there could be any number of reasons for that, and if this were a detective story there could be a lot of abstruse and complicated mileage in it – but in real life, I tend to find, the simplest and most obvious solutions are more usually correct than otherwise.

'I was looking, basically, for someone who could know my movements in every detail, but at the same time wasn't quite *good* enough to have first-rate people working for him – someone who was, basically, just that little bit naff . . .

'I've done a little bit of digging into your life, Volan, and guess what I found. Large lumps of Pseudopod funding have been parlayed through your political connections here on Thanaxos into a number of anonymous private accounts. It's been going on for years quite happily – but, with the Dellahan situation disrupting Pseudopod interests, you knew that they'd be sending one or more heavy-duty and free-ranging operatives, and that in all probability they'd stumble on your personal scams. Setting those two jokers on me was your attempt to lead me off the scent or kill me – but you did it so ineptly that, in the end, they led me straight back to you.'

Volan was looking at me sardonically, having gone into method-acting mode to cover up any sense of dismay he might be feeling.

'Essentially correct,' he said, 'barring one or two particulars. The particulars in question being the details of my escape upon being found out. Here – *catch*.'

With that, he threw what seemed to be a silvery globe about the size of a clenched fist, using the resulting confusion to step backward through a hatch that rose and lowered with a clash and the electromagnetic chunking of deadbolts.

I'd instinctively ducked when Volan had thrown the object – but now I saw that it was floating in mid-air. It began to spin, slowly at first, and then accelerated.

'My Goddess,' breathed Bernice. 'What is it?'

'Not good news,' I said softly. 'I recognize it from researching Grabor and Sleed. He must have got it from Sleed at some point. It's a stupid grenade.'

'A *what*?' exclaimed Jason Kane.

'You've heard of a smart bomb, right?' I said. 'This operates on a completely different principle. A certain sub-sect of the White Fire used it to, in quotes, improve the race. It's thrown into a room and, once primed, it hunts down the stupidest person in it and detonates . . .'

'Well, I personally think that certain tropes and themes to be found in *Finnegans Wake* were rather overdone,' said Bernice, instantly and brightly.

'And the *X*-factor, in the Special Theory of Relativity could be better described as Universal Consciousness,' cut in Jason Kane, almost as fast, 'as opposed to some anthropomorphic Mind of God.'

'Time flies like an arrow,' called out Mira, from where she was still looking after Emile, 'but fruit flies like a banana . . .'

Around the room, all the members of the Council were suddenly trying to make intelligent-sounding noises. Then they stopped and, slowly, inexorably, every pair of eyes in the room turned towards Prince Jimbo.

'Hello, chaps.' He beamed back at them. 'I had eggs for tea.'

There remains little more to tell, so far as it directly concerns me. I feel I have to add a small personal incident, though, in the interests of completeness – and not for any kind of fictive roundness, which I have no truck with, in any way, shape or form.

After the dust and various other things had settled, I needed to go and clean up – and realized that, on Thanaxos, I had nowhere left to go. The private rooms of the House

Royal weren't open to such as me, and the ablutionary facilities of the *Star of Afrique* were a bad joke. In the end, with nowhere else to go, I settled on the hotel where I'd stayed with Sela Dane.

I found her in the room, miserably packing an even dozen of identical suits in her bag. I'd noticed that she'd gone, after the spell in the Council Chamber had been broken, but I'd had no idea where.

She turned to look at me, with eyes that seemed to have been crying quite recently.

'Jeez, guy, but you look a mess. What the hell is that?'

'Just a bit of blood,' I said. 'It's not important. It's not mine.' I glanced towards her travel cases. 'Where are you going?'

'I don't know.' Abruptly, there were tears in her eyes again. She dashed them away, angrily. 'I've pissed on my chips with DataDay, I know that. I'm gonna be a laughing stock. How could I put out shit like that?'

'Hey,' I said. 'It wasn't your fault. People are going to know that.'

'Yeah, but shit sticks. They're never gonna take me seriously again.'

It wasn't a big thing or anything. I just gave her a hug to try to make her feel better – but she laid her head against my slightly blood-spattered chest without caring, and I knew the spark and light were there. They had never, really, gone away.

'Don't worry about it,' I said. 'I know a few people. We can sort something out.'

ATTACHMENT (TENTATIVE CONCLUSIONS):

It's not my job to draw any real conclusions from any of this – and I don't think I'd dare. Nothing really ends in life – you feed some drugs to a laboratory rat and, two hundred generations down the line, the monsters start being born. Drawing conclusions is for those who have to deal with them *then*, somewhere down the line. All I can do is be as honest as I can, tell you what I can, and say something about how the lives of myself and those with whom I was involved have carried on.

Was the Entity inhabiting Prince Jimbo one of the All-High Gods of Dellah? Did it really die, locked up in his head as it was, when he did? Neither I nor anybody else can be completely sure, but I *think* the answers are, in order, yes it was and yes it did. There was nothing to suggest otherwise, then or later. Nobody suddenly acting strangely and out of character – at least, no more than to the extent that real people, as opposed to *characters,* in the holomovies of the New Frontier Adventures, do. In the times when I've been bothered to look, I haven't seen anything to do with Thanaxos that would suggest an outpouring of mass religious mania, any more than any other planet with its fair share of religious monomaniacs.

In any event, if this Entity still somehow survives, it'll have a job getting out of the lead-lined casket in which

Jimbo was buried, with full State Honours. On the one hand, in the larger sense, this helped diffuse the vestigial Belief he had engendered in his last days. A combination of this Belief and a refusal to *really* believe how much of an embarrassment he had been at all other times, converted him into a state of instant martyrdom. The mass Thanaxon grief at his death, and subsequent interment in a specially commissioned tomb – visitors permitted at a reasonable price – went some way to displacing and dispelling the warlike emotions that had had Thanaxos turning its eyes to Dellah. For the moment, the Earth-imposed blockade of that planet was safe, from the Thanaxon quarter at least.

I've mentioned how ultimately nebulous my work for Pseudopod Enterprises was – and playing a part in achieving this fragile stability meant that my work was done. At least that's what the *original* Volan assured me, when he called me at my and Sela's hotel room (a different one from the one we'd shared before: this one had been rented by me on the Pseudopod expenses that would not be curtailed, and that had been replaced by what Volan called 'a commensurate sum' of actual pay).

I wasn't so sure. Not about my work being done – but about just *what* that actual work might have been.

'I get the feeling that all this "preserving the stability of the Sector for Pseudopod interests" stuff was just window-dressing, wasn't it?' I said. 'Correct me if I'm wrong, but wasn't it *really* about rooting out the iffy things your local counterpart was doing and fingering him for them?'

'Not at *all*, my dear chap,' Volan said. 'Though I must admit that, in that particular respect, that was a little and completely unexpected bonus for us all. Such a pity you couldn't actually catch him, but at least he's well out of harm's way now . . .'

That and his tone told me all I needed to know. 'So all the other things that happened, all the good and all the bad, were just incidental details to your own personal agenda?'

Volan appeared to change the subject. 'Do you know that one of the circles of Hell contains a table, laid out with the most sumptuous banquet imaginable?'

'OK,' I said, 'I'll bite. What the hell does that have to do with anything?'

'Seated to either side of it,' said Volan, 'are the Selfish Damned. They're all of them starving, but their elbows are splinted. They can't put a scrap of this luxuriant repast into their mouths . . .'

'And it never occurs to them to feed each other across the table,' I finished for him, sourly. 'Very deep. Very apposite. Very moving.'

'Enlightened self-interest, occasionally harnessed to the greater good, is one of the few things we've got going for us,' said Volan sternly. 'In the end, I sometimes think it's one of the few good reasons for having human beings in the galaxy in the first place.'

After those last fateful events in the House Royal, Bernice Summerfield, Jason Kane, Kimo Ani and Mira had taken the *Star of Afrique* and conveyed a slightly punch-drunk Emile back to his sinecure, before exposure to all the potential Thanaxon victims broke the fragile control he had achieved over his own Entity. They then, presumably, went their separate ways, Jason's people to carry on doing whatever it was that they did, and Benny to recover from the rigours of the past few months and then get on with whatever she was going to do next.

There are a few odd, nebulous rumours about her. Personally, I'm waiting for the next Adventure of the New Frontier in which she stars – so I can work out what she's doing, by the simple expedient of taking what it says and inferring the precise opposite.

Sela Dane, having blown her reputation so spectacularly

with DataDay while under the influence, is going to make a comeback – though not quite in the usual way. A couple of months from now, half the galaxy is going to wake up to find a hot new interstellar reporter, beautiful and elegant and, with the guts and steel-trap mind to take the datastream by storm, someone everybody's going to be talking *about* and wanting to talk *to*. She might look a little like Sela, but hardly anybody's going to make the connection, the tags and identifiers and memory of celebrity being incredibly mutable, given the right amount of torque. The girl's gonna be huge. I know this for a fact. I know this 'cause I'm going to have a hand in it. And anybody mentioning the immediately obvious will be shot.

As for me, I'm just going to fade. The people who know me know who I am, if you get what I mean – and for the people who don't I'm not gonna let anything slip even by implication. In writing this out, I've done my own impromptu and informal Mary-Sue – changed my fundamental aspects of persona, my personality, the basic facts of my life and history, my entire manner of speaking. The gist of events is here, but there is nothing to tie the man in the centre of it all to who I truly am. I could be anyone, basically.

But you'll never know.

ALSO AVAILABLE IN THE NEW ADVENTURES

OH NO IT ISN'T!

by Paul Cornell

ISBN: 0 426 20507 3

Bernice Surprise Summerfield is just settling into her new job as Professor of Archaeology at St Oscar's University on the cosmopolitan planet of Dellah. She's using this prestigious centre of learning to put her past, especially her failed marriage, behind her. But when a routine exploration of the planet Perfecton goes awry, she needs all her old ingenuity and cunning as she faces a menace that can only be described as – panto.

DRAGONS' WRATH

by Justin Richards

ISBN: 0 426 20508 1

The Knights of Jeneve, a legendary chivalric order famed for their jewel-encrusted dragon emblem, were destroyed at the battle of Bocaro. But when a gifted forger is murdered on his way to meet her old friend Irving Braxiatel, and she comes into possession of a rather ornate dragon statue, Benny can't help thinking they're involved. So, suddenly embroiled in art fraud, murder and derring-do, she must discover the secret behind the dragon, and thwart the machinations of those seeking to control the sector.

BEYOND THE SUN

by Matthew Jones

ISBN: 0 426 20511 1

Benny has drawn the short straw – she's forced to take two overlooked freshers on their very first dig. Just when she thinks things can't get any worse, her no-good ex-husband Jason turns up and promptly gets himself kidnapped. As no one else is going to rescue him, Benny resigns herself to the task. But her only clue is a dusty artefact Jason implausibly claimed was part of an ancient and powerful weapon – a weapon rumoured to have powers beyond the sun.

SHIP OF FOOLS
by Dave Stone
ISBN: 0 426 20510 3

No hard-up archaeologist could resist the perks of working for the fabulously wealthy Krytell. Benny is given an unlimited expense account, an entire new wardrobe and all the jewels and pearls she could ever need. Also, her job, unofficial and shady though it is, requires her presence on the famed space cruise-liner, the *Titanian Queen*. But, as usual, there is a catch: those on board are being systematically bumped off, and the great detective, Emil Dupont, hasn't got a clue what's going on.

DOWN
by Lawrence Miles
ISBN: 0 426 20512 X

If the authorities on Tyler's Folly didn't expect to drag an off-world professor out of the ocean in a forbidden 'quake zone, they certainly weren't ready for her story. According to Benny the planet is hollow, its interior inhabited by warring tribes, rubber-clad Nazis and unconvincing prehistoric monsters. Has something stolen Benny's reason? Or is the planet the sole exception to the more mundane laws of physics? And what is the involvement of the utterly amoral alien known only as !X.

DEADFALL
by Gary Russell
ISBN: 0 426 20513 8

Jason Kane has stolen the location of the legendary planet of Ardethe from his ex-wife Bernice, and, as usual, it's all gone terribly wrong. In no time at all, he finds himself trapped on an isolated rock, pursued by brain-consuming aliens, and at the mercy of a shipload of female convicts. Unsurprisingly, he calls for help. However, when his old friend Christopher Cwej turns up, he can't even remember his own name.

GHOST DEVICES
by Simon Bucher-Jones
ISBN: 0 426 20514 6

Benny travels to Canopus IV, a world where the primitive locals worship the Spire – a massive structure that bends time – and talk of gods who saw the future. Unfortunately, she soon discovers the planet is on the brink of collapse, and that the whole sector is threatened by holy war. So, to prevent a jihad, Benny must journey to the dead world of Vol'ach Prime, and face a culture dedicated to the destruction of all life.

MEAN STREETS
by Terrance Dicks
ISBN: 0 426 20519 7

The Project: a criminal scheme so grand in its scale that it casts a shadow across a hundred worlds. Roz Forrester heard of this elaborate undertaking, and asked her squire to return with her to sprawling and violent Megacity – the scene of her discovery. Roz may be dead, but Chris Cwej is not a man to forget a promise, and Bernice is soon the other half of a noble crime-fighting duo.

TEMPEST
by Christopher Bulis
ISBN: 0 426 20523 5

On the wild and inhospitable planet of Tempest, a train is in trouble. And Bernice, returning home on the luxurious Polar Express, is right in the thick of it. Murder and an inexplicable theft mean that there's a criminal on board; the police are unable to reach them; and so the frightened staff and passengers turn to a hung-over, and rather bad-tempered, archaeologist for much-needed assistance.

WALKING TO BABYLON
by Kate Orman
ISBN: 0 426 20521 9

The People – the super-advanced inhabitants of a Dyson sphere – have a problem: to stop an illegal time-travel experiment they must destroy ancient Babylon and all its inhabitants. If they do not, war will break out with the dominant power of the Milky Way, and whole galaxies will be destroyed. Their only hope is that Bernice can travel back to the dawn of civilization, and find the culprits – or Earth history will never be the same again.

OBLIVION
by Dave Stone
ISBN: 0 426 20522 7

A man called Deed is threatening the fabric of the universe and tearing realities apart. At the heart of the disruption, three adventurers, Nathan li Shoa, Leetha and Kiru, are trapped. Their friend Sgloomi Po must save them before they are obliterated, and in his desperation he looks up some old friends. So Bernice joins her feckless ex-husband Jason and her old friend Chris on the rescue mission; but then Sgloomi picks up someone who should really be dead.

THE MEDUSA EFFECT
by Justin Richards
ISBN: 0 426 20524 3

Medusa, an experimental ship missing for twenty years, is coming home. When one of the investigation team dies mysteriously, Bernice is assigned to help discover what went wrong. But to do so she must solve a riddle. Somehow the original crew are linked to the team put on board – their ghosts still haunt the ship. And the past is catching up with them all in more ways than one.

DRY PILGRIMAGE
by Paul Leonard and Nick Walters
ISBN: 0 426 20525 1

Thinking she has been offcred a blissful pleasure cruise on Dellah's southern ocean, Benny gladly accepts. After all, she has some time on her hands. But, trapped on a yacht with an alien religious sect who forbid alcohol, she soon discovers that all is not well. And, as the ship heads towards a fateful rendezvous, she must unmask a traitor or risk the system being torn apart by war.

THE SWORD OF FOREVER
by Jim Mortimore
ISBN: 0 426 20526 X

Forced to leave her home on Dellah for Earth, Bernice finds work on an Antarctic dig. Once there she uncovers a link between an ancient reptile race, a secret society and a desperate megalomaniac – as well as the fabled Ark of the Covenant. A desperate race has begun, and she soon realizes her deadly knowledge affects not only her own life, but the destiny of the entire human race.

ANOTHER GIRL, ANOTHER PLANET
by Martin Day and Len Beech
ISBN: 0 426 20528 6

Lizbeth Fugard, an archaeologist working on the backwater planet of Dimetos, is in trouble. Someone is following her – watching her. Terrified, she calls on an old friend to help. On arrival, however, Bernice becomes involved in politics, gun-running and a centuries-old love affair, and soon realizes that unless she can find the truth a cycle of violence and hate will jeopardize more than one planet's future.

WHERE ANGELS FEAR

by Rebecca Levene and Simon Winstone

ISBN: 0 426 20530 8

Something very odd is happening on Dellah. A long-ignored religion is rapidly gaining recruits as the faithful talk of their god walking the land once more. It is a time of faith and miracle. But behind this rebirth lies a dark secret – a secret that has terrified the great powers of the galaxy and left Bernice and friends to face a terrible menace on their own.

COMING SOON

Dead Romance
by Lawrence Miles
ISBN: 0 426 20532 4
15 April 1999

Seventies Britain holds no thrills for Christine Summerfield. Nothing exciting happens. The world never changes. That is until ritualistic murders rock the city of London – murders that draw Chrissy into an unreal world of bizarre monsters and threats from another dimension. And at the heart of it all is a handsome enigmatic stranger called Christopher Cwej.

Tears of the Oracle
by Justin Richards
17 June 1999

Jason Kane, Bernice's one-time husband, thinks he's found the fabled Oracle of the Lost on the obscure planetoid known only as KS-159. Legend says the Oracle can tell the future and answer any questions. But when Bernice and friends arrive, they discover the answers are rarely helpful – and that certain knowledge can kill.